PSYCHOTROPIA

VOLUME 1

PSYCHOTROPIA

MAESTRO'S CREED

BILL REINERT

PSYCHOTROPIA

Copyright © 2024 by Bill Reinert

Cover Copyright © 2024 by Bill Reinert

Cover Design by Damonza

Edited by Krysta Winsheimer

Publishing Service provided by Edits by Stacey

Published by BillReinertWrites

All rights reserved.

This is a work of fiction. Names, characters, businesses, places, events, locales, and incidents are either the products of the author's imagination or used in a fictitious manner. Any resemblance to actual persons, living or dead, or actual events is purely coincidental.

No part of this publication may be reproduced, distributed, or transmitted in any form or by any means, including photocopying, recording, or other electronic or mechanical methods, without the prior written permission of the publisher, except in the case of brief quotations embodied in critical reviews and certain other noncommercial uses permitted by copyright law.

For permission requests, write to the publisher BillReinertWrites.com

Library of Congress Control Number: 2024901880
Paperback 979-8-9898977-0-4
eBook 979-8-9898977-1-1

Printed in the United States of America

*For Joan the Loner
You made the desert bloom.*

LETTER TO THE READER

After Martha, my beloved wife of thirty-two years died of cancer in 2019, she was cremated. I decided to place the beautiful Southwest-themed crock that contained her cremains on a pedestal in the garden that she so lovingly tended. I thought she'd enjoy being among the showy gladiolas and other blooms she'd nurtured. There she remained for a little while.

My neighborhood website teems with accounts of doorbell trolling, porch piracy, vandalism, and other urban woes. While I was happy seeing her in her garden, I had nagging anxiety concerning someone possibly stealing the crock and incidentally, or otherwise, her ashes. I brought her cremains back inside and set them to rest, secure once more, on the fireplace mantelpiece.

As writers of fiction do, I imagined what I might have done had the crock been stolen, not to mention what in God's name might motivate someone to intentionally swipe its contents, as opposed to simply the crock itself.

Ouroboros and his El Camino cult, which are at the heart of my novel, *Psychotropia*, are the product of those ruminations, and entirely fictional.

Please refer to the glossary at the end of the book to find definitions of unfamiliar words you encounter. Their meanings will be evident in the course of your reading, but you do have a place to go for a quick fix.

I hope you enjoy reading the story as much as I enjoyed writing it.

CHAPTER
ONE

Sparrows mobbing the suet feeders and birdbath wheeled off as Liam parted the faded dining room curtains, closed against the building heat. Blinking in the harsh sunlight, he gawked at the garden in disbelief. He looked to the left and the right as the AC hummed and the ceiling fan stirred the dusty air.

Gone.

Joan was gone.

No urn.

No ashes.

What the flying fuck?

An image of a half-waking dream jarred him. Joan had

vanished without a word to him. He'd woken up sweating. Now, she was, again, stolen from him.

He rubbed his stubbled cheeks with his right palm.

Shit never ends…

He checked the mantelpiece. The dust-free circle remained from when he'd decided—the day before—to move the ceramic vessel into the garden. Joan would surely want to be out there among her gladiolas, which his neglect—coupled with the heat dome baking the region—had withered to husks. A hundred-year event that had occurred two of the past five years, the dome was frying anything and everything with roots.

At a quarter to eight, it was already 85 degrees—in the shade.

Coffee in hand and his arthritic, graying beagle Daisy hobbling gamely at his heels, Liam hustled out the back door to the garden. He kicked at the rock-hard laurel tree pods that littered the deck.

His phone streamed *Morning Edition* updates to his hearing aids—the Election Day Quake and its aftershocks, along with the easing surge, wildfires ravaging the West, and the increasingly lethal water wars in the Southwest.

Barely perceptible in the baked soil, sneaker prints circled the coyote-shaped pedestal. Liam glanced at the blinking red light embedded in the eaves-mounted security camera. Not for the first time, he'd forgotten it was there.

His next-door neighbor Miriam (Joan called her Miri-him, which Miriam, who was trans, found hysterical), a security consultant, had somehow snowed Liam and some other neighbors into chipping in for a collective home-security "net."

"Like a mutual defense pact," she pitched it. "Everybody's invested."

Miriam, who went by M, hosted an open house for neighbors at which she screened a slick presentation featuring local news coverage of El Camino and Nextdoor posts decrying the rise in porch piracy and vandalism. A cutting-edge hologram guided them through her AI system's 24-7 monitoring of her clients' digs, including sensors that could distinguish between the sound of a breaking window and a breaking plate.

M passed around and touted a trove of wireless indoor and outdoor cams and sensors; all of them issued piercing sirens and communicated autonomously with their owners' digital devices, as well as a flourishing private security firm owned and operated by some of M's retired associates.

Capping the production with a clamorous panic-button demo, M offered a 30-day trial with no obligation.

After signing a confidentiality agreement, participants received a steady stream of photos, videos, and texts concerning would-be thieves, B&Es, yard shitters, and other local miscreants. After bemoaning the cost and the loss of privacy when the trial expired, most of the participants eventually ponied up. The growing frequency of brownouts and internet crashes, not to mention the smoky air, had everyone on edge. The pandemic and rise in violent crime had decimated the Neighborhood Watch, whose existence, M opined, probably couldn't "do any harm."

Watching Liam fret all this, Joan had snarked feebly on her deathbed that paranoia was M's side hustle.

Thus far, the only image Liam's sec cam had captured of any real interest was of a leathery, racially indiscriminate non-dom, probably schizo. Grinning and singing maniacally, she hoisted layers of filthy fabric above her ass and hosed the sidewalk in front of his house with piss. Having finished her business, she resumed her foraging for redeemables with a rickety Dollar Store shopping cart.

Tears slid down Liam's stubbled cheeks as he turned his attention from the cam to stare at the coyote, its head thrown back and jaws agape in a silent, frozen yip. Two of a trio of spray-painted quail sculptures lay on their sides, legs poking out of the dirt.

Fuck!

Sweat from Liam's forehead mixed with his tears as he tugged open the back door, still sticky in its frame from the earthquake; a good fix was beyond his meager skills, and such skills were in short supply in the wake of the "Big One." In the kitchen, Liam handcrafted a fruit smoothie, dropping in half the blueberries, strawberries, blackberries, and kiwis to which he was accustomed; between the years-long drought and the critical farm worker shortage, the prices had tripled in the past few weeks.

He could easily afford them but denied himself out of a sense of solidarity.

I'm full of shit…

Breakfast in hand and AC humming, he planted himself at his dining room table, laptop before him.

"Access security video," he said while wiping his face with a napkin. He swept aside a jumble of papers with his free hand.

What kind of lunatic would have walked off with Joan's ashes?

Roused from his nap, Vonnegut lazily raised his orange tabby head. Abandoning his window-side rattan perch, he hopped up into Liam's lap, headbutting him.

"Somebody stole Mommy," Liam cooed, scratching the cat's ears. "Can you believe this shit?"

He fought off more tears. "Play," he muttered at the video that appeared on his screen. The time stamp read 05:21 07-17-28. About two hours earlier.

Tired of fast-forwarding, he muttered, "Search motion."

He pumped his fist as a big raccoon lurched into view. Liam held his breath as the ring-tailed culprit sniffed and pawed briefly at the crock before moving on to more alluring scents.

It occurred to him that he'd missed the alert because he'd fallen asleep listening to an audiobook about coping with grief. M had offered to provide microchips that triggered a pulse pattern in the recipient's brain in such circumstances.

She had no takers that he knew of—*yet*.

"Next motion," he ordered. Liam stiffened, wide-eyed, as the feed lurched to a figure skulking into the scorched garden.

The intruder wore a baggy black hoodie drawn tight around his face, black sweatpants and sandals, and, to Liam's surprise, what looked like a high-end NVG. The back of the hoodie bore a tattered logo. He (or she) glanced furtively to the left and right, shot a bird at the camera, and circled the pedestal and its burden appraisingly. Picking up and hefting it, he lifted the lid with one hand while cradling the vessel against his chest with the other.

He peered inside.

Poking his index finger into the vessel, he withdrew it quickly and held it up to his face. After thrusting the finger skyward for a moment, as if in offering, the thief replaced the lid and strolled out of camera range carrying Joan's ashes.

Night vision goggles! What the fuck!

On the chance a neighbor might notice something telling, Liam uploaded the footage to the Nextdoor website, captioning it with what little he knew. He included a good photo of the urn, the centerpiece of his makeshift mantlepiece shrine to his genius, departed spouse.

Ending his absence from the site since Joan's cancer diagnosis, Liam found himself scrolling through page after page of grievances and video footage ranging from shootings to surly panhandlers to public indecency.

Anarchists and Ludds, or Neo-Luddites, were blamed for random tire slashings and other assaults on self-driving wheels, or AVs, in particular, that were trickling into higher-end neighborhoods.

Some of the hooliganism, Liam noted, was blamed on displaced Idunnoans and such who found themselves trapped by circumstance in "Bloregon," as PNS, Patriot News Service, had nicknamed the state. Liam couldn't decide whether the PNS talking heads snarked that Oregon was boring, or that Oregon blew, or blows, as it were, or both.

Youth Party posers considered it virtually obligatory to torch or toss acid on cars whose owners had sadly neglected to strip them of Idaho plates.

Portland's threadbare police department, depleted for years by vax mandates, aggressive scrutiny, and bad shootings, had recently announced it would respond in person only to reports of violent incidents involving at least two persons. Pols being pols, the authors provided little guidance on how to define "violent incidents," leaving it largely up to local law enforcement.

So much for calling "the man" regarding the theft of Joan's ashes…

Tearing himself away from his laptop screen, Liam downed his meds with the last swallow of his tepid coffee.

DAILY NEWS

BREAKING NEWS

The Patriot Congress unanimously passes a resolution supporting national "Stand Your Ground" legislation

CHAPTER
TWO

M stood in her driveway sporting a baggy, printed sundress and a dime-store sombrero. Vaping weed, she monitored the descent of an Amazon quad schlepping a microwave-sized carton to a white circle in her driveway. Humming quietly, the drone released its cargo on the pavement, rose a couple of stories into the air, and cruised southwest.

"Yo," she said as she extended her hand holding the vape.

Liam waved off M's offer of a hit.

M glared at the retreating device. "Fifteen minutes behind schedule," she griped. Walking over and kicking the carton as if it were a tire, she deftly slit it open with a key and removed a receipt.

"Bitch, bitch, bitch," Liam chided.

"Second time in three days," M retorted.

"More spook stuff?"

M, who actually loved talking "spook stuff," put a hushing, black-tipped index finger to her scarlet lips as if the departing drone might eavesdrop. She (*Merle*, at the time, named after the country music legend) was outed as trans while serving in Army intel in Texas and given a general discharge during the Trump years.

After toiling for years—ultimately successfully—to have her discharge upgraded, she found work as a contract security analyst for the NSA under Biden and began transitioning.

"Never mind that," Liam said. "Some non-dom asshole—*I'm assuming*—stole Joan's ashes early this morning."

"Stole her *ashes?*"

"Word."

"From your house?"

"From right there," he indicated the pedestal on the other side of the chain-link fence. "I moved 'em out here a couple of days ago."

"So she could fry in tropical Portland, Oregon?"

"They're *ashes.*"

"Right," M muttered, turning back to her Amazon receipt. "When?"

"Little after 5 a.m."

"Got the video?"

"Pirate in a hoodie," Liam said. "Night vision goggles. No face, obviously."

M side-eyed him, nodding her satisfaction. "Told you the security would pay off."

"Night vision goggles, huh…?" she mused after a pause.

"Uh-huh."

"Lot of that gear out there since the quake and break if you know where to look," M said. "Lots of people worried about looting and rioting."

"What looting and rioting?"

"The ones Patriot News cites from junk sources and passes off as reporting."

"Right. Anyway," Liam interjected, "the hoodie has some kind of logo I can't make out. Incidentally, my garden gnome dissed your redeye." He jerked his thumb toward the eaves.

"Dissed?"

Liam thrust out his middle finger.

"The *audacity*."

"I tried zooming," Liam noted. "Still too blurry."

"I got this," M uttered a cryptic command to her phone. "Come over here in the garage, out of the sun. We can see the holo better."

"Liam security footage, 7-17-28, with motion," she told the phone.

"Holo?" Liam mused as he trailed M into the dark, cramped, sweltering box. "Don't you have to access my thingamajig to do that?"

The raccoon flickered to life, faltered momentarily, and stabilized. M chuckled.

"Next motion," she ordered. "The app automatically enables access to the installer for troubleshooting purposes. Expedites everything. 10G stuff."

"Uh-huh…"

The intruder appeared.

"Sweet, huh?"

Liam watched the device and its owner warily. "So, you can access anything on my devices?"

"You're my bitch, sweetheart," M said with a grin. "Good thing we're so close."

Liam scowled.

"Not if it's encrypted," she added.

Liam said nothing.

"You're *such* a Luddite."

"Were I a Luddite, I would have slit my own throat a long time ago," Liam said. "I *really* need to get Joan's ashes back."

M patted his shoulder, "We're working on it." She slow-moed through the video.

They lingered over the remnants of the logo on the back of the hoodie.

"Looks like a circle, some kinda wheel," M noted.

"And scaly."

"Like a snake."

"The head's missing," Liam said.

"Ring any bells?"

"Reminds me a little of the snake on the 'Don't Tread on Me' symbol," Liam ventured.

"Yeah," M agreed. "What is it with snakes?"

"They speak with forked tongues."

"There's the AMA logo with the snake coiled around a staff, too," Liam said.

"This one's been showing up as graffiti on Roberta," M noted.

"That's where I've seen it!" Liam exclaimed. "There's a big plywood sign by a non-dom camp next to the I-5 ramp to Tubman Avenue. There's a picture of a snake swallowing its own tail."

"Right," M said. "I've seen that somewhere."

"Any idea what it means?"

"Something to do with rebirth," she said. "Or death."

"Or fertility," Liam ventured.

"Or all of 'em," M concluded. "Hmmm…"

"What the hell would anyone, let alone some curb hugger, want with someone's ashes?"

"Maybe they liked the crock?"

"Then why not dump out the ashes?" Liam considered. "He looked inside…"

"Dunno," M said. "Maybe he likes ashes. Maybe he's following orders?"

"Orders?" Liam said. "*Whose*?"

"The voices in his head?"

"You think those voices in his head sprang for those fancy-ass goggles?"

M scrutinized the device anew. "Could have stolen 'em."

"The plot thickens," Liam said.

M advanced the video frame by frame.

"And look at the way he looks up," Liam said, with an unconscious skyward glance. "Like he's looking toward Heaven."

"You believe in Heaven?"

"I believe it's a long haul," Liam said, "but the relevance escapes me."

"Mmm…"

"Like it's a gift from God," Liam said, still taken with the image.

They fell silent, watching the looping image.

"Save the file as 'Liam ashes theft,' and quit," M muttered. The holo vanished into the gloom.

M looked thoughtful for a moment. "You know that Ouro-something guy who runs El Camino preaches some mumbo jumbo about people's ashes."

Liam gazed at his neighbor with renewed interest.

"Or so I've heard," she qualified. "Calls 'em cremains."

"*Cremains*," Liam said. "That rings a bell. Ouro *who*, now?"

"El Camino Ouro asterisk," M told her phone.

"The name you're seeking is Ouroboros," the phone replied in a masculine British accent. "Ouroboros is spelled O-u-r-o-b-o-r-o-s. Ouroboros is—"

"Shut it."

The voice stopped.

"Ouroboros?" Liam pondered. "Sounds like a Star Trek alien or some Greek monster."

"Where have you *been*?" M retorted. "The one and only Ouroboros is a street preacher who stirred up an army of non-doms to occupy the school after the quake, toward the end of the last surge."

She glanced skyward at a couple of quads cruising in the distance. "Way into psilo therapy. Seems to be licensed and all. But he also talks some voodoo poppycock about people's cremains containing psychic energy or something.

"'It was all over the snooze and Nextdoor last spring."

"Well," Liam said pointedly, "I was preoccupied last spring."

"Right," M looked at the floor. "You had your shit show."

Liam had been too consumed with getting Joan through the last surge to keep up with the Nextdoor site; he'd been marginally aware, however, that the mayor and the school super had ceded control over, and responsibility for, the building and grounds to somebody who'd emerged as a voice for the legions of the city's homeless. Rumors spread that the leader had cut a deal with the city to digitally track his followers' movements.

"Anyway," M continued, "he managed to calm things down after, you probably remember, the cops shot two of his followers. One of 'em died on the spot."

"Hmmm…"

M absently thumbed through something on her phone. "Anyhoo, he showed up at the school toward the end of the last surge. Got the cops, useless as they were, to slink off in the wee hours."

"Some of that rings a bell," Liam said. "What about the psychic energy?"

"Ouroboros claims psilo therapy—"

"Shrooms," Liam uttered knowingly. "Joan tried that to deal with the cancer."

M waited expectantly, but Liam fell silent.

"Anyway, he says psilo will cure just about anything if experienced properly, in other words, under his close supervision. And sometimes he cuts the psilocybin with cremains," she said. "Ritualizes it somehow. Again, so I *hear*."

"Seriously?" Liam queried after a lengthy pause. "The psilo part, I get, but where the hell do they find cre—" his voice trailed off. Assuming M's scuttlebutt was sound, Liam realized Joan's ashes could be headed for the blood of a total stranger.

Liam accepted the offered vape hit this time as he considered it all. This Ouroboros guy was touting the benefits of ingesting a hallucinogenic mixed with human ashes. *Is it possible?*

"So, you think the guy who took those ashes is connected to Ouroboros."

"Given the evidence," M said, "that's my best guess."

Liam raised a hand in farewell. "Thanks for the help, dudette."

"Where you goin'?"

"To get those ashes back."

"You want company?"

"Not right now, thanks."

"Entonces vaya con Dios."

"Gracias!"

DAILY NEWS

BREAKING NEWS

SCOTUS delays decision on whether to hear Florida case banning interracial unions between trans partners.

CHAPTER
THREE

Vonnegut batted at Liam's hand with an orange paw as the cat dad scrutinized the pirated aerial Amazon footage of El Camino that M had sent him.

Visible from the air were hundreds of tents and other makeshift shelters. In one area, an apparatus moving on a track appeared to be pouring concrete into patterns resembling the walls of tiny buildings. In another, workers assembled prefabricated, shipping container-sized sheds.

The grounds occupied a few blocks, including a city park, now avoided by many resentful rezzies. Along the margins stretched a motley collection of junk cars, lean-tos, and storage sheds, which sheltered the unchipped and unvaxxed; they took what handouts were available from El Camino and sympathetic neighbors.

The tents were in reasonably orderly rows, with avenues between them leading to the school and the portable classrooms, most of whose roofs boasted solar arrays.

The throngs cleared a path for a threesome, rolling slowly through the grounds on what appeared to be Segways. flanking them was what appeared at a distance to be a pony.

The leader, whom Liam guessed was Ouroboros, stopped at intervals to chat with or instruct workers. Occasionally, Ouroboros appeared to chastise or harangue them, waving his fist around and pointing toward various points around the site.

The roofs of the main school buildings—the original, thirty-year-old footprint—hosted raised gardens with an accompanying tangle of hoses.

Scattered throughout the footage were odd, indistinct blurs he couldn't identify.

A team of workers appeared to be shoveling earth onto a huge mound of what he guessed was garbage. It resembled an anthill from the air.

Others sorted through a huge bin of what looked like recyclable materials, and still others tended a large garden.

What has this guy Ouroboros managed to pull together since the quake? And what might he be doing with Joan's ashes?

It was time to check out El Camino in person.

<u>DAILY NEWS</u>

BREAKING NEWS

Isolation from loved ones driving older Americans to join cults.

CHAPTER
FOUR

Clutching a liter of ice water, Liam, with Daisy tottering at his Teva'ed heels, navigated garbage, bagged and otherwise, as they set off down the rapidly warming sidewalk. Piles of unsolicited goods Amazon had donated to El Camino, and, in turn, Caminos had left for whoever wanted them, expanded the obstacle course.

Amazon began donating returns too costly to process in the wake of a shuttle crash at its Bezos Lunar Research Station—a disaster that killed several employees and guests. Jeff Bezos himself, who was visiting, was seriously wounded, according to unconfirmed reports. Conspiracists questioned whether he hadn't tried to fake his death, replacing himself with a clone in the public sphere. A special Space Force commission was investigating the lunar disaster, which Bezos, in turn, blamed on saboteurs from the rival Chinese base.

Cynics accused Bezos—assuming he was still alive—of using his loudly trumpeted largesse to rehab the company's reputation. An epic antitrust suit, and the scores of employees killed or maimed when the earthquake destroyed several warehouses, had ravaged the company's image.

In any event, Liam decided that the custom of residents placing unneeded goods—some of them new—on the sidewalk had gotten out of hand. A few kids scrambled on, jumped off, and fashioned forts from the abandoned merch and refuse.

What wasn't carried off spilled into the streets, where passing cars tossed, crushed, and scattered it further. Scavengers had staked out territory at busy intersections to peddle goods for whatever they could squeeze out of passing drivers and pedestrians, many of them tourists; such soft touches may not have cared or been aware that the same shit was available for the taking just a block or two away.

An AV 'piloted' by an earsplitting Ye holo rhyming behind its dummy wheel plied the street behind him, jouncing over potholes stubbornly undetectable to its tech. Turning to gawk, Liam laughed as the twenty-something passengers, whose detached, plush, swiveling back seats faced each other, grimaced at the jolts.

They flipped him off as their ride cruised by.

He and Daisy passed a partially fenced-off vacant lot where rezzies had taken to dumping earthquake debris: broken concrete, glass, and various fractured, buckled, and shattered building materials. Adding to it all was the regular garbage, which the besieged city was struggling to pick up monthly. Yellow police tape lay trampled on the ground.

Liam wrinkled his nose at the ambient stink of baking rot, which hadn't reached his block—*yet*. At least most of the non-doms now had the use of the school's restrooms.

Little boys and girls played among the rubble, broken

furniture, and filthy mattresses. One sat crying on the flat surface of a mini-fridge-sized concrete chunk, rubbing his bare foot. Seeing no red, Liam figured the kid was okay.

But where the fuck are their parents, or whoever is responsible for them? Are they El Camino kids? In this heat?

"You guys have water?" he called.

Three dark-skinned, dark-haired boys turned to look at Liam and nodded vacantly.

"Are you all right?" he called to the crying kid, who now stood like the others, staring at him. After glancing at the others, he nodded without expression.

Pint-sized zombies…

The amplified tootle of some type of flute met Liam's ears as he and Daisy hung the final left onto 19th Street toward the school. Drones hovered or flitted about overhead, apparently watching for —*what?*

An enticing aroma drifted to him from a bicycle-propelled food cart selling insect snacks. Ground Bounty, the sign read, boasting Chocicadas, TerBites, BBQ Chirps, Redantz, Cricketacos, and Bugburgers. From a card table, Caminos plucked paper cups containing samples that they readily popped in their mouths. Most passersby, as the law required, tossed the cups straight into a garbage can after hefting them for a glance at the contents. A flyer on the table stated that 20 percent of Ground Bounty's proceeds went directly to El Camino, adding that all the products were farmed and prepared locally.

Munching on some salty Chirps—*better than kale chips*—Liam pondered the odds that the discards got recycled into some other kind of snack.

A few feet away, smiling Caminos staffed another table dispensing El Camino T-shirts, baseball caps, and other souvenirs. Abutting them were sheer eye masks that they boasted would filter out particulates from the pervasive if not always clearly visible, smoke and ash.

Banners affixed to a six-foot cyclone fence surrounding the

grounds promoted local businesses that sponsored or supported various El Camino activities and programs.

Behind the fence rose the brick facade of what had been Martin Luther King, Jr. Elementary School, closed by the district six months earlier; structurally condemned in the wake of the Election Day Quake, the building rose three stories above the street in front of Liam.

An array of security cams worthy of a North Korean embassy clung to every location in sight where it made sense. *If you were paranoid, perchance.*

What compelled Ouroboros to such vigilance? And who paid for all this hardware?

The school's east exterior brick wall, facing the street, boasted an LED mural, the focal point of which was a slogan, in capital letters as tall as a man:

FREEDOM LIES HERE!

HERE LIES HOME!

Scrolling, Star Wars-style, off the top of the screen, the text gave way to idealized images of what Liam assumed were individual, smiling Caminos, some in groups of different ages and skin tones. It ended as an artful composite shot of the earlier photos, the subjects chorusing, "Freedom lies here! Here lies home!"

It reminded Liam of a giant holo next to a Dallas, Texas freeway he'd seen in another lifetime. Promoting a nearby super church, the image was of a beaming, pompadoured minister bumping fists with a smiling, bearded shepherd.

Jake Jones Presents Jesus, the sign had boasted.

"Jesus!"

Liam gaped at the painting, next to the slogan, of a coiled snake, about ten feet in diameter, swallowing its tail.

Men, women, and children with hand trucks shuttled cartons from the back of a pickup outside the receiving door to a loading dock at the far end of the wall. A man sporting I-Ware examined uncrated parts of what appeared to be a high-end power loader akin to the one made famous in *Aliens*.

A power loader in a homeless camp?

He recalled having read that Activelink/Panasonic proved eager for the goodwill engendered by funding fancy pilot tech projects at El Camino.

Some of the workers paused their efforts to stare blankly at Liam as he snapped photos with his phone. They continued staring robotically for a moment after he, noticing the attention, slipped the phone into his back pocket.

In the distance, past makeshift avenues snaking through yurts and tents of all descriptions, loomed the mountain of garbage he'd seen in the drone footage. About twenty-five feet high, it occupied roughly half an acre. Another LED billboard mounted at its foot conveyed animated kids frolicking on a huge playset on the crest of a grassy hill. That image bled into large, scrolling text explaining the project was the brainchild of Portland State University's noted urban planning department; grad students in the Homeless Studies Department were conducting a pilot project involving converting urban waste to biofuel and providing green space in the bargain.

Could a nutty, mushroom-addled street preacher really pull all this together?

Sheermasked laborers, a mix of White, Black, and Latino men, women, and children, presumably Caminos, muscled wheelbarrows heaped with donated soil up the slopes from a huge pile that lay near the fence. More laborers raked and smoothed the dumped dirt over the trash.

He'd read on Nextdoor that Ouroboros (with the blessing of the El Camino Commission, which he chaired) had ordered that the dear leader's Orwellian "Freedom Lies Here" assertion be blasted across the campus several times a day. Drones equipped with speakers ensured the broadcast reached everyone, including unhappy neighboring rezzies.

In response to a flood of complaints on Nextdoor, Ouro explained on his webcast that the curious broadcast was an indispensable component of his El Camino regime; that regime, he noted, was keeping the homeless legions off the city's busiest, most touristy sidewalks.

Liam's searching eyes settled upon a scrum of Sheermasked Caminos beneath a shady covered area near the fence; the group was parting ranks to clear a passage, as he'd seen captured in the drone footage.

The Stars and Stripes fluttered from poles affixed to the vehicles, along with other banners he couldn't make out. It appeared to Liam, whose view was obscured, that the leader was eerily floating through the air; his swarthy legs remained still as he advanced. Liam gawked when he realized, momentarily, that the man was astride a Onewheel.

On the rider's head rested a neon-red hard hat nestled atop a black durag that veiled the back of his neck.

So, the notorious Ouroboros is a hipster, OG wannabe.

The man's elevated perch lent the illusion of height, but Liam pegged him at around five-seven. He sported a navy mesh tank top straining against a broad chest that sloped into a paunch. On his nose perched a tinted, granny-framed EYERis. Liam thought he spied a receiver tucked inside Ouro's left ear. Tattoos of the freedom mantra and the circular snake jostled for real estate across his neck and sternum.

Close by his mouth, and integrated into his Sheermask, a water line snaked to a Hydrant Liam had noted was strapped to his back.

Similarly equipped and clad, save for the hard hat, Ouro's red-bereted deputies trailed him at a respectful distance, as if to emphasize that they were present more for crowd control than to ensure Ouro's personal safety. Flanking the threesome was a pony-sized Neapolitan mastiff, ropes of drool dangling from his maw.

Liam wondered why Ouro's deputies weren't entitled to hard hats. Not to mention everyone else near the school. The city, after all, had condemned the building post-quake.

But then again, why would they need them when Ouro insists the building is perfectly safe?

Liam had seen on Nextdoor a clip of Ouro presenting a video at a school district meeting that juxtaposed post-quake photos and footage showing cosmetic damage to the school's exteriors with those showing near ruins. With the blessing of the school board, Ouro ranted—with no real evidence—that the superintendent had deepfaked the images to maximize the appearance of destruction, thus justifying the board's decision to level it.

Ravenous, of course, to expose the freshest civic freak show, influencers and cable news hosts seized on the woke-versus-woke angle; juxtaposing ready-to-air, cherry-picked sound and video bites, they competed to render the players cartoonishly craven, petty, and corrupt.

A CNN Poll suggested the country was split down the middle over which footage was genuine; those who thought it wasn't said they assumed Ouroboros had faked it himself to throw off the city.

Whoever posted the video on Nextdoor included an apt, pithy caption: "UNREAL!"

Stunned by what they denounced as outrageous lies and deepfakes, the board chair cut off Ouro's microphone mid-sentence and had him removed from the meeting. The incident generated footage that looped endlessly for a couple of days on PNS, CNN, Metaverse, local stations, and, of course, Ouro's carefully curated webcast.

When the district released its engineers' dry, clinical footage and analysis a few days later, it ran once on the local news without a tease and vanished.

In an appearance on PNS's "Talking Patriots" segment, Ouro railed against the city's so-called propaganda.

"These haters will do anything to keep us from getting a step up here," he charged, noting that his own engineers had declared the building "seaworthy," as he put it.

"No question," the Patriot interviewer concluded with a sly grin, "there's something going on out there in Bloregon, friends…"

The segment wrapped with Ouro tootling the network's theme on his flute and, to his hosts' delight, crushing a potty-mouthed bobblehead of PNS host Jared Jeberische in his prosthetic hand, which he'd dubbed Nic (short for bionic).

Why were the red berets, who evoked the similarly red-bereted and unpaid Guardian Angels of yore, forced to get around on dorky, mall-cop Segways while Ouro held forth perched heroically on his Onewheel?

Ouro barked something in Spanish over the still looping, mystical flute air—*hell was up with that music?*—to two men still unloading the truck. They weren't in Camino tank tops and, in fact, were shirtless. They gave no sign of hearing him. Frowning for a moment, he turned and continued on his way to where Llam and Daisy lingered.

The two men locked eyes as Ouro guided his flashy little ride close to the fence. Somehow, he balanced himself stock-still on the device.

How does he do that?

Swiveling smartly in concert on their Segways, his deputies backed up to within a few feet of Ouro, facing the milling, tank-topped denizens mere feet away. Their right hands rested lightly on what appeared to be holstered Tasers.

Tasers!

DAILY **N**EWS

BREAKING NEWS

Neighboring metros overwhelmed by refugees flooding in from the submerged city of New Orleans. #New'tlantis

CHAPTER
FIVE

"Welcome to El Camino, friend!" Sweeping off his hard hat with his shiny bionic hand, Ouroboros swiped the back of the other across his brow and beamed at Daisy.

The mastiff by his side watched them neutrally.

"Warm this morning, init?"

Init?

"So, what else is new?" Liam replied.

Ouro tilted his head as if viewing a curious object, "Have we met, friend?"

Friend?

A mellifluous FM radio voice.

"I reckon not."

"Ah," Ouro considered Liam appraisingly. "Well, it's felicitous that you flagged me down."

Flagged him down?

"I fear my production duties are intruding on my managerial obligations."

"Production duties?"

"Freedom Lies Here."

Liam shook his head ponderously.

"Freedom Lies Here," Ouro explained, "is my webcast."

"Right…"

Ouro appeared dubious. "What shall I call you, friend?"

"Vitali."

"Liam, it shall be, friend."

"I said, *Vitali*." Searching the surrounding faces for signs of corroboration, Liam found only more vacant stares.

"My sources are impeccable, Liam," Ouro said with a dry smile before muttering something under his breath.

"Impressive," Liam replied, as he might comment on a conjurer's antics. Splaying his hands on his hips, he tilted his head. "So, how are we friends if we've never met, Mr.… Ouroboros?"

"All," Ouro said, a dramatic sweep of his arms taking in the eerily quiet gathering, "are my friends."

"So, all your friends are homeless?"

Ouro's plump lips curved into an ironic smile. "I see you're enamored of wordplay. A worthy pursuit, indeed."

"I try."

"These homeless friends, or non-doms, as some demean them, *have* a home—*here*!"

"El Camino."

"El Camino, indeed," he replied. "For as long as they need it."

"Long as they're vaxxed."

"Indeed, friend, as long as they're vaxxed," Ouro said. "I think that's little enough to request of someone who wants what I, and of course, El Camino, have to offer."

"What *do* you have to offer?" Liam ventured.

"The best way to get acquainted with me, Liam—and El Camino, of course—given my present time constraints, is to watch *Freedom Lies Here*.

"Agree, or otherwise, with my methods," he added, "I have no secrets."

"God forbid…"

Quads jostled like paparazzi for sightlines overhead. Some of them bore the CNN logo, others PNS, others appeared generic.

Where the hell do all the pictures and sounds go? Is my face being pixelated out somehow? What about waivers?

Ouro's gaze followed Liam's to the attentive drones. "You see, these 'spies,' as it diverts me to call them, track me day and night," Ouro explained. "Patriot News is shooting a segment about us."

"Us?"

"El Camino. And CNN is keeping an eye on us *and* the Patriot crew."

"A reality show," Liam ventured.

"A show within a show of a sort," Ouro agreed. "It certainly wasn't my idea, but it brings needed attention to this neglected minority of temporarily unhoused. Submitting to constant monitoring is challenging, but given the benefits that accrue to my friends here, I believe it's the least I can do."

"My wife always said I do the least I can do," Liam shared.

"It appears we're on the same page," Ouro offered, thrusting out his arms inclusively.

"I thought as much," he added. "Excellent."

Liam considered asking Ouro if all this surveillance was legal, consensual, or otherwise, but tacked instead.

"So, what's a non-dom, anyway, *friend*?" he inquired instead.

"Surely you're well aware, Liam, that it's shorthand for non-domiciled, a demographic euphemism for the homeless," the leader explained with a thin smile, "that, of course, was co-opted.

"I suppose it's easier, cleaner, and meaner to simply call them non-doms."

"Which rhymes with—"

"Condoms," Ouro acknowledged with another fake smile and a shrug. "Props, Liam, for your lexicographical insight. Reprehensible it is how the American tongue, one of humankind's greatest achievements—a million words and counting thanks to those motivated to migrate to our shores—is violated merely to cast aspersions and divert the undeserving."

He sipped from his water line. "I trust you're staying hydrated in this challenging climate." Ouro nodded his apparent approval as Liam waggled his water bottle. "So, surely you didn't brave this heat just to sample the Chirps, my friend, delectable as they are," Ouro ventured. "What business brings you to our humble, if proud, collective this morning?"

"Not sure it's business, per se," Liam replied. "My wife died of cancer just before the quake, and I lost track of what was going on in the 'hood' while I was caring for her."

Ouro nodded with a solemn expression, as though sadly familiar with this information.

"El Camino being famous now," Liam continued, "I thought I'd pay a visit."

"My heart aches for you, brother." Ouro, who sported a purple soul patch, stripped off his EYERis with a flourish and swiped at his dark eyes and mocha cheeks. He took a moment to compose himself.

"Joan, her name was?" He reseated the high-tech spectacles with care.

Liam nodded pensively, wondering what Ouro was tracking with the AI specs even as he messed with his visitor.

"Your channel suffices to enlighten me that she was an extraordinary soul, now at peace in the expanse."

"Not to differ with you, but my *what*?"

"Your channel, Liam," Ouro explained. "It's like an aura, for lack of a better word."

"My *aura*?"

"Honing the ability to seek out channels of the people we encounter is an essential element in my psilocybin therapy."

"Right." His reporter's instincts told Liam bluntly that straight-up asking this verbose, psilo-addled con what, if anything, he knew anything about Joan's ashes would be akin to sparring with a handful of smoke.

Seductive as the circumstantial evidence—the Ouroboros symbol on the perp's sweatshirt and the El Camino mural, along with the rumors about human ashes—might be, he had no *proof* that Joan was there.

"If you'll bear with me asking, Liam, where do you suppose your beloved life partner is?" Ouro queried with a kind smile.

"In a good place, I presume."

Ouroboros's curious appearance and demeanor stymied any meaningful estimate of his age or ethnicity. He was fit enough and, judging from his facility with his transport, extraordinarily agile for any stage of life. Penetrating, deep-set blue eyes set in an olive complexion only enhanced the mystique.

Ouro pulled a treat from his pocket and held it up to the fence to entice Daisy.

"Here, baby," he cooed. He glanced at Liam as if seeking his assent for the dog treat. Liam nodded. Daisy toddled over uncertainly, sniffed Ouro's hand, and finally gobbled the treat.

The great mastiff lay on his side, panting in a bit of shade cast by Ouro's mute attendants. A little girl appeared with a bowl of water that she set down before him; she beamed as he lapped at it eagerly until a woman's stern headshake banished the smile.

"Good girl, Daisy!" Ouro scratched the beagle's nose through the fence.

Liam's eyes widened. "How do you know her name?"

Ouro smiled sadly. "The *world* must be known before it can be changed, Liam."

"That's not an answer."

As if unhearing, Ouro placed his hard hat back on his crown with a performer's grace.

"Well, I'm about my morning rounds," Ouroboros said. "Freedom calls."

"Freedom?"

"Lies here. Google it!" Ouro joshed, gesturing toward the mural. Swiveling nimbly on his precarious ride, he rolled off in the direction of the mountain, his red berets falling in line behind him. The convened Caminos dispersed robotically back to their toil.

Liam failed to grok how dispensing prosaic mumbo jumbo while spinning around on a Onewheel nourished freedom.

"Ouro?" he cried. "A word about cremains?"

Ouro's receding bean might have twitched. Stopping, he craned his head around to meet Liam's eyes, his own inscrutable. "Sweet dreams, friend."

Sweet dreams?

As if on cue, Ouro and those near him suddenly chanted, "Freedom lies here. Here lies home."

Amplified by means Liam couldn't detect, the mantra suddenly boomed across the sprawling grounds, accompanied by an eerie, echoing chorus of Caminos. Holos of Ouroboros appeared at intervals across the campus, echoing the words.

Beckoning to his deputies, Ouro zigzagged his way through the milling workforce and out of Liam's sight.

DAILY NEWS

BREAKING NEWS

The governor of Texas signs into law a bill banning homelessness and any references to it in primary schools.

CHAPTER
SIX

Tate Truman pulled his exterminator van ahead of Liam and Daisy as they traipsed back up the hill from El Camino in the heat. A small Stars 'n Bars fluttered from either side of the windshield. Rolling down his window, Tate poked his broad, beady-eyed mug out into the heat. A Sheermask dangled by a strap from his rearview mirror, and what looked like night vision goggles hung from the passenger-side hand grip.

Night vision goggles!? Nahhh, Tate is way shorter and stockier than the perp in the video. And what would he want with cremains?

Strident voices issuing from Tate's dash screen sparred about Idunno sheriffs under fire for auctioning off confiscated firearms—

no registration required—to help address a shortfall in public safety funds.

"You been down in brown town?" Tate inquired pointedly.

Tugged firmly over Tate's close-cropped scalp was a red gimme cap exclaiming, "Kill 'Em All, And Let God Sort 'Em Out!" Curled up on the passenger seat was Tate's brindle pitbull, Ranger, whose muscular rear end partially obscured the butt of a handgun. A small quad lay on the back seat.

"You asking me or tellin' me?" Liam replied drily. He savored the rush of cold air from the cab against his sweaty face. "I saw you roll by while I was taking pictures.

"Are you stalking me?"

"Ha, ha." Tate spat in the street, triggering a twitch from the white rat perched on his shoulder.

"I don't sneak around," Tate retorted. He muted the raucous audio.

"I'm exercising my rights, is all," Tate said. "You know they started a needle exchange program, for fuck's sake!"

"More power to 'em," Liam replied.

Tate was aghast. "It's a school, for chrissake!"

"It *was* a school, Tate," Liam noted.

"It's still a school," Tate insisted. "They just changed the name."

Liam ignored Tate's point of fact. "You want addicts Oding for want of a clean needle? Haven't the quake and the pandemics killed enough people?"

"Fuck the quake and the so-called pandemics," Tate replied with an extended, twitchy middle finger. "They're just excuses for the city to roll out the red carpet for druggies until *we* give up and leave. *Then* guess who takes over?"

Liam pursed his lips.

"Ever think about that?" Turning his gaze to Daisy, Tate tossed the beagle a treat. "'S'up, girlfriend?"

Liam rubbed his chin thoughtfully through his Sheermask before finally stripping it off.

"Dunno," he said. "This guy Ouroboros has 'em slaving away on all kinds of shit."

"*Ourobozo?*" Parroting a Nextdoor influencer's moniker for Ouro, Tate spat again. "He's a commie and a druggie. He even *calls* the place a commune."

"Collective," Liam said, although he might easily have missed the usage of the commune label.

"He's a *fuckin' commie!*" Tate ranted. "He hands out free drugs!"

"You mean mushrooms?"

"Hell yeah, I mean mushrooms!"

"Tate," Liam replied gamely. "They're *legal*—"

"Free eats!" he squawked. "Free cribs! You want that in *your* neighborhood? You want *bug eaters* in your backyard?"

Liam laughed.

"I'm serious," Tate declared. "Idaho's not down with this shit. You know, they actually help people arm themselves."

Liam rolled his eyes.

"You want residents to shoot curb huggers now, now that they piss and shit in the school … in the commune bathrooms instead of in your yard?" he countered. "That makes no sense, Tate."

Daisy whined and tugged at her leash.

"Nobody knows *what's* goin' on in that school since that con took it over," Tate continued. "And now my taxes—*our taxes*," he qualified with a nod to Liam, "are paying for an army of losers who can't pull 'emselves out of the gutter. They won't work. They've turned this place into a shithole! How much is *your* house worth these days?" Tate concluded with a scowl.

"Happy trails," Liam replied, raising his hand in a feeble farewell. Nodding toward the weapon in the passenger seat. "That thing loaded?"

"Always!"

"Don't shoot anyone I wouldn't shoot."

Chuckling, Tate flipped off Liam and sped off down the street.

Florida senator slams proposed resolution condemning urban vigilantism.

CHAPTER
SEVEN

Sweaty from his round trip to El Camino, Liam dumped a bin of ice cubes in a stainless-steel pot of cold water he placed on the kitchen floor. Daisy and Vonnegut sprawled on the cool tiled surface, panting as the ceiling fan stirred the air.

Clutching his water bottle, he resumed his investigation.

"Nextdoor, Liam ashes theft post," he prompted his aging Lenovo.

In response to the video he'd posted earlier, there, sure as shit, was the villain: Darth Vader, flowing black cape and all, a barely visible Sheermask stretched over his respirator. Next was Donald Trump, risen from the (allegedly) dead and still replete in a blue suit, red cartoon tie, and antique MAGA hat. Vladimir Putin, the Grim Reaper (*why would he be collecting ashes?*), Loki, The Joker, and last, but not least, disgraced Texas Sen. Ted Cruz, in a prison jumpsuit, brought up the rear.

So much for the crowd-sleuthing idea.

He chuckled despite himself at the inane imagery and the fact that people had taken the time to create it. On the other hand, a clever fourth grader could conjure credible fakes with the latest apps; some of the deepfake porn he'd viewed actually looked like it could have been shot by a little kid, *God forbid.*

Still, he was dismayed at the utter obliviousness of or disrespect for the emotional gravity behind his plea for help.

It was someone's—a neighbor's in this case—ashes, for Christ's sake.

He scrolled through more coverage and video of the neighborhood, particularly around El Camino. When brownouts hampered his laptop efforts, he turned to his phone. He was going to learn as much as possible about Ouroboros and his weird-ass homeless cult before starting to figure out how to retrieve Joan's ashes.

The school district, Liam was reminded as he read, had targeted what had been Martin Luther King, Jr. Elementary for closure during the first Covid pandemic, citing plunging enrollment in an aging facility. The board had just transferred the iconic name to a new school in a whiter neighborhood—much to the dismay of many residents—when the Election Day Quake knocked scores of schools and medical facilities offline. Structural engineers eventually declared MLK a total loss and urged the school district to condemn it and the neighboring Cesar Chavez Middle School, erected around the same time.

The temblor left a few houses sitting askew on their foundations. The city condemned such residences, leaving families to find other housing if they could. Financial help from the remnants of FEMA's post-quake ops remained a forlorn hope. If they were indigent and squatted in their own shaken, if marginally habitable homes, they could find support from El Camino in exchange for labor and hosting non-doms.

Ouroboros raucously prayed and advocated for the homeless at city and school board meetings; he accused both bodies of lying about the schools' conditions.

"Freedom Lies Here, Ouroboros," Liam cued the laptop.

The first webcast to appear opened with Ouro playing some kind of indigenous music on his flute, which appeared to be fashioned from a bone. Following that came a report on vaxx street clinics, a slick Sheermask infomercial, and man-in-the-street-style interviews with colorful non-doms conducted by an attractive, polished young redhead, Sheermasked, of course. Ouroboros, Liam noted, had a penchant not merely for lurking around but often chiming in during the interviews.

The ten-minute segment concluded with more flute tootling.

"Freedom Lies Here, Ouro, after Election Day Quake," Liam uttered.

This one opened with a clip of Ouro ranting at a school board meeting that MLK Elementary was fully functional. A skateboard slung across his back and dreads undulating beneath his bulging rasta cap, Ouro lectured his audience that the schools had been extensively and *expensively* retrofitted to weather an earthquake only five years before.

"I have in my hand incontrovertible proof," he thundered, brandishing a fistful of papers at his dour listeners, "a smoking gun, if you will, that the superintendent and the mayor forced, commanded, and conspired with these so-called engineers to condemn this edifice. It's obvious they're trying to keep us, the persecuted, the citizens, many undomiciled by the earthquake, from sheltering in the building. They are violating our constitutional right to decent housing.

"*This is bullshit!*" the leader exclaimed.

Liam shook his head.

The leader's charges, whatever their merit, found traction on local talk radio. Members of Ouro's suddenly swelling flock began pushing shopping carts crammed with their belongings down the middle of busy Martin Luther King, Jr. Boulevard at rush hour.

"He just sayin' what a lot of homeless folks are afraid to say," said a leathery, gray-haired, Black man pushing an ancient tricycle bearing garbage bags full of redeems. "'Cuz we don't want the city comin' down and sweeping us away like trash. At least those white nationalist motherfuckers left for Idunno."

"Amen!" chimed in a nearby woman, pulling a wagon bearing food bags and a listless, morbidly obese French bulldog.

Outnumbered and leery of violent confrontations, the Police Bureau brass opted to look the other way as long as no one got seriously hurt.

The parades led to the school grounds, the far-flung athletic fields of which already hosted a cluster of tents, tarps, and derelict vehicles. The encampment quickly expanded along the campus's fenced margins. Aroused curb campers marched and biked in protest around the neighborhood.

Liam recalled the cacophony of chanting marchers, blaring air horns, car horns, and brass instruments. Akin to the BLM marches of years earlier, they choked the streets as he and Joan, helpless as an infant in her living room hospital bed, sought precious sleep.

Ouro appeared on another webcast playing his primitive instrument as, coasting on his one wheel, he led such a procession like the proverbial Pied Piper.

Neighborhood merchants who had weathered the pandemic, the quake, and the wildfire smoke tried with little success to immunize themselves against broken windows and graffiti by posting Freedom Lies Here signs in their unbroken windows. The procession's unsolicited antifa escorts spray-painted security cam lenses as they marched.

Local TV news crews launched a fleet of drones to capture the story, literally, from every angle. Ouroboros, meanwhile, demanded on Nextdoor and his webcast that the school be handed over to his ragtag minions. He thundered that he had evidence the city was overstating the quake damage to keep out the non-doms; he cited a poll, whose origins he neglected to mention, suggesting that 87 percent of their swelling ranks agreed.

The city, of course, was eviscerated on the cable shows, many of which featured, if not teased, sound bites of Ouro's colorful diatribes. Even more irresistible to the talking heads was his side hustle as a psilocybin therapist.

"Tell me about your best-ever hallucination in the thirty seconds we have left!" a PNS interviewer demanded.

"Uhh…"

"Any past lives?"

Past lives?

"Well, there was Charlemagne," Ouro deadpanned.

"Charlamagne Tha God of The Breakfast Club!" the host exclaimed with glee. "Got shot, didn't he? *Luuvvv* it!"

A holo of the deejay rhyming appeared beside him.

Wrong Charlemagne, moron.

"Didn't know he'd passed," the host mused.

He didn't.

Ouro had smirked.

A week-long armed standoff between a thin blue perimeter of cops and an army of non-doms ended when a patrolman working his third double in four nights emptied his Glock into two occupiers, killing one and paralyzing the second. CNN, PNS, Russia Today, Metaversity, the *New York Times*, and other mega-platforms parachuted in their own drones and virtual talking heads to usurp the coverage.

Peeved and outgunned, the local stations stalked crusading, news-bombing celebs and their avatars and mocked the cable kahunas' butchering of local names.

"It's the WilAMmette River, NOT the WILLamette!"

Families of the shooting victims sued the city over civil rights violations and, while they were at it, demanded more cuts in police funding. A sneering Patriot Vice President Tom Cotton called for "sending in the troops," during a "Talking Patriots!" segment on Patriot News.

Unfucking believable.

Tearing himself away from the ever-widening rabbit hole into which he'd plunged, Liam did some sloppy asanas on the carpet. He teased Vonnegut with a toy and caressed Daisy's ears as she snored contentedly beside him.

Rising, he stood before the mantelpiece, ran his fingertips across the photos of Joan he'd placed there, sobbed, then reread, for the umpteenth time, the document she'd downloaded from Satirev. The cedar keepsake box in which she'd stored it flanked the space where he'd placed the urn.

His desperation for some agency in Joan's final hours had driven him to rifle through her drawers for anything that might comfort her, if only infinitesimally. When he found the box she'd harbored among other treasures on a bedside table, he'd fumbled it, spilling out a heavily creased page of text.

Curious, he'd been astonished to glean from a glance the gist of an abstract of a Senate investigation into a secret CIA Op, the so-called Project EXTRACT. The program had culled children aged six to ten from around the country who had scored off the charts on certain indicators for high potential for introversion, servility, and "intuition."

Intuition was a euphemism for extra-sensory perception—telepathy, in particular.

Overcoming grave reservations, he'd asked her why she'd kept it from him.

"Why didn't you tell me about this?"

"I barely looked at it," she said, closing her eyes after a weary glance. "I put it away to read later, and I got sick and forgot about it."

As certain as he was that it was bullshit, pressing her on it was out of the question. Speaking had become a trial for her. She'd tried to protect him from his own prospective recriminations, given his dismissive treatment of the nightmares she'd shared of injections, examinations, interrogations, and isolation.

"Read it to me now," she whispered.

He met her exhausted gaze.

"You sure?"

She nodded wearily.

"Okay."

At a low-profile Senate Intelligence Committee hearing decades after the project's abrupt termination, CIA chemist and behaviorist Joseph McCarrihy took the fifth concerning whether the young test subjects had ever been administered mind-altering drugs with the intent of enhancing their evident extra-sensory perception. As the families had been compensated at the time and waived any rights to future legal action, none of the participants were invited to testify and learned of the hearing only afterward.

Citing Cold War fears that the KGB was conducting its own paranormal youth experiments, McCarrihy protested he was being scapegoated. In his seventies at the time of the hearings, he'd shot himself in the head a few weeks after the report was quietly released and then buried, a circumstance, Liam conjectured, that probably prompted the leak.

When Project EXTRACT was quietly terminated, the children were returned to their families, per the agreement, after being subjected to unlimited cognitive testing. McCarrihy's agents hectored parents and children to sign nondisclosure agreements, ensuring they never spoke about their time in the program.

Among the twenty children who made the final cut, some of whose families changed their names, three had ended their own lives in the ensuing years, and a few others had died under indeterminate circumstances.

Evidently, someone had wanted him held to account, if only posthumously.

Liam was compelled at times to wrest Joan awake when she was screaming about being spied on, monitored, stalked, but he'd never taken the dreams seriously, apart from half listening to her detailed recounting. Given her profoundly weird upbringing, he thought it normal she'd have weird, awful dreams, just as he had.

Such accounts made him feel powerless.

Ferreting a magnifying glass from a drawer, he inspected the black-and-white headshot of McCarrihy that accompanied the text. Something about it held his eyes for a moment, but he was too weary to pursue the thread.

DAILY NEWS

BREAKING NEWS

Majority of Americans believe they live in a 'surveillance state'.

After they stripped and had sex in the dark on the grassy shore of Lake Ray Hubbard, Joan removed the engagement ring Liam had slipped onto her finger as he proposed to her and handed it back to him.

"It's a little too big," she said with a smile, wiggling it to show him. "I don't want it slipping off when I'm swimming.

"I'll take it to a jeweler this week."

Moonlight washing her spectral flesh, she waded into the still tepid water. Splashing herself and giggling, she gingerly immersed herself up to her neck in the moon-speckled surface and dog-paddled away from the shore.

"Be careful," Liam called.

He thought he heard her laugh.

She disappeared from view as a cloud obscured the shimmering moonlight. He felt a chill.

"Joan! Sweetheart!" he called. "You're out too far. Come back!"

"Where do you suppose Joan is?" came a voice from behind him.

Liam froze.

"What the fuck are you doing here?" he finally managed. "You *can't* be here!"

"I'm here, there, and everywhere, Liam," said Ouroboros. "Like the Beatles. Joan is journeying to the expanse, where pain and sorrow are mere ephemera. She's transcending…"

"*Fuck you!*" Liam screamed, waking himself with a jolt as he writhed in his sweat-soaked sheets. "*Jesus!*"

Traipsing downstairs with Vonnegut after he collected himself, he poured himself coffee, did some stretching, and grimly returned to his research.

Citing extensive quake damage elsewhere, the city had finally yanked the handful of cops at El Camino under cover of night, drones shooting infrared footage notwithstanding. A profane farewell between Caminos, including Ouroboros, and the departing cops led local newscasts. Clips of the shootings' aftermath, including the maestro eulogizing his lost assets, looped endlessly on cable.

The mayor and the school superintendent announced at a presser the following day that the building, after all, was vacant and the homeless needed shelter. Eager to rid themselves of a massive headache, the school handed over the keys to the building in exchange for $1.

After bitching about the cost, Ouro paid up symbolically on behalf of El Camino for a photo op before taking a victory lap on the infotainment circuit.

"Drug doc schools Portland libs," read a PNS teaser.

DAILY NEWS

BREAKING NEWS

Support for psychotropic therapy mushrooms in Blue states.

Returning from his evening bike ride, Liam found M vaping and examining some VR gear on her front steps in the light from a headlamp. A soothing breeze tickled the cranberry-hued ponytail that tumbled down the front of her sundress. Scarlet toenails poked from her sandals.

Locking up his bike on the porch and collecting Daisy from the house, he strolled next door.

M's black cat, Sam, lay curled up in her lap. "Hey."

"Hey."

"So?"

"So what?"

"Did you see Dr. Feelgood?"

"I did," Liam replied. "Think he could hack Nextdoor?"

"Ouroboros?"

Liam nodded.

Guffawing, M glanced down at the beagle panting at their feet. "*Daisy* could hack Nextdoor."

The dog poked her head up expectantly at the sound of her name. M tossed her a treat from the bag she kept on the steps to greet friendly, bypassing pooches.

"Security's a joke on most noncommercial sites." She glanced up at him questioningly.

"I wonder how he might use it to fuck with people."

Liam was wary of betraying too much of his thinking. M was a handy tech wiz, but Liam was eager to plop himself down in front of his laptop and determine his next move on his own. M was, or had been, after all, some kind of espionage pro; she was cagey about what they got up to in her basement, which they called the office. Liam assumed it was related to her drone deliveries and security gigs.

He imagined a bank of computer screens and audio gear monitoring people and tracking global crypto rates.

"You know Tate?" M asked.

"Tate Truman?" Liam squelched his urge to flee at the mention. "Sawed-off Trumpie? Beady eyes? Exterminator? Gun nut?"

"That's him."

"Never met the guy," Liam said.

"Funny."

"As it happens, I ran into him coming back from the school yesterday."

M's eyes tracked another descending drone headed across the street this time. "You have all the luck," she said.

Following his companion's gaze, Liam wondered if the device was at least theoretically capable of picking up their conversation.

Who might be listening?

"His .38 rides shotgun when he patrols, you know," Liam said. "He's a frustrated vigilante."

"Surprised he didn't hightail it to Idunno before they slammed the door."

"He told me a while back that he wanted to," Liam recounted, "but his Filipino bride, Imelda, slammed that door shut. Said no way he was dragging her and her mother to live in patriot country."

M guffawed anew. "I hacked his Nextdoor account and posted a bunch of legit vax info on it under his name. I wrote, *as him*, that I'd finally seen the light," she continued, "and apologized for all the anti-vax garbage and racist, homophobic shit I'd posted earlier."

"What racist, homophobic shit?"

"Oh, I just made that up," she said. "Call it counterintelligence."

Liam chuckled. "That's brutal," he said. "You should be ashamed of yourself. And this after he just came back from a suspension."

"Yeah, and then he went apeshit and just quit the site," M noted with a satisfied grin. "After he posted a final rant about Caminos replacing rezzies."

"The great replacement theory?"

"Which, of course, was the point of the fake apology."

"Ah," Liam said, taking a sip of water.

"Anyway, why would Ouro waste his time on Nextdoor?" M asked. "He's all over Instagram and TikTok and he has his own webcast. He's even showing up on Patriot News now."

Liam nodded. "Apparently, they're shooting a doc about him," he said, "which he took pains to assure me wasn't his idea."

"Course not."

"I watched a few of his webcasts last night. He really works the camera."

"The novelty wears off fast," M opined. "He plays his weird flute, describes his 'sacred' visions, does vaxx updates, and interviews his friends."

"Friends?"

"Caminos," she said, "who all sing his praises."

"Imagine…"

"El Camino would be a great subject for a sociology thesis," M said with a smirk. "Or maybe cultural anthropology."

Liam stared for a moment. "What'd you just say?"

"Cultural anthropology," she said, looking at him curiously. "You know, the—"

"Thanks," Liam muttered. "C'mon, Daisy. Gotta run."

DAILY NEWS

BREAKING NEWS

Portland State University becomes first in the nation to offer a degree in Homelessness Studies.

CHAPTER
TEN

"The world must be known before it can be changed," Liam recited from his steno pad. He shifted his solid weight uneasily on the plush green couch on which he perched in the office of his longtime therapist, Mariposa Gideon.

"Based on what you've learned about him," she inquired, "what do you think he means by that?"

"Seems to me," he considered, "the subtext is that psilocybin and its cousins along, allegedly, with a shot of cremains, will lead everyone under his guidance to enlightenment. And save the planet."

Neither spoke for a moment. Liam plucked a tissue from the

floral printed box on the table before him and wiped his glasses irritably.

"What a load of shit," he concluded, shaking his head.

Gideon laughed. "Can you elaborate on that?"

"For starters, his so-called 'slash therapy' seems to require monitoring people," he replied. "He knows my name, my wife's name," Liam muttered. "He *must* know where I live."

"And as such, where Joan lived."

"Right."

"Odds are—"

"For some reason, I half *expected* him to know my name," Liam said, shaking his head. "Never would have guessed he'd know my fucking dog's name."

She nodded sympathetically.

"Creepy," he declared. "And he probably stole or had someone steal the ashes to use in his weird-ass mission to create a master race or something."

"Sounds like Ouroboros is on his game," Gideon said, sipping her fragrant, steaming tea. Smiling, she added, "He told you himself that his sources are *impeccable*."

Liam grunted and leaned back on the sofa. "What else does he know about me?" he muttered. "For that matter, what does my neighbor, the spook, know about me?"

"What do you *think* they'd be interested in knowing about you?" she asked.

He shrugged vacantly.

"And Ouroboros?"

"He probably knows I was a journalist," Liam said. "Maybe he wants to ingratiate himself with me. He'd probably also want me to know he knows my background. But if he thinks I suspect him of having her ashes, he'd want to persuade me otherwise." He took a swig of water.

"Have you considered just asking him about the ashes outright?"

Meeting her questioning gaze, he leaned forward again.

"I *know* people," he declared, thrusting his right index finger toward the ceiling. "I *know* how they are. I spent thirty years talking to people and writing stories about them. I watched his pods and all the local news videos. I did my homework. This guy *lives* to fuck with people."

"Okay."

He nodded fervently as if reassuring himself.

"Other than that, they were... accessible," Gideon ventured. "What in particular might he think was special about your wife's ashes?"

"Oh, my god, like I've told you, she was a fucking genius," Liam exclaimed. "She was a champion debater, ace problem solver. Eidetic memory. A mathlete. She could recite Shakespeare flawlessly for twenty minutes at a time."

"Wow."

"Yeah," he said. "And, scarily, she read my mind, like I've told you, and many a lesser one, I imagine... that caused big problems. I've always obsessed about women and sex, and I watched porn, and she obviously was aware of all that. But I was never sure *how* aware."

"Uh-huh."

"And you'll recall that wild story I shared with you," he continued, "that she told me that as a little kid, she was a subject in what she later found out was a Cold War-era CIA program experimenting with kids they recruited who showed off-the-charts potential for extra-sensory perception.

"Given that she had a dissociative disorder," he continued, "I assumed, or hoped, maybe, that it was some kind of weird delusion."

Gideon nodded.

"I figured she had enough psychic and weird genius shit to contend with that she didn't need me interrogating her about some crazy paranormal conspiracy.

"And then I found that report I told you about that someone

sent her about a Senate investigation into just such a CIA program that had been killed."

Her eyes widened. "How would your friend Ouroboros know about all this?"

"If he had a little personal data and knew what he was doing, he could learn all that with a few keystrokes," he added. "Maybe he reads Satirev."

"So, it follows he'd covet her genius ashes for his, shall I say, unorthodox therapeutic methods?"

"If he can convince people who are tripping that they'll inherit the abilities of people whose ashes they swallow," Liam continued, "it seems like he'd be *very* interested in hers."

They fell silent for a moment before Liam's head snapped up.

"*That's* what he means," Liam said as if seized by an epiphany. "The deceased's talents are indispensable assets in human progress."

"The end justifies the means." she ventured.

"Something like that," he said. "So, he's on the lookout for potential assets."

"Interesting theory." Taking another sip, she languorously scratched the ears of her calico, Netty, curled up on a tower beside her.

Liam snapped his fingers at the feline, who stared at him.

"He probably has as much access to drone footage as anyone," Liam said. "For all I know, he has a dossier on the whole fucking neighborhood."

"Your neighbor or Ouroboros?"

"Either... both."

"Do you think you're getting paranoid, Liam?"

Liam rubbed his stubbled chin in silence.

"Do you think you're more upset about the theft itself," Gideon asked, "or the prospect of being spied on?"

"I'm upset," he replied through clenched teeth, "that I've fucked up my ability to carry out the one big thing my wife asked of me before she died."

"And what was that?"

"I promised to scatter her ashes at the place where I proposed to her," he said.

"How did you fuck that up?" Gideon absently swished the dregs in her mug and crossed her long legs, tugging the hem of her skirt over her knees.

"I left her outside," he said. "Where anybody could see her. *It.*"

"And why did you do that?"

"Why did I leave her outside?" he asked. "So, she could be in her garden. With her gladiolas. Her favorite flowers."

"You acted from your heart, Liam," she said.

Liam grunted.

"Did she ask you to place her outside when she died?"

"She asked me to scatter her ashes," Liam said, staring at the ceiling. "She shut down after she entered hospice. We really never broached the elephant in the room."

"That she was dying?"

Staring at his feet, he nodded.

"To protect you."

"To protect me," Liam nodded. "I tried to return the favor by being as matter-of-fact as I could about the whole fucking shit show."

"So, there was no closure..." she said.

He stared at the ceiling.

"How could you possibly guess that some person would notice the urn, let alone be invested enough, if you're correct," Gideon queried, "in some mystical belief about cremains to steal it?"

"That was a long-ass question," Liam noted.

She laughed.

He snapped his fingers again. After staring at him for a moment, Netty poured herself off her tower, sauntered over to the sofa, and sniffed at his proffered hand.

"Do you think it's possible?" he asked.

"What?"

"That consuming someone's ashes could somehow enable you

to assume their abilities?" he asked. "I can't stop thinking about somebody actually swallowing her ashes."

"I think a charismatic practitioner who actually believes that could certainly convince suggestible people that they're inheriting powers," she replied. "Certainly, if they're under the influence of psychotropics."

"Stoned."

She shrugged.

"The stoned ape-man."

She shrugged again.

"And people who join cults are kind of inherently suggestible?"

"People who join cults are generally searching for meaning."

"A reason to exist."

She nodded.

"By taking drugs?"

"That's one path," she said. "Remember, guided psilocybin therapy is aimed at helping people deal with trauma, PTSD, depression, and addiction."

Liam nodded his head irritably.

"Could he have ordered this guy to steal the ashes?" he asked as he petted the calico's silky coat. "Could he have known I put them out there?"

"You said he has drones flying all over the place," she said.

"Doesn't everybody?" he said. "I don't know why it didn't occur to me before now, but odds are there *is* footage somewhere of me putting the ashes out there."

"There may also be footage," Gideon noted, "of the funeral home people picking up Joan from your house."

Liam fell silent for a long moment.

"Are you okay?" she asked at length.

Nodding, Liam remained silent.

"Tell me what the ashes represent to you."

"They're the actual physical, tangible presence of her," he said after a moment. "I don't think of myself as sentimental, but a friend of mine told me after seeing my 'shrine'"—he made air quotes—"to my wife that I am. I have to keep that promise. That's why I have to get those ashes back."

"Understood."

"I'm flummoxed," he said. "I rejected long ago any notion that privacy still existed. But I was so focused on making my wife's last weeks as comfortable as possible that I completely lost track of what was going on in my neighborhood.

"Now it seems like everyone's spying on everyone else."

"Ever seen *The Lives of Others*?" Gideon asked.

"Don't think so."

"It's about the Stasi bugging and eavesdropping on ordinary citizens 24-7 in the old East Germany."

"Sounds like a riot," he said. "How does it end?"

"A woman who's being sexually blackmailed throws herself in front of a bus."

"*Nice.*"

"It's *very* human."

"And how does that help me?"

"You could review all the intel you have and maybe find a prospective, maybe disgruntled, inside man or woman to tell you more."

Liam stared.

An inside man!

DAILY NEWS

BREAKING NEWS

Texas governor declares Jan. 6 as Great Republic of Texas Patriots Day, a state holiday.

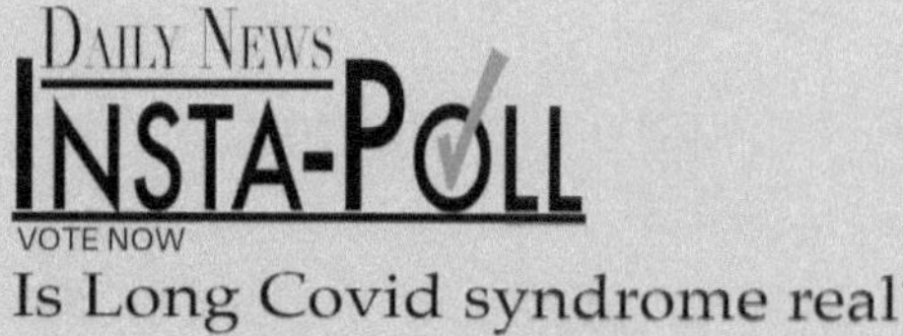

Liam and Daisy arrived at Roberta Park early the next morning. Jessie leaned heavily on her hickory walking stick and rubbed her temples as she lectured her Norwegian elkhound, Magnus, on the matter of not annoying her. They stood on the margin of the leash-free area, far above swayed a thick canopy of Douglas firs in the park's native flora patch, outer boughs browned from the heat.

"You're *late,*" Jessie snapped as Liam detached Daisy's leash. The pooches made straight for each other's butts, tails whipping in unison.

"Another migraine, Sis?" Liam queried sympathetically.

She grunted. "Don't change the subject."

"I thought I'd give you time to find a discreet place to liaise." Nodding approvingly, he added, "I'm down with the shade."

"They can't see us through the trees," Jessie said. She fished a matted green tennis ball from a tote with a latex-gloved hand.

"Who?"

"The drones."

"I don't see any drones."

"Exactly," she replied, wiping the ball with a towel. "I don't think they can hear us, either."

"I reiterate," he said. "I see no drones."

"Keep your voice down," she admonished without looking at him, putting a slim index finger to her thin lips. "I read they're experimenting with cloaking devices."

"They?"

"Those in positions to benefit from such a capability."

"*OMG!*"

"NFK," she replied.

With a downward stroke of her Chuckit, she snatched the ball off the ground and launched it feebly. The dogs flung themselves after the yellow orb, Magnus bounding ahead of the arthritic Daisy. A black lab pup joined the chase momentarily before yawing off.

"Honestly, you're so naïve," Jess lamented, rocking gently on her feet. "By the way, you didn't reiterate. You altered your original statement."

"Whatever," he said. "How's the plague?"

"Same shit, different day," she said. "Headaches, insomnia, joint pain, mental fog."

"You shouldn't have come," he said. "The smoke can't be good for you."

She grunted. "Magnus needs the exercise."

"How you feeling right *now*?"

"Comme ci, comme ça."

"I'm really sorry, Jess," Liam said. "You'd think they'd have it figured out by now."

"New strains keep coming," she said wearily. "Viruses truly are the gifts that keep on giving."

"Heard anything from Ellie?" Liam inquired.

"What's your plan to retrieve Joan's ashes?" Jess asked, ignoring his question as, sidling closer to him, she clasped his arm firmly. "I'm wounded, incidentally, that I had to hear about that on Nextdoor," she chided.

She stared at a black Newfoundland taking a huge shit nearby.

"Nothing for you to do," Liam replied, looking downward. "Anyway, I knew you'd see it when I posted it."

"Because I'm unemployed?" Jess stared as the Newfy's owner summoned the dog. "Because I have so much time on my hands?"

"Unemployed?"

"College is laying off half of the adjuncts," she replied. "Declining enrollment. Chat's writing the curriculum now. School is offering to pay laid-off staff peanuts to 'fine-tune' the output."

"Fine-tune?"

"Make sure the content passes the woke smell test."

"Wow."

"Where do you suppose *that's* headed?"

"Well," he said, "I told you I took a buyout after being advised my content was generating insufficient clicks."

"No, you didn't tell me that," she intoned.

Liam sighed. "Maybe not," he muttered.

"Definitely not," she insisted. "I would have remembered."

"Okay," he said. "Anyway, when did all this happen?"

"Hey, excuse me!" Jess cried to the Newfy's companion, a young man sporting threadbare harem pants, a wispy red beard, and a top knot above his shades.

He looked at her questioningly.

"You need to pick up after your dog, sir."

"It's none of your business, lady," the man replied, "but I'm following his therapist's instructions."

"So, your dog's therapist told you not to pick up his shit?"

"He's a rescue with dominance issues," the man replied.

"Picking up after him makes him think he's the alpha, which is a real issue."

"That's insane," Jess replied.

"Forget it, Sis," Liam muttered.

"Shut up, Liam," she snapped.

Pointing to Magnus, who was attempting to mount a protesting poodle, the sneering man said, "Looks like your rapist friend over there could use some couch time."

"*Rapist?*"

"Quit while you're behind, lady," the man said. "Gotta bounce. Hamilton!" The massive canine peed on a tree and trotted after his companion.

Jess scowled at the man's retreating figure. "Smug fucking hipster!"

Liam chuckled. "Is there any other kind?"

Jess rubbed her temples. "*Magnus!*" she barked. Startled, the dog turned and meandered toward them, and Daisy tailed him.

"They announced it last week."

"Announced what?" Liam asked. "Who?"

"The layoff," she snapped, rubbing her temple. "Try to keep up."

"Right," he replied. "Why didn't you tell me?"

"I knew you'd see it when I posted it," she said drily. "Nothing for you to do..."

Liam sighed anew.

"*Had* you contacted me," she said. "I could have told you that the picture on the back of his hoodie looks a lot like part of a mural they painted on the school."

"I saw that yesterday," Liam noted. "What do you know about El Camino?"

"Have you been there?" she asked. Pulling a vial from her pocket, she tapped out and swallowed a couple of pills, chasing them with a swig of water and a grimace. "A lot of peculiar shit occurred when you were occupied caring for Joan."

"Yeah, I've been reading about it."

Her almond-colored eyes closed, she rocked gently and nodded her approval.

"I actually met Ouroboros yesterday," he said.

"Ouroboros," she echoed, still rocking. "He has the city eating out of his hand. He could sell snow to an Eskimo."

"You mean Inuit."

"That doesn't rhyme with snow," she said. "And did you just call Eskimos 'nitwits?'"

Liam shook his head sadly.

"Ouroboros," she announced, "a.k.a. narcissist, sociopath, court jester, trust-fund baby."

"*Stoner*," Liam chimed in, "and don't forget accomplished Onewheeler."

"Onewheeler," she echoed, shaking her head. "A pathetic clown."

"I got that vibe from a five-minute chinwag with him," Liam said. He scooped up the drool-slicked ball Magnus dumped expectantly at their feet.

"He's a snake," she said.

"A *snake*, you say… like the snake in the mural."

"Yes, swallowing himself," she said. "*Full of himself*. That's Ouroboros."

"What do you mean, that's Ouroboros?"

"That's where he got the name, from the snake," she said. "It's an ancient symbol depicting a snake, or serpent, if you will, eating its own tail."

"What does it mean?"

"Researchers say it signifies infinity and the cycle of birth and death," she noted.

"Whoa…"

"Whoa, indeed," she said. "Ashes signify death, destruction— *obviously*. Powerful stuff." She shrugged.

"How do you know all this?"

Side-eyeing him, she said, "What I'll tell you is that it was astute of you, Liam, to not raise the subject of Joan's ashes when you met him."

"Uh, thanks." *Rare praise indeed from Jess.* "And how the hell did you know about that?"

"I'm a savant—remember?" she replied with a *Mona Lisa* smile.

Liam stared at his half-sister. "Why does everyone seem to know about everything I do?"

"You said yourself that privacy is obsolete," she said, feebly chucking the ball again. "I happen to know him."

"Know who?"

"*Ouroboros,*" she growled. "*Really,* Liam."

"You know Ouroboros?"

A woman cleaning up after her panting husky glanced in his direction.

"Actually, his name at the time was Ignatius Adler."

"Ignatius?"

"Made a point of mentioning that his mother named him after a wildly eccentric anti-hero character in—"

"*A Confederacy of Dunces.*"

"You read it then?"

"A hundred years ago," he replied. "You recommended it to me."

"I seem to recall that, yes."

"One of your better ones."

She smiled. "Glad to hear it."

"Anyway—" he prodded.

"He took my comparative religion and cultural anthro classes a while back." Scrolling absently on her phone, she continued. "Told me he was a rich brat searching for meaning and authenticity in his life. Supposedly he had an epiphany while he was tripping on psilocybin—*therapeutically,* of course. Said his granddad was a pioneer in psychotropics research."

"Really?"

"He also told me he served in the Peace Corps in a Guatemalan village, where he became acquainted with curanderas, women folk healers, who harvested and used psychedelic mushrooms in their healing and spiritual practices.

"In certain instances, they also ingested the cremated ashes—"

"Cremains!" he exclaimed, his eyes wide.

"If you like."

"Whoa."

Magnus and Daisy panted heavily in the shade by a water bowl.

Jess glared at two spry, unleashed dachshunds bounding from the back seat of an AV, followed by a young man launching a small drone among the trees.

"Asshole," she muttered, retreating to the other side of the tree.

"Yes, he's an asshole," Liam concurred urgently. "And you were saying…"

Her eyes still fixed on the intruder, Jess continued. "Because he helped them out with a new latrine and some repairs, they allowed him to partake in a psilocybin rite but refused him ashes. He was furious, thought they'd humiliated him."

"Surely the Peace Corps doesn't sanction that type of activity."

"He went AWOL, so to speak," she said, "and sought out more psychedelic experiences. Picked up the name Ouroboros from their tattoos. State Department tracked him down and keelhauled 'em back here."

"I'll be damned."

"No doubt," she joshed. "Are you familiar with the book *How to Change Your Mind*?"

"My therapist mentioned it."

"Read it," she directed. "It's all about therapy with psychotropics, such as for PTSD or anxiety disorders. Ignatius told me about a guided session in which he turned into a pair of scissors that cut out perfect little paper houses that stacked themselves up in little columns. He said a gust of wind scattered them into little diagonal rows, on the inside of each of which a two-dimensional family sprang to life.

"There was a lot more," she continued, "but you get the gist."

"Hardly…"

"He concluded from this vision, or channel, or whatever, that his destiny was to guide these unblemished paper families, if you will, to transcendence, perfect them in a way, via the sacrament of psilocybin and cremains."

Liam said nothing. And nothing after that as his mind raced.

"Are you still with me, Liam?" She tightened her hold on his arm.

"Cremains, again…" he said ponderously. "Unblemished paper families."

"Which are, of course," she said, "metaphors for the conventional, hopeless, nuclear family unit."

"I'm speechless."

"Good," she said. "Anyway, he got himself qualified as a therapist through an online cert mill to spread his hallucinogenic gospel."

"He told you all that?"

"I couldn't fabricate such—excrement."

"Naturally." He shook his head in wonder.

"He wouldn't stop talking about it," Jess said. "He asked me what I thought about, quote, 'spiritual dimensions of hallucinatory epiphanies,' end quote. I told him that teaching anthro and comparative religions doesn't make me an expert on psychotropics."

"Fair enough."

"I wondered what would become of him," she said, peering skyward, "but he seemed harmless enough."

"Odds are someone said that about Hitler when he was young, or maybe Attila the Hun," Liam answered. "Or Sir Elon Musk."

"I've read extensively about psilocybin and so-called primitive cultures that ingest ashes," she said. "I have never read about anyone combining the two."

"Until now, that is," Liam noted. "If, in fact, that's what he's doing."

"That appears to be the case," she noted. "So, what's your plan to get the ashes back?"

"Uhhhh."

"That's not an answer," she noted.

"The evidence all points to El Camino."

"You could *say* that," she snarked.

"I can't go sneaking around that fucking circus searching for ashes I'm not even sure are there," he said.

"They're *there*," she said.

Liam stared. "And you know that how?"

"I *know*," she said. "El Camino is a cult. Ouro probably sends his neurally manipulated avatars to find ashes for him, wherever it is you'd *find* human ashes."

"Isn't eating ashes sorta cannibalism-y?"

"Probably not unless they consume the actual flesh, as well," she said. "But it could have been both. The tribes I've read about only ingest the cremains."

He winced sympathetically as she paused to shake out and gulp down a couple more pills.

"The cremains impart the essence of whoever's remains they were, shamans believe," she added. "Including nonhumans."

"The essence?"

"Their innate abilities," she said. "Their genetic assets and malfunctions, perhaps."

"You're blowing my mind."

She rubbed her temples more vigorously.

"I see you have incoming," Liam murmured with an arm around her shoulder. "You need your cave."

Eyes still squeezed shut, she nodded.

"We'll try breakfast next week," he said. "You know, it's been a while."

"Call me when you have a plan, Liam."

Leashing up Magnus, she waved the Chuckit at her brother and set off limping across the park toward her apartment.

BREAKING NEWS

Idaho governor vetoes bill decriminalizing recreational psilocybin use.

Lugging a case of cat food he'd bought on his way home from the gym, Liam came upon a grizzled Black man of medium build lying in the gutter. The man's large hands were clasped across his chest as if praying. He wore a dirty tank top and a rolled-up jacket cushioned the back of his head from the pavement. His chin was stubbled, his eyes closed to the sky. Wrapped around his sinewy left arm was a blood-flecked ACE bandage.

He looks like a corpse.

Liam wearily donned a Sheermask.

"What up, man?" he murmured as he gingerly took a knee by

the curb. "You need a hand?" The textured sidewalk dug into his knee.

The man didn't stir.

He shook the man's arm gently, with no response, and then more vigorously. "Wake up, man, you're in the fuckin' street!"

The man didn't stir.

Oh my God.

Liam craned his head around. Two people sporting neon framed I-Ware sat at the bus stop a few yards away, seemingly staring into space. One of them glanced blankly in Liam's direction for a moment and then back at God knew what metaverse thief of time.

Probably gaming.

Liam was about to dial 911, at least to have a record of the incident—there was virtually no chance of speaking to anyone—when the opening soprano sax notes of John Coltrane's "My Favorite Things" burst from the vicinity of the man's worn, dirty jeans.

The man's eyes fluttered open. Squinting against the sun's glare, and with a hand shielding them, he reopened his eyes sufficiently enough to warily and wordlessly size up Liam.

"Ah, shit," he rasped. Without moving his head, his eyes still locked on his unsolicited companion. He pulled a scuffed device from his pocket and raised it to his ear.

"Thaddeus speakin'."

Liam heard a muffled, disembodied voice.

"Been better," Thaddeus testified. "I musta passed out. Some white dude here checkin' me out on the sidewalk. Probly thought I was roadkill." He chuckled. "'Bout how I feel."

Diverting his eyes from Thaddeus, Liam rose gingerly from his uncomfortable stance.

"Hold up," Thaddeus said to the phone. He held up a long-nailed index finger, apparently beckoning to Liam.

"You got sumpthin' I can write with, brother?"

Chuckling, Liam dug in his pocket and handed the man an American Family promo pen and some Post-its.

Nodding to him, the man vigorously shook the pen before scribbling what looked like a phone number on the pad's first sheet; peeling it off, he tucked it in his shirt pocket before handing the pad back to Liam.

"Much obliged, brother," he said. "You came by at exactly the right time, which tells me this meetin' is no accident."

"Oh," Liam said, musing on this fresh intel. "Glad I could help."

He waggled his water bottle at the man. "Thirsty?"

"Nothin' personal, bro," he said, shaking his head, "but I don't drink used water."

"No offense," Liam said with a grin.

Alert as he now appeared, the man made no move to alter his position.

"You okay?" Liam asked. "You need a hand?"

"What I need's a new phone," the man rasped. "These burners the school hands out ain't worth shit."

The school?

"What school?" Liam asked delicately.

"M-I-fuckin'-T, bro," Thaddeus said with a snort. "I'm lyin' in the street. What school you *think* I'm talkin' 'bout?"

"You live in El Camino?"

An inside man!?

"Live-*duh*," Thaddeus replied. "No more. And not *in* El Camino, *at* El Camino, to be specific." He extended a thin hand to Liam, who helped him sit up and then to lift, swivel, and plant his sagging-blue-jeaned ass on the curb. He groaned with the effort.

"What's the difference?"

"Privs."

"*Privs?*" *Privileges?*

"Name's Thaddeus, BTW."

"So I heard."

"That's right."

Thaddeus. Local color. Is that racist?

"So, what's your name, brother?"

"I'm Liam," Liam replied. "Live down the street."

"'Sup, Liam?" They bumped fists. "Thanks for checkin' on me."

"De nada," Liam replied. "Haven't seen you out here before."

"It's your white privilege not to see me out here."

"Ouch!"

"I'm fuckin' with ya," Thaddeus said, laughing. "Anyhow, being *in* El Camino means easy access to the buildings, which means followin' orders, toein' the line, and all. I wasn't down with bein' chipped. Ya feel me? But like I said, I figured it might be worth three hots and a cot, showers, clean bathrooms, burners—"

"Burners?"

"You know, dealer phones," Thaddeus said. "Tossers, *The Wire*, *Law and Order, bum, bum bum bum bum BUM*. You feel me?"

Liam laughed. "Capiche."

"Capiche?"

"You know, like in *The Godfather*."

"The Godfather?"

A sweat broke on Liam's brow. *Is it racist to assume minority non-doms have seen* The Godfather, *or is it racist to assume they haven't?*

"I didn't mean…"

"You didn't mean to ascribe certain levels of pop culture sophistication to an old street nigger?" Thaddeus scowled before momentarily breaking into another grin. "I'm still fuckin' with ya. This is the best convo I've had since before I got chipped. BTW, I don't think anybody actually said 'capiche' in *The Godfather*.'"

"You want some coffee?" Liam asked.

"Yeah, and a chocolate croissant, and I need to piss like a racehorse."

"Given existing heat and particulate levels," Liam's phone cooed in a silky register, "I suggest you go indoors. As you probably already know, Le Petite Boulangerie is right around the corner."

"*Whew*," Thaddeus commented. "That's a sweet-ass voice. Your phone married?"

DAILY NEWS

BREAKING NEWS

Reports of shooters targeting drones on the rise in big cities.

Liam and T, as Thaddeus now bid Liam call him, lounged at an umbrellaed sidewalk table outside Le Petite Boulangerie, sipping their iced lattes with an extra glass of ice and nibbling day-old chocolate croissants. The bistro's brick facade was still in disrepair, and the broken windows were still boarded up after the earthquake. Qualified carpenters, masons, and so on, were swamped with work and demanding top dollar. Even they struggled to obtain critical building supplies given transportation challenges, including several key bridge collapses during and after the quake.

A welcome easterly bent the ephemeral spray from a mister in their direction and the forest fire smoke away from Portland for the moment.

"Can't remember the last time I had one of these babies," T said, waving the pastry in the air. "Reminds me of Montreal."

Montreal?

"So—?"

"So, the psilo was a bridge too far," T continued. "Never done hard drugs, and never will. I didn't buy Ouro's bullshit, so they kicked me out."

"Wow," Liam said. "You mentioned chipping."

"I did." T side-eyed his companion questioningly.

An unleashed Australian shepherd interrupted him, nosing at both of them. Its companion, a young, Sheermasked woman in a sports bra and threadbare Daisy Dukes, bade her wayward charge return to her side.

"He's supposed to be leashed on the sidewalk, ma'am," T chided with a fake smile.

"It's all good," trilled the smiling, aqua-tressed woman as she slipped the dog a treat. "He's a teddy bear."

"No, ma'am," T countered, "he's a dog, and dogs *s'posed* to be leashed."

The woman scowled at the pair as she led her companion away. Having crossed the street, she took a moment to leash the dog, giving them an elegant, ebony-tipped middle finger as she strode away.

"Ten to one, she'd a called po-po if we were both Black," T said, making air quotes for a reason Liam couldn't discern.

"Po-po?" *Cops*, it occurred to him—a second too late.

"Cops, PF, cops," T affirmed.

"What cops?"

"Amen." They bumped fists again.

"And what the fuck is PF?"

An older woman sitting nearby glanced at Liam.

"Ooh, *language*, paleface," Thaddeus chided. "Good thing this place is French. They won't understand you. Ils ne comprennent pas."

"Parlez-vous français?"

"Oui, un peu," Thaddeus replied. "Did I not mention Montreal?"

"*Paleface*," Liam intoned after a solemn moment. "Ah. Capiche."

Chuckling, T raised his latte in salute and continued his story.

"So, I marched down to the school with the rest of 'em," he recounted. "We all followed that crazy fuck, Ouroboros, with his stupid Onewheel and his flute. He's not bad with the flute."

"The microchips," Liam prompted.

"I'm gettin' there," his companion informed him. "Anyway, I was already vaxxed and boosted." He locked eyes with Liam. "I ain't stupid."

Liam nodded agreeably.

Biting off some chocolate from the croissant, Thaddeus chewed it thoughtfully, his eyes closed.

"So, the question was, do I go along with this plant business and eat?" he asked. "Or do I maybe go hungry?"

"Plant?"

"Implant. Microchip," Thaddeus said. "Try to keep up, bro."

"I'll try," Liam said. "Please continue."

"Anyway, my health ain't what it was," Thaddeus said. "I'm borderline diabetic, so they keep tellin' me. I figured, what's more important? The loss of privacy? Hell! I live in a fucking tent—when I'm lucky—so how much privacy I stand to lose?"

"If you're planted?"

"Implanted!" T exclaimed.

Ah. "The chips are actually implanted under your skin?"

"Where else would they put 'em?"

Liam shrugged. "In your head?"

"Which is covered with skin." Shaking his head, T eyed Liam dolefully. "Everybody who wanted in or at—*at* bein' the grounds, you dig, but not the school itself—had to be chipped."

"How did they insert them?"

"Guy did it with some kind of injection gun," T said. "Word was that numbnuts paid a tattoo artist to shoot 'em into our arms. About the size of a grain of rice."

"Hurt?"

"Nah, it was strawberry shortcake, man," T sneered. "Course it hurt. Like hell."

Wincing, he stared at the bandage on his arm.

"So—"

"So, hell, yeah, man, I got drunk and cut the fuckin' thing out myself," T explained, "with a kitchen knife."

"*Jesus.*"

"Smarts like a mother, but good riddance," he continued. "Cut it out the night I left. Got infected, uh course, but the ER patched me up and gave me some antibiotics and Tylenol. Said they couldn't give me anything stronger."

"Jesus."

"Coulda been worse," he said. "I was only there eight hours."

"Eight hours!" Liam exclaimed. "Where?"

"St. Vincent," Thaddeus said. "Walked over there."

"Walked?"

"They said I was lucky," he added. "Coulda gotten gangrene."

"God *damn*," Liam said. "What do the chips actually do?"

"Track everything."

"Like the military."

"A-*fuckin'* men," T said. "That's why I left. I miss a meal here and there, but I'm used to that. At least I'm free," he said before popping the last bit of croissant into his mouth.

Free to go hungry?

T started wiping his fingers on his pants before grasping the paper napkin in his lap.

"So, what's the point of the implants?" Liam asked.

Thaddeus took a subtle, thorough look around the other tables and up at the sky, a hand shading his eyes, where a couple of quads cruised high up. A server followed his glance for a moment before turning his gaze elsewhere.

More paranoia?

"Like I said," he continued, lowering his voice, and leaning toward his companion, "the plants tracked and recorded everything we did, along with our vitals. Some computer somewhere crunches the numbers and awards points based on how you measure up."

"Measure up?"

T shrugged. "Behave and produce."

"Where do the points come in?"

"You redeem the points at the store."

"I saw that on his webcast," Liam said. "Store have a name?"

"Freedom Buys Here."

"No way."

"*Word*," T said, his head bobbing. "You can earn better digs, better food, burners, burner minutes," —he held up his phone— "and better jobs. Numbnuts preaches that when you're planted, you don't gotta worry about your next meal, or where you're gonna crash, or if the po-po will fuck with ya, or if somebody's gonna mug ya, or if you're gonna get sick."

He stopped talking as a ponytailed waiter whisked by with an order.

"They gotta work, yeah," he continued, hunched over the table, "but they know they're gonna eat, so they can think about what all they're gonna spend their precious fuckin' points on. Top earners get to live in one of the schools. AC's spotty with all the brownouts, but it's better than nothin'."

"Top earners," Liam mused. "Sounds like a sales contest."

"It's a fuckin' cult," Thaddeus declared. "And besides the plants, I wasn't down with the deefs."

"Deep fakes," Liam muttered.

"Ouro fucks with people by showing clips of 'em in his webcasts."

"How does that fuck with them?"

T gravely fixed his eyes on Liam. "A lotta Caminos in those clips weren't *in* those clips."

Liam stared. "What do you mean?"

"They weren't there when the pictures were taken," T declared. "They were deef'd in."

"You can't be serious!" Liam slumped back in his chair.

"Serious as a heart attack, bro."

A woman seated at the bar looked at the pair for a moment before returning to her conversation with an unseen listener. T looked around to see if anyone else was peering in his direction.

"Fuckin' A," he told Liam in a near whisper. "Our homie Ouro gets his assets stoned and cooks his videos to fuck with their heads."

"Assets?"

"What he calls his followers, his *clientele* in private, or so I've heard," T explained.

"Wow."

"Anyway," he continued, "people who were in the original vids vanish. He changes other people's faces around, so you lose track of who was there with you. It's seriously messed up, bro."

"They start questioning reality," Liam said.

"Somethin' like that," Thaddeus said. "I knew I hadda leave when I saw myself standin' on top of that fake hill, waving at a drone."

"You weren't really there?"

"I never set foot on that garbage heap," he said. "Other people said the same thing, but kept it under their hats."

"Didn't want to upset the gravy train?"

"Didn't know what to do," he said with a pensive shrug. "Some of 'em was freaked out. Some of 'em decided they musta been there after all. Most of 'em just kept their heads down and clammed up. They figured numbnuts must know what he's doing," he continued. "Figured maybe he is crazy, or they are, but either way, they were better off than they'd been before."

"So why make a stink?"

Wide-eyed, Liam leaned in on an elbow, chin in hand.

"The ones who've had the psilo just didn't give a shit about the vids," T continued, clearly reveling in his narrative. "They weren't gonna cut off the gravy train, either. They tell everybody else how they should be grateful to numbnuts for feeding and housing them. Said he gives 'em hope and helps 'em past their fear of the future, fear of death."

Liam shook his head pensively.

"If Ouro's treatment 'rechannels your essence' sufficiently," T continued with air quotes. "You're eligible for slash. He claims slash gives you power that only he can teach you to use optimally."

Liam gaped and continued to gape at the sight of what appeared to be the rear end of Tate's exterminator van cruising past the bistro. He didn't catch the plate.

Is Tate keeping tabs on me?

"What's up, bro?" T asked, following his gaze quizzically.

"Nothing," Liam replied. "Do you still talk to Caminos?"

"Sure," T said. "They can buy off-rez time, and they don't seem to care that he can locate 'em and maybe eavesdrop on 'em any time."

"Maybe?"

"Nobody knows for sure," T said. "That's his game. Keepin' people off balance."

A long silence followed.

"Want another croissant?"

"Split one?" T asked with an eager grin.

"Fine."

"Why are you so interested in this wack shit?" T asked.

"My wife died a few months ago."

"I'm very sorry to hear that, bro." He met Liam's gaze expectantly.

"Thanks," Liam said. "She asked to be cremated, which I did. Found a perfect urn that she would have loved to put her ashes in."

"Nice."

"Had her, or them, on my mantelpiece for months, with some pictures and other mementos."

"Uh-huh."

Thaddeus shifted in his chair and looked skyward again. The drones had disappeared.

"Anyway," Liam said, quickening his telling, "she was a gardener, and I decided she should be in the garden with her flowers, scorched or not, so I put her outside."

"Nice."

"Then somebody wearing a hoodie with an Ouroboros logo on the back stole the urn with the cremains in it."

Another long silence.

T laid a weathered hand on Liam's wrist. "That is so messed up, bro."

Liam shrugged and nodded his thanks. He swiped at the beginnings of a tear.

T looked thoughtful for a moment. "You think her ashes ended up in El Camino?" he asked.

Liam met T's steady gaze. "Tell me everything you know about slash therapy."

DAILY NEWS

BREAKING NEWS

Diagnoses of paranoid schizophrenia rise sharply in U.S.

Tate's van slid up to the curb next to Liam, who was striding home from the gym. "Hell you doin', man?"

"What?"

"Don't play dumb," Tate declared. "Why are you kissing up to that asshole, Ourobozo?"

"First of all, cool your jets," Liam advised, his eyes narrowing to slits as they met Tate's. "Secondly, what're you talkin' about? Thirdly," he concluded. "How would you know about it if I did whatever you're talking about?"

"I *saw* you on his webcast!" Tate declared.

"What?"

"Get in the van!" The back passenger door slid open. A faint, pesticidal odor met Liam's nostrils.

Liam stared.

"Front's occupied," Tate noted, glancing at Ranger and a large plastic bag full of envelopes with which he shared the seat.

Liam stared.

"I *just* need to show you something," Tate pleaded.

"You need to show me this webcast I couldn't possibly be in?"

"Just get in—*please*."

Torn by an uneasy feeling in his gut, Liam was just intrigued enough to comply after a moment.

"Play," Tate told his I-Dash.

They watched in silence as aerial footage of Liam's encounter with Ouroboros played across the screen. At what Liam recalled as the end of the odd encounter, he was astonished to watch Ouroboros ceremoniously invite him onto the grounds and embrace him warmly. They whispered something into each other's ears before letting go, shook hands heartily, and parted.

"Well?" Tate snapped.

"Well, even if this wasn't complete bullshit and that was actually me in the video, it's none of your business."

"It was *you*."

"*Course* it's me," Liam said, struggling to keep his shit. "But it wasn't me. I mean, the first part was me. The huggy-kissy shit was fake."

"Deep faked?"

"Apparently," Liam snapped. "I don't fuckin' believe he did this."

"Oh, he did it all right," Tate gloated. "I warned ya."

"What happened to the audio?"

"It's haywire," Tate replied. "I think somebody's jamming it."

"You can't be serious."

"If somebody can freeze Trump's supposedly dead body and insert you into fake videos," Tate retorted, "then somebody can jam the sound on webcasts."

Liam snorted. "Or maybe you'd rather believe conspiracy theories than shell out to fix your fucking dash screen."

Tate's beady eyes flashed, but he said nothing.

"What's with the envelopes?"

To Liam's surprise, Tate chuckled. "Oh, I hand those out to curb huggers and panhandlers," he said.

"What's in them?"

"Open one up."

Shaking his head dubiously, Liam obeyed, ripping open the cheap paper to find a tri-folded sheet of paper. Turning it over, it appeared to be a generic job application at first glance. He looked at Tate questioningly before scanning the text, which included one inane, offensive question after another.

Are you acquainted with people of different races and/or ethnicities?

Have you ever stolen more than $20?

Do you trust your neighbors?

Do you receive any kind of government aid?

Have you ever lived in El Camino?

"What is this garbage?"

"I downloaded it from a website," Tate said triumphantly. "I hand 'em out to street trash who're probably stupid enough to think I'm giving them money!"

"That's messed up, Tate."

"They want something for nothin', so I give it to 'em," Tate replied, turning his gaze to a tiny, ancient, fully masked abuela approaching them on the sidewalk. She towed a large camp cooler in an old child's wagon bearing a homemade sign announcing her wares.

"Tamales!" she called in a heavily accented rasp. Side-eyeing Liam shyly, she said, "Fresh tamales for sale."

"No gracias, señora," Liam replied with a polite smile.

The old woman turned her expressionless eyes to each of them in turn. She scowled at Tate, who waved at her mockingly before she turned heel and continued down the street trailing her cooler.

"Cabrón," she muttered.

"Adiós," Tate called after her. Turning to Liam, he asked, "What did she say?"

Liam laughed. "She said she'll pray for you."

Tate guffawed. "Sure, she did. Nice mouth!" he called after her, but she appeared not to hear.

Shaking his head, Liam considered the flyer, grateful at least for the relatively cool air in the van.

"Take a few," Tate said solicitously. "You can hand 'em out to non-doms that hit you up on the street."

Again, Liam narrowed his eyes and stared, recalling how he'd thought he'd seen Tate's van cruise by the bakery the day before.

Daily News

Breaking News

Companies increasingly turning HR functions over to AI.

CHAPTER
FIFTEEN

Liam rubbed his bleary eyes as he stared at his laptop screen. He was on his seventh straight half-hour episode of *Freedom Lies Here*, seeking any clue whatsoever as to the whereabouts of Joan's ashes.

Patriots and Friends-style "Amigos" segments featured a garrulous, socially distanced panel of "assets," all of whom deferred to their illustrious host. Most of them headed one project or another underway on the campus; judging from their reports, all the efforts were going gangbusters, thanks mostly, of course, to Ouroboros's visionary leadership.

Acknowledging their contributions with a nod of approval, the influencer cued a round of hearty fist bumps.

In another segment, Liam noticed T—who'd said he wasn't there—among several Caminos waving to an aerial camera from the top of the anthill.

"Zoom max, black man." Enlarged several times, the fringes of T's face became more pixilated.

It was fake, all right.

T's face in the frame was raised in an expression of such transcendence that Liam couldn't fathom it on his new friend's actual visage. On closer examination, he noticed others were also pixilated.

It was all, as Bush II had said of Trump's inauguration speech some ten years earlier, some weird shit.

Elsewhere, Ouro did stunts on his Onewheel, showcasing his prosthetic appendage with stunning, one-handed card and coin tricks. (Coy on the matter of why he'd needed and how he'd acquired the intricate AI device, he mentioned merely that he'd 'seen action'). He bragged that the device had a direct line to an electrode implanted in his brain; it "anticipated his needs," he said, and he often found himself with the correct implement in his hand before he was even aware that he needed it.

He riffed on recent headlines and commentary, spoofing PNS newscasts even while he shared conspiracy theories into which the network leaned to keep viewers hooked.

"The latest from PNS is *aces*, amigos!" he crowed to launch one segment, stressing the initials to sound decidedly like the male organ. "Our red friend China's scientists have developed a means of controlling the weather using satellite networks!"

"Cuz, like, how else *would* they do it, y'know?" he asked with a theatrical shrug.

"I also have word that in response, the great Patriot Congress is supporting subsidies for arms-dealing billionaires eager to beef up the great U.S. Space Force," he said, "which brings to mind the classic *Seinfeld* episode—you *do* remember *Seinfeld*—in which Elaine notes to a famous writer, hilariously, that *War and Peace* was originally titled 'War: What is it Good For?' They don't write 'em like *that* anymore!"

What a wack job.

There were split-screen rants, juxtaposing footage of Ouroboros railing at a microphone with images of the city council or the school board or their individual members listening raptly, looking at their phones, or napping.

On what remained of Nextdoor, haters opined that the footage was staged, with clips of Ouro ranting in his makeshift studio spliced with footage of random meetings of either governing board. Having read about members of Congress crankling out sound bites in a deserted House or Senate chamber in the wee hours, Liam smirked. Utter, obvious rot, but lots of constituents and local newscasters scarfed it up back in their home districts.

Enough resulting clicks and likes and the wee-hour ranters might snag some PNS Facetime.

A soft, persistent dinging broke his concentration and spurred a feeble protest from Daisy, snoozing at his feet.

"Sec cam motion," Liam muttered. An array of views from the cams mounted around his house appeared on his screen, two of them enlarged to display alternate perspectives of a quad depositing a parcel on his creaky back deck.

He pumped a fist. Relishing the break, he hadn't realized he needed, he stood, stretched, and fetched his purchase from outside the back door. Because of theft concerns, he no longer accepted deliveries to his front porch; he'd even installed a mail slot in his front door after the quake when looting and porch piracy soared.

Back at the table, he slit open the shoebox-size parcel with a key and pulled out the receipt. Yup. It was the top-shelf, portable DNATek he'd ordered. The company claimed the device, about the size of a hardcover book, could identify DNA from bone fragments in human ashes.

Morbid, perhaps, but how else would he identify Joan's remains among those of God knew how many others, particularly if they'd been disinterred, as it were, from their home in the urn?

The company mostly catered to those combing through the rubble of disastrous fires for incinerated victims, "guaranteed" 98.3 percent accuracy in IDing remains.

It lightened his wallet by about five grand, but it would be well worth it if it delivered—within the 1.7 percent chance it would be mistaken.

Returning to his toil, he viewed again the aerial footage Tate had shown him in the van of his and Ouro's hearty embrace, which, of course, was phony. As the camera followed Ouro's departure, Liam was shocked momentarily, to notice an odd, if barely discernible, bulge in the rear of his white culottes or whatever the fuck he was wearing.

"Zoom rear end, white pants."

Liam gaped. It looked like the outline of a small handgun. He was shocked for a moment before the logic hit him. From all the evidence, Ouroboros was a power-crazed, if outwardly benevolent, cult leader.

How would he *not* be armed?

That could certainly muddy Liam's nascent plans to reclaim Joan's ashes.

The thought evoked his recent therapy session. Did whoever was responsible for all this insanity know whose ashes they had? Apart from his garden, how *were* they sourced? How many (much) ashes had they obtained?

Did the thief steal the ashes on Ouro's orders or initiative, or did he snatch them to curry favor?

Something in the background of the video caught his eye as he pondered all this.

Reversing the imagery, he replayed the moment in slow motion.

Blurry but discernible, there it was again: an outthrust arm, pointing, just within the camera's line of sight, apparently to a spot near the desk behind which Ouro was mansplaining how human consciousness expanded exponentially after some hungry ape-man gobbled a bunch of magic mushrooms and hallucinated God only knew what.

How better to explain such an experience to his friends without language than to share it with them?

Suddenly, a graphic appeared on that part of the screen, blocking his view of the arm. Backing up again, he zoomed in as much as the video would allow and replayed it frame by frame.

There it was—a tattoo of the theater's iconic laughing and crying masks. The image was too blurry for him to be positive, but it closely resembled one adorning the back of M's forearm. The scarlet nails visible at the end of the pointing hand all but closed the case for him. M adored the ink, which, she'd confided to him and Joan, symbolized her repressed life as a trans and the liberating joy of her decision to transition.

What the fuck was she doing in Ouroboros's lair? During a *webcast*, yet...

He racked his weary brain to recall what she'd told him about Ouroboros when he'd shared his story of Joan's ashes with her in the driveway just two days earlier. It already seemed like weeks had passed.

He couldn't recall having asked her if she'd ever met him. He was almost certain she'd never mentioned it if he had.

It was discomfiting, to say the least. Even if she hadn't met with him, what was she doing there? If she were being coy about her association with Ouroboros, whatever it represented, it was probably best not to confront her directly.

But if she hadn't shared this info with him, what else might she not have mentioned?

DAILY NEWS

BREAKING NEWS

Membership in U.S. 'death cults' swelling: report.

CHAPTER
SIXTEEN

"MLK elementary school post-quake visual."

After a final adjustment to the quaint, bulky E-ZVR eyewear he'd positioned over his eyes, Liam suddenly found himself, or rather his avatar—the first moments were disorienting—facing the school's main entrance.

As part of a trial run of the software it was considering buying, the school district's engineers had dispatched drones and bots with infrared cameras to map the exteriors and interiors of both schools digitally, which they inspected to assess earthquake damage. To boost its claims that the buildings were irreparable after the quake, the district made the map available to the public on its website.

As far as Liam could see, he was only the second person to have viewed it.

He was mildly surprised that Ouro hadn't somehow sabotaged it. Perhaps he was giving him too much credit.

"Wadda you see, boss?" T asked.

"Don't call me boss," Liam chided his companion. "And don't look at me. Look at the screen."

"Right," T replied.

"Just entered," Liam said. "Office to the left. Hallway in front of me."

T nodded attentively as he stared at Liam's computer screen. "Gotcha, bro."

The virtual environment reminded Liam of his first VR experience, part of a high-tech, traveling Van Gogh exhibit in Seattle. The headgear, quaint by 2032 standards, nonetheless swept him off his feet from the artist's depiction of his room, down a rickety staircase, out the front door, and into a seamless travelogue through the artist's sunflower phase in Lille.

All this while sitting on a stool, spinning at will, and craning his head around to immerse himself in Van Gogh's impression of the glorious French countryside. The kicker was when he suddenly burst through a wormhole and was transported into *The Starry Night*.

He advanced the graphics in fits and starts, following his curiosity; he'd thought he'd be able to move around at will, but this app was limited to forward and reverse play, so he began fast-forwarding through the tour. T cautioned him to slow things down as his avatar descended the stairs into the basement.

"All the way to the end of the hall, bro," T muttered. "Been a while. I need to get my bearings."

The structural damage was extensive, if not necessarily obvious. The sim highlighted x-rays of dozens of small fractures in the building's masonry. It had lost only a few bricks and broken windows at the time of the temblor.

"Wow!" T exclaimed. "Now I'm really glad I split."

"Amen," Liam replied. "Wonder what it would take to bring down that ton of bricks."

"A good shake."

"A big sneeze."

"I'm pretty sure the lab is at the end of the hall," T said. "I hadda fetch sumthin' down there when I worked in the kitchen. They actually sent a guard down there with me."

"A guard?" Liam asked.

"They didn't trust me enough to let me go myself because I said no to the psilo."

"Wow. Why not just send the guard?"

"That'd be too easy," T said. "Ouro loves to overcomplicate shit."

Liam considered this. "Interesting."

"He always gotta be the smartest MF in the room, know what I mean?"

"I feel ya."

T laughed. "His boys all be trying to impress him with how useful they are."

"I'm surprised they let you in the building if you wouldn't do psilo."

"I'm a good cook," T replied. "I was a Navy culinary specialist, a military chef. I made the school kitchens *work*!"

"Wow," Liam muttered. As interested as he was in T's history, he tried to steer the chat back to the task at hand. "So, where's that vault you mentioned?"

"It's an old portable rubber room they moved from another wing," T said. "They used to lock crazy little kids in there in the good old days until they got their shit straight."

Liam shook his head. "Sounds like a veiled threat."

"Now that you mention it," T said pensively.

"Is that where he did the psilo therapy?"

"Nah, they converted the janitor's workroom into a little lab," he said. "I think that's where they keep the cremains."

"Where did they get the cremains, anyway?" Liam asked. "They can't be stealing them all from people's gardens."

"Well, I heard Ouro claimed the ashes of some non-doms who died in the quake and the last surge," T said. "I guess nobody else wanted 'em."

"That's fucked up."

"Amen, bro."

Liam arrived at the door in question, which swung open before him. Indeed, it contained a workbench and storage shelves full of parts.

"Where's the lab?" Liam demanded.

"Remember, bro, this was taken after the quake but before the Caminos moved in," T noted. "I'm just showing ya how to get there."

"Right," Liam said.

"They partitioned off a little office where numbnuts does his psilo and slash therapy," T explained. "Has 'em drink some magic tea, then lie down on couches, two at a time, just him with them, playin' music, and talkin' to them about their trips, and helping guide them into their—"

"Channels," Liam interjected. "Like new horizons."

"I guess," T said. "Most of 'em come out saying they never felt better, their lives suddenly make sense, and weird shit like that. They're not supposed to talk about that stuff, but 'course they do," he continued. "Said Ouro tells them stories about the people whose ashes they're supposedly swallowing, tells 'em about the new powers they'll have if they believe."

"*Believe*?" Liam mused.

"I think he does want 'em to talk about it," T ventured. "Like it adds to the mystery, makes people more curious—especially the real mental cases, schizos and addicts and such who want real help."

Contemplating the virtual enclosure still before his eyes, Liam was silent for a moment.

"We should do a dry run," he said at length.

"I reckon you'd like some ideas about how to get around security," T ventured.

Removing the primitive headgear, Liam blinked repeatedly and took a moment to reorient himself before meeting T's eyes again.

"I reckon I would."

DAILY NEWS

BREAKING NEWS

Texas legislature proposes substituting "involuntary servitude" for "slavery" in school textbooks.

CHAPTER
SEVENTEEN

"Hello." Jess never IDed herself when answering the phone, an annoying quirk to which Liam had long ago resigned himself, factoring in her Asperger's. Of course, the syndrome hadn't been classified as such until relatively recently, before which those so afflicted were considered wildly eccentric or even touched.

"It's Liam."

"Yes?"

Declining to torment his sister, as was his habit, by insisting on pointless pleasantries, Liam cut to the chase.

"I have a plan."

"Concerning Joan's ashes?"

"Exactly."

"*Finally.*"

"Uhhh…"

"Meet me at 8 a.m. tomorrow at Boulangerie."

"Uhhh…"

"I know this goes without saying, but tell no one about this," she said. "Be prepared, on time, and alone."

Silence.

"Please confirm."

After pouting for a moment, Liam replied, "I'll be there. Alone."

"Until then, Liam."

Dᴀɪʟʏ Nᴇᴡs

Bʀᴇᴀᴋɪɴɢ Nᴇᴡs

SCOTUS nixes appeal of 50% water rationing in Texas state prisons.

CHAPTER
EIGHTEEN

T woke up on a wicker couch on Liam's spacious front porch with M looking down at him.

"What up, T?" she chirped. She leaned against the peeling white railing that walled off a tangle of rose bushes.

"M?" he replied, blinking in the harsh sunlight. "Hell are you doing there, starin' at me?"

Liam stepped onto the porch from the open door where he'd been standing, and looked expectantly at M.

"Well, what *are* you doin' there, staring at him?" he asked. "And how do you two know each other?"

T shook his head slowly. "She didn't tell you she worked for numbnuts? Used to see her all the time. Ask *her* if I can cook."

Liam locked onto M's eyes.

She shrugged.

"You lied?"

"I didn't," she replied. "You asked me what I knew about El Camino."

"Oh, my *fucking* God!" Liam exclaimed. "You didn't think to tell me you *know* that crazy fuck?"

"A. You never asked, and B. It's none of your business, Liam," she said. "I don't discuss my clients."

"Your *clients*?"

"Wouldn't have many if I did. Cool your jets," she admonished. "I no longer work for him."

"What did you do for him?"

"I designed his security system."

"*Seriously?*"

T chuckled.

"You *know* what business I'm in."

"I'm not sure I do."

"You didn't grow up poor and an outcast, Liam."

"And that has what to do with the issue at hand?"

"I'm sure you've had to work for people you didn't like," she said. "You know what kind of legal bills I had from that NSA litigation?"

"Well, I was gonna ask you for help," Liam said, "but now I don't know *what* to do."

"Understood," M replied, "but I did nothing illegal, and I'm your best bet for getting in and out of that school with the least trouble."

"How did you know about that?"

T looked at his feet.

Liam turned to eye him. "*You* told her about this?"

M snorted. "You told me yourself, Liam, that privacy's extinct."

T nodded his vigorous assent.

"Ran into her on the street the other day," he said, nodding toward M. "She bought me a croissant."

"And a smoothie," M chimed in.

"And a smoothie," T agreed. "Goddamn good smoothies there."

"And the *security*?" Liam persisted.

"She set up the sec lab—the bridge, numbnuts calls it—right off the mess, the kitchen, so we saw each other a lot; we dialogued. Just trying to do you right, boss," he continued. "She's an ace."

"Now *you're* an expert on security systems?"

"Lighten up, boss," T said in a low voice. "I was there. She knows the sec inside and out."

"Like the back of my girlie hands," M boasted, thrusting out her palms in a pushing motion. "I installed it, and I supplied the drones."

T chuckled.

Liam pondered this. "So, you can hack into it," he mused at length.

"Unless he's fucked with it a lot since I left," she said. "He knows just enough to be dangerous, thanks to me." She mock-curtsied.

Liam rolled his eyes.

"Anyway," she concluded, "I *should* still have a back door into the code."

DAILY NEWS

BREAKING NEWS

Majority of Americans in Dem-led cities say they feel unsafe in their homes.

Two or three drones with blinking red lights cruised the skies over El Camino at night, T explained to Liam as they sat at his dining room table; the remainder of the fleet roosted on charging platforms and were serviced as needed in a portable with a retractable roof hatch. The small aircraft entered and exited as their AI dictated.

Two guards equipped with Night Eyes, Tasers, and receivers patrolled on Segways. More guards stood vigil over the front and rear entrances of the schools.

T's grasp of all these details—assuming they were accurate—impressed Liam.

Other school entrances were locked from the outside, with no one in or out. Liam wondered what the fire marshals would think about that. Mindful of the cops' experience, they had adopted a hands-off policy with the community and didn't involve themselves other than issuing unheeded warnings about the buildings' fragility.

Under cover of chaos and darkness, if everything went according to plan—a shaky prospect—they would leap into a waiting, darkened, plateless AV of which M was in remote control. They would all rendezvous at the nearby home of Jess's estranged wife, Ellie, among the most rational people Liam had ever met, not to mention an ex-police K9 officer and journalist, to debrief.

T's El Camino co-asset Rhiannon, a Navy vet whom he had trained in the kitchen, had agreed to get them into the school after T shared with her the mission. She insisted, however, on deniability. T said Rhiannon, a thirty-something, baby-faced Haitian émigré, discouraged potential abusers by feigning schizophrenia and packing on weight, a task made easier by working in the kitchen. A refugee from Florida, she shared on Ouro's webcast an account of seeing "do-gooders" being clubbed and arrested for handing out water and coffee to voters suffering in Florida's brutal heat and humidity.

Meanwhile, M would hack the system and direct the patrolling drones to awaken their counterparts to stage an aerial laser show above the school, complete with music. According to the security protocols, the guards would summon Ouro wherever he happened to be.

Once Ouro left whatever he was doing to investigate, Rhiannon would cut power to the school. Liam and T would slip inside under cover of darkness and their light-bending Fade-A-Wear suits, which rendered them virtually invisible, at least at night.

M had tipped Liam a while back to a tech breakthrough in "invisible fabric" that the military had under wraps. When he shared his nascent plan with her, she offered to rent him two beta suits she'd snapped up at a Patriots convention for a cool $5,000 each.

"It's only for a couple of hours," he griped.

"Take it or leave it," she replied. "They're awesome and awesome ain't cheap."

Thus camouflaged, he and T would locate the vault, find, and secure the correct ashes in Liam's Invisitote, and sneak back out.

Liam allowed himself ten minutes to accomplish all this.

That was the plan, in any event.

Plan B?

Improvise.

DAILY NEWS

BREAKING NEWS

U.S. Senate Majority Leader Mike McDonnell, 102, found dead at his desk in the chamber during roll call vote.

CHAPTER
TWENTY

Liam and T hunched behind a beige van parked on the rezzie side of the street across from the elementary school. One of the few streetlights left functional by the earthquake flickered eerily. A scattering of school windows was dimly illuminated.

Posted outside the school's main entrance, a sentry stared at their softly glowing phone.

"You really think this is gonna work?" T whispered. Shoulder to shoulder, they sat on the sidewalk in the 2 a.m. darkness, leaning against the vehicle.

Sweat coating his flesh, Liam grunted. The non-breathing

Invisiwear in which they were cloaked was sweltering even on the relatively cool night; they could do nothing but endure it.

"Think we got enough gear?" T fingered his NightEyes nervously.

Watching a cat dart between cars, Liam grunted anew at what he construed as T's lame attempt at levity.

"What if—"

"Shut *up!*" Liam hissed. "We're supposed to maintain radio silence. We did the dry run last night. I paid your gal to leave the door open when she leaves. We have five seconds to get in the door without tripping the alarm." Glancing over his shoulder yet again, he added, "That assumes the diversion works."

T nodded doubtfully.

Liam smacked T lightly on the shoulder with a hand. "You can back out now, man," he said. "No harm, no foul."

T was silent for a moment. "Fuck it," he said at length. "I'm in. You and your missus got a raw deal."

"Good," Liam replied. They bumped gloved fists. "Thanks. Now we wait for the fireworks."

"If you two don't shut the fuck up," M growled over their receivers, "there may not be any fireworks."

T chuckled.

"Roger that," Liam muttered.

"Cut the commando shit, G.I. Joke," M said. "You never served."

T chuckled again.

"Sky is clear," she muttered. "Stand by."

The pair rose creakily to a half stoop.

"Ah, shit, that hurts," T groaned.

"Shut it!"

They peered over the hood of the van in a crouch, craning their veiled heads and infrared Night Eyes to the skies above El Camino.

The blinking red lights of three drones wove a leisurely aerial ballet one hundred feet above the campus. Liam felt his neck starting to crick. He wondered if the flies' routes were fixed.

"What's *taking*—"

Suddenly, the drones formed a loose circle and began eddying in an apparent dance. A fourth, then a fifth, and finally, a parade of other drones rose to join them in their aerial ballet. A score or so of them had gathered when they simultaneously sprouted lasers, some of them red, others blue, and still others white.

Ouroboros, Liam had heard, enjoyed staging such nocturnal displays for the benefit of Caminos, "tourists," and, of course, all manner of cams. This one, though, was M's creation.

The guard at the school's entrance lowered his phone and gawked upward at the display. Wondering, perhaps, if the show wasn't one of his eccentric leader's whims, he did nothing.

Wagner's "Ride of the Valkyries," immortalized as the anthemic accompaniment for U.S. gunship raids on North Vietnamese targets in *Apocalypse Now*, exploded from the drones' speakers.

Lights blazed on in tents, shelters, and the schools themselves across the campus.

"Holy shit," T muttered.

"A-fucking-men, bro," Liam replied. He imagined tracers exploding from the lofty bot parade.

Light washed through the former MLK Jr. Elementary's front doors, illuminating the guard, who stood aside to allow a figure resembling Ouroboros, accompanied by a huge canine, to sprint from the building.

"What the fuck?" It was Ouroboros, all right. His gaze turned skyward, his evident rage echoing through the amplifiers posted on poles around the campus. Across the grounds, Caminos poured from their tents and shelters and streamed from the condemned school buildings.

Holos of the leader sprang from the turf at intervals, relaying and amplifying his profanity.

Like babies crying, a chorus of shrill, eerie coyote yips broke out from what sounded like mere blocks away. Caminos and Rezzies beefed about non-doms and others who insisted on leaving dog food out for the "invaders," even as a ragtag local pack steadily expanded its ranks.

"Get ready," T muttered.

"Roger that," Liam said. His headband was already saturated, so he tugged on his goggles to swipe at the sweat stinging his eyes.

"Gate open," M muttered.

The pair dashed across the street to the remotely unlocked passage, which gave way before them, and dashed to the corner of the school, a few yards from the entrance. Seconds later, the school went almost completely dark.

"Rhiannon's on it," T said, chuckling.

"Let's go!" Liam snapped.

They dashed to a spot immediately to the right of the doors. Seconds later, a heavyset figure exited the doors, stopped, flicked a penlight on and off three times, and fled into the cacophonous chaos washing over the grounds.

"Now!" T exclaimed.

Liam was already moving quietly and quickly into the school lobby, with T on his heels. They trotted down the dark hall, down the stairs into the basement, to the door that had swung open for Liam in the VR program.

The door, thankfully, was ajar, a sign, Liam conjectured, of a rapid, careless exit.

Liam swept his penlight over a few urns of various descriptions scattered on shelves of an aluminum rack bolted to the wall. There was no sign of Joan's ashes, nor any ashes. Scanning each quickly with his DNATek, he found nothing.

"What the fuck?" Liam exclaimed.

"Well, *damn*, bro…"

"Where else could they be?" Liam demanded.

"I dunno, man."

"*Hurry up!*" M snapped in their ears.

"They're not here," Liam whimpered.

"You need to leave!" M barked. "He's gonna remember the override any minute."

Override?

"Oh, *shit*," T muttered.

"Maestro?" A plaintive, frightened girl's voice issued from the dark behind them.

Daily News

BREAKING NEWS

Fireworks company owner arrested for bombing at drone expo.

CHAPTER
TWENTY-ONE

Liam winced when something snapped in his thigh as the pair lurched around on their haunches.

"Maestro, no te veo!" the girl bleated. "I'm scared. What are those lights?"

"What in Jesus fuck?" Liam gaped at the monochromatic, pleading teen standing within arm's reach of him.

"Who is that?" M asked. "What's going on?"

"Maestro, am I dying?" she pleaded, sobbing. "I hear voices, but I can't see anyone."

"Maria," T said. "It's Thaddeus. From the kitchen."

"Thaddeus?" she cried.

"Sí, chica, *Thaddeus!*" he said. "T."

"Get out now!" M barked in their ears. "Leave the kid."

Liam's stunned gaze careened between T and the girl.

"No te entiendo, Thaddeus."

"You're OK, Maria," T murmured. "You're high on psilo."

"Si, si!" she replied. "Maestro gives me té."

"He was getting her high in the middle of the night?" Liam asked indignantly.

"Told ya, the dude don't sleep," T said. "Claims it's one of his powers."

"Ask her about the ashes!"

"She's stoned, and she's scared shitless, man."

Lights flickered in the hall beyond the room, revealing a silhouette of the tiny girl's swollen belly.

"Oh, my God," Liam exclaimed, "she's pregnant!"

"Yeah," T muttered. "Forgot about that."

"Bastard had her tripping while she's knocked up," Liam snapped. "Jesus!"

"*Aces*," M sniped. "I'm done, gentlemen. Way to screw the pooch! Rotsa ruck." She went dark.

Rising to a stand, T took the girl gently by her arm.

"Maria," he said, "Tu ven conmigo."

"Pero, el maestro," she protested, weeping.

T steered her into the hall.

Liam gaped. "Are you *crazy*?"

"Can't leave her here with looney tunes," T said. "Gotta move, bro. Grab her other arm and be ready to tase."

"Wait," Liam said on an impulse. "Where was she before?"

"She was in Idaho before she wound up here with her boyfriend."

"I mean, where was she before she walked in on us just now?"

"She was in the tank," T said.

"The '*tank*?'"

"Where numbnuts drugs 'em," T elaborated. "Some people call it the tank. He calls it the 'TLab.'"

"'TLab?'"

"Transcendence Lab."

"What bullshit," Liam snorted. "Where is it?"

"Through that door." He used the beam of his penlight to outline the frame of a door, slightly ajar, at the rear of the room. Liam hadn't noticed it.

"Show me."

"We *don't have—*"

"The ashes might be in there!"

Striding through the door, Liam swept his penlight beam along one wall until it fell on a file cabinet tucked under a rectangular table set against the wall. Atop the table were three 3-D printers.

Before Liam could ask him, T had jacked open the lock on the cabinet's top drawer with a large screwdriver.

"Jesus!" Liam exclaimed. He poked his light inside.

"We gotta bounce!" T hissed, keeping a close eye on Maria.

"Holy shit!" Liam exclaimed.

"What?"

"Open up your bag!"

T stared as Liam shoveled plastic ghost guns and rounds by the handfuls into T's and his own unfurled InVisitotes.

"Enough!" T exclaimed. "Allez, allez, allez!"

French…?

"Estoy asustada!" Maria cried.

"I *know* you're scared, chica," T murmured.

"Me están persiguiendo," Maria said. "Nos van a matar me and Jesús!"

Unable to keep up with her rapid Spanish, Liam turned to T.

"Her English is actually pretty good," T said. "She's defaulting to Spanish 'cuz she's rattled."

Makes sense…

"Nobody's killin' anybody, chica," T replied. "We'll keep you and the baby safe. Now close your eyes and silencio, por favor. Es muy importante!"

"Sí."

Voices reached them from down the hall.

"Jump on my back and hold on tight," T ordered her.

She didn't move.

"Give her a boost, bro," T said.

Gently hoisting the slight girl, Liam laid her, belly down, on T's back. The voices grew louder as they bolted up to the top of the steps. T pulled her arms together tightly around his neck and turned his back to the steps to block her visibility.

Two men in tank tops cast cursory glances in the trio's direction as they raced down the hall, brandishing Tasers.

"Hah," T muttered approvingly. "Maria, it's gonna get real loud in a second. Entiende?"

"Sí," she whimpered.

"Muy bien," T murmured. Turning to Liam, he said, "We're going to cut through the kitchen and out onto the loading dock."

"Roger that!" Liam replied.

Two more men appeared at the top of the steps. One continued past them, but the other stared in their direction, appearing mystified. Liam held his breath.

Maria moaned.

"What the fuck?" the man exclaimed. He took a tentative step toward them before collapsing and writhing in agony as T's Taser found its target.

"Pull that alarm behind you and follow me," T ordered, gesturing to the red bar at Liam's shoulder.

Liam obeyed, triggering strobe lights and an ear-piercing siren. Maria screamed. Liam bolted down the hall behind T toward another tank-topped man heading straight toward them, brandishing a weapon.

Juking past him, T yelled, "Take him!"

"What the fuck?" the man cried as he turned to gawk at the girl hurtling past him atop a moving blur. Liam wheeled around to tase the amorphous target, and the man collapsed; his flopping head slammed against the antiquated lockers lining the walls before thudding against the floor.

Alarmed by the man's lifeless appearance, Liam stooped down

to slap his face softly and then harder. The man's eyes fluttered open, and he stared at Liam vacantly for a moment.

"Sorry I hurt ya, man," Liam pleaded, "but where are the ashes?"

The man's eyes suddenly rolled back in his head and went white; his face slackened as Liam shrank from him.

"Sorry, dude," Liam muttered, staring back at the prone form with the dart tail jutting from his sternum.

Please, God, don't let him die.

He followed T through a door into the school kitchen, where lingering greasy food odors met his nostrils.

Dashing out the back door onto the loading dock, they were greeted by a clamor of screams, shouts, thudding footsteps, opening and closing doors, chants of "Freedom Lies Here, Here Lies Home," coyote yips, Goliath's booming, enraged vocals, and the blare of the fire alarm.

Dogs barked and howled their fury up and down the neighboring streets as houses lit up.

Hands propped on his knees, T bent double, panting heavily under the burden of the pregnant teen on his back.

"Can you take her?" T asked, wheezing. "My spine's 'bout to snap."

"Uh, ok." They transferred Maria to Liam's back after a brief struggle. Exhaustion took hold of him, reminiscent of his state after a couple of sleepless nights while caring for Joan in hospice.

Overhead, blinking drones careened across the sky, smoky from distant—for now—wildfires to the east. A wave of fresh sweat poured into Liam's eyes thanks to his sudden burden. All sound, save for canines and approaching voices, suddenly ceased.

"Clear!" Men's voices issued from inside the school, each successive cry getting closer.

Projected by a hovering drone, a shimmering holo suddenly materialized before them, hovering near and slightly above them.

"You have no idea what you're doing, you self-righteous assholes," Ouroboros's seething avatar informed them.

"Invisibility cloaks are slick, but I will find you. And then," he screamed, "Adiós, motherfuckers!"

"Jesus," T muttered through his heavy pants.

Amen.

Barely had the echoes of the bellowed threat, amplified by the speakers across the campus, faded when Goliath's enraged baying grew louder.

Goliath doesn't need to see us to find us.

They dashed across the street into the darkness, settling under a sprawling maple tree, its foliage crisping from the heat. Screaming in Liam's ear, Maria flailed against his awkwardly grasping arms as she tried to free herself.

"Stop!" he cried.

"Where's the fuckin' car?" T bellowed.

Across the street, the giant mastiff launched himself over the fence and, fleetingly, into the sweeping spotlights of the drones overhead.

Running behind a car, Liam cowered.

Taser ain't gonna stop that monster.

Daily News

BREAKING NEWS

Idaho legislature passes resolution declaring English official state language

CHAPTER
TWENTY-TWO

Seeking in vain a couple of telltale headlight blinks, the gasping men scrambled up the contours of a curbside SUV with their limp burden, triggering a car alarm as Goliath closed the gap between them.

"Step away from the car, step away from the car," the audio alert commanded beneath their feet.

Motion lights splashed across the front yard of a small house to their left. The front door burst open momentarily, throwing off a bleached halogen glow.

"What the fuck is going on out here?" barked a man backlit by the light from the house.

Liam was poised, reluctantly, to tase Goliath (*poor brute didn't ask for this)* when a large, snarling German shepherd raced by the man on the porch toward them. He made a beeline for Goliath, who snapped at Liam's heels as he kicked wildly at the massive head and jaws while trying to aim his weapon.

"Frederick, get back here!" screamed the man in the doorway.

Distracted by a fresh foe, Goliath pivoted his dish-sized paws from the car's hood to plant his front legs on the pavement and face his adversary. The dogs snapped at each other indecisively.

"Get off my car, you assholes!"

The dogs' barking suddenly turned eerily shrill.

The ground beneath them shuddered for an instant, triggering a symphony of neighboring car alarms that further pierced the air. Clawing for holds, the two men clung to the vehicle's roof.

An aerial spotlight washed across a posse of Caminos on the other side of the fence, most gingerly recovering their feet following the fleeting aftershock; a couple of others, undeterred by the shaking, were scrambling over the fence.

Two thunderous cracks in quick succession triggered another round of frantic barking from the snarling dogs, not to mention others up and down the street, setting off a robust coyote chorus.

The end of the world?

Liam and T looked skyward to see not drones, of which Ouro had apparently regained some control, but a smoky shower of debris. Goliath and the Caminos sprinted down the street, away from the gunfire, toward the school entrance.

Frederick, the German shepherd, bolted back into his yard and around the side of the house, out of sight, as the front door had already slammed shut.

Liam gawked at the marksmanship display. How the hell?

"C'mon, c'mon!" a familiar voice implored them. "Get in the van!"

A black ski mask concealing his face, Tate waved what appeared to be an assault rifle in their direction. Heaving the vehicle's rear doors open, he motioned the threesome forward to the extended van, larger than the one Tate had driven previously.

T shot Liam a questioning glance, to which Liam nodded.

Do it.

Sliding gingerly off the scratched and dented SUV with Maria still on Liam's back, they hobbled over to the van. T hopped in first, reaching back to help wrestle Liam and his cargo to safety.

Liam was only halfway in with Maria when Tate gunned the surprisingly peppy van up the hill and away from the school. T barely managed to reel in his companions and pull closed the rear door before collapsing across a double seat behind Tate, his chest heaving.

Gasping for air and drowning in sweat, Liam tugged off his stifling headgear. "What the fuck are you doing here?" he barked at Tate. After catching his breath, he wrestled Maria into the second seat behind T, who Liam suddenly noticed was clutching his chest with a hand.

"You're welcome," Tate replied.

"You okay, T?" Liam queried, leaning over him. "Need a doc?"

Panting hard, T waved him off with his free hand. "Just need a minute, is all."

Liam turned back to Tate. "Thanks for the ride, yes," he said testily, "but what are you doing here?"

"Go ahead and laugh at me and my carry," Tate declared, waving around his Colt just as the van hit a big pothole; the revolver's barrel jounced against the ceiling with a thud.

Opening her eyes at the noise and surveying her surroundings, Maria wailed like a banshee.

"Fuck me!" cried Tate, who apparently hadn't noticed her in the darkness. "Who the hell is that?"

He twisted his hooded head around to stare at Maria, who screamed and lunged toward the van's rear, fumbling for the door release. Liam lunged after her, wrestling her away from the rear as gently as he could and grasping her firmly; he begged her to calm down. She went limp in his arms and resumed sobbing.

"This is Maria," replied Liam. "She's pregnant, and she's high as a kite, so be nice."

"Maria, the stoned, knocked-up Mexican," Tate muttered, shaking his head.

"Chapina," Maria retorted before burying her head in her tiny hands.

"Chapina?" Liam mused.

"Guatemalan babe," T explained. "What the chicas call themselves."

"Can you *please* lose your hood?" Liam implored Tate. "You're freaking her out."

"Oh, so it's *my* fault," Tate grumbled before complying.

Reaching out, T took one of her delicate hands in one of his beefy ones.

"Did you guys fuckin' *kidnap* her?" He gaped at Liam.

"Just drive."

"Sure, I'll drive," Tate carped. "It's only *my* fuckin' van."

"All right then, we'll walk."

"*Sure*, you will," he replied. "Incidentally, since I *am* driving, where do you want to go?"

Digging out his cell phone, Liam texted Ellie's address to Tate.

"Incoming."

"Copy that."

It occurred to Liam that the three men in various stealth camo, for lack of a better word, must look nightmarish to the terrified, psilo-addled—and yes, *kidnapped*, at least technically—young woman.

Now what?

"Hoo, that could've been nasty," Tate said with a laugh, still hefting the gun in his right hand.

"Put that fuckin' thing down!" Liam snapped.

Ranger, whom Liam hadn't noticed until now, growled his disapproval from the front passenger seat.

"Easy, bud," Tate muttered.

"Please," T pleaded from behind Tate, "put it down. Things are fucked up enough already."

Tate considered his passengers in turn as if weighing a reply before slipping the gun into a large glove compartment with a magnetic keypad.

"Thank you," Liam and T chorused.

"I figured you were trying to get your wife's ashes back," Tate said after a pause. "I wanted to help but knew you'd never ask me."

"So, you *stalked* me?"

"I looked *out* for you," Tate countered. He patted the dash with a victorious grin. "I figured this rig might come in handy."

"Christ," Liam muttered. "Is anyone *not* spying on me?"

Tate patted the rifle. "He ain't gonna send any more drones after us," he said with a grin. "I still can't believe that," he added.

"Believe what?"

"That I actually nailed those fuckers."

"Yeah," Liam acknowledged, "that was amazing." He shook his head.

"It was weird," Tate said, warming to the topic. "Crazy as everything got so fast back there, I wasn't even thinking about shooting at 'em. And then…"

To Liam's amazement, Tate fell silent.

"And then what?" Liam prompted after a moment.

"You're gonna bust my balls," Tate began tentatively, "but I can't explain it. It's like something got inside my head and took over my body. Like somebody else picked up the gun, aimed, and shot. Then I was standing in the street, watching the debris, and I couldn't believe it myself."

Liam stared, at least as impressed by Tate's apparent sincerity as he was by the feat itself.

"Wow."

"Yeah," Tate echoed pensively. "Wow."

"I wonder if that aftershock did more damage to the schools," Liam mused as he surveyed his new surroundings.

The cool air in the van bore traces of carpet shampoo. Strapped to the extended cab's left wall were stacks of bins and boxes of what appeared to be food. Folded flat against the opposite wall was a hinged Army cot and sleeping bag. Abutting them were a tiny sink and microwave. Stretched across the tops of both was what appeared to be a padlocked, Army-green gun locker, above which a drone perched on a rack bolted to the ceiling. A folding platform about the size of a laptop clung to the wall opposite the cot.

Sweet little setup for a survivalist.

"I almost forgot," Tate broke the momentary silence. "Did you get 'em?"

"Get 'em?"

"The ashes."

"We couldn't find 'em," Liam lamented after a pause.

"Any idea where they are?" Tate persisted.

"I dunno," Liam muttered.

"*Idaho?*" Tate said quizzically.

"Sí," Maria suddenly piped up. "*Idaho!*"

Liam turned to Maria. "What *about* Idaho?"

"Si, si," she exclaimed. "Idaho. We are there? I see monstruos." She stared, wide-eyed, at the black rear of Tate's round, swiveling, behooded bean.

"Monsters?" the driver muttered. "She's stoned all right,"

More English. She's calming down…

"Shut up, Tate."

"¿Dónde is Miguel?" she asked.

"Miguel?"

"Si," she cried. "Mi novio."

Her boyfriend.

"Me siento tan raro. Tengo miedo."

"We don't know where your boyfriend is," Liam replied with a shrug. "And we know you're scared, but you're safe with us."

"Speak English," Tate jabbed.

"Go to hell," she snapped.

T roared with laughter before groaning with the pain it evidently provoked.

"That's better," Tate replied with a chuckle.

"Tate!" Liam exclaimed. He turned back to the girl. "So you're married, or you're getting married?"

"We marry," she replied between sobs. "We need be together para el bebé."

"Está tu novio in Idaho, Maria?" He glanced questioningly at T, who shrugged and groaned.

"Él está en camino."

"He's on his way," Liam translated aloud. "What for?"

"Maestro lo envió a comenzar un nuevo El Camino."

Ouroboros sent him to start a new El Camino.

Liam and T eyed each other in disbelief as the van rolled to a stop a block from Ellie's duplex.

Daily News

Breaking News

Study shows dogs suffering from feelings of inadequacy.

CHAPTER
TWENTY-THREE

Tate gawked at the distinctive, lush images of vaginas, breasts, and curvaceous, insouciant nude women that dominated Ellie's living room decor. Sitting at her kitchen table drinking coffee, Liam squelched a laugh, recalling some of the artwork that had decorated Ellie's cubicle at the shop. The old white boys weren't wild about it, but Ellie was the best editor in the building.

"Don't like it, don't look," she'd respond to raised eyebrows, daring them to comment.

An air purifier, AC unit, and ceiling fans stymied the pernicious, smoke-fouled air.

Jess scowled at Liam from her post by the sink. Her

spectral hands tightened visibly around her walker's aluminum handle.

"I'm sorry I stood you up, Jess," he said, "but you would have taken over the whole show."

"You mean the whole shit show?"

"Shit show is right," T chimed in from his prone position on a floral sofa.

"If we'd met like you agreed to, Liam," she said, "you wouldn't be in this situation."

"Shit happens, Jess," he replied. "I knew you'd argue with me about everything."

"And it would have gone so much worse?" she jabbed.

"I repeat: Shit happens," he replied. "You know, apart from the fact that the ashes were missing—and how could we have known *that*—it actually went all right."

"And apart from the fact you may have critically injured or killed someone," his sibling countered, "and that this homophobic Trumpie" —she nodded toward Tate— "woke up the whole neighborhood playing Rambo?"

"Hey, fuck you, lady!" Tate retorted. "I saved their asses."

Liam rubbed his temples. "Anyway, we're meeting now."

"This is getting us nowhere," observed M, who sat across the table from him.

Jess stared. "And you are?"

"This is my neighbor, Miriam," Liam said.

"M," M interjected.

"Ah," Jess said knowingly. "Mirihim."

Their eyes met for a long moment while the others watched nervously.

"Speaking," M said drily.

"She knows Ouroboros, too," Liam noted. "She installed the security system at El Camino."

"How *interesting*."

"It's a living," M replied lightly, meeting her gaze before turning back to Liam. "So, where are the ashes?"

"The ashes?" asked Maria, who sat quietly on a beige loveseat with Ellie, sobbing.

"I'm trying to get my wife's ashes back," Liam pleaded.

She stared at him. "No te entiendo."

"Las cenizas de su esposa," T translated.

"No!" She looked at Liam in horror.

"Sí," Liam replied quietly. "That's why we ran into you in the school. I was looking for the ashes when you showed up."

T translated again.

"Oh, señor," she cried. "Lo siento mucho!"

"It's not your fault, honey," Liam replied, "One of your neighbors from the school stole an urn from my yard with my dead wife's ashes in it."

Swiping at tears, Maria blinked questioningly.

Ellie stepped in to interpret.

"Oh!" Maria shook her head in evident dismay.

"So," Jess interjected. "Where are the ashes?"

"I think Miguel has them," Maria replied meekly.

"You *think*?" Jess exclaimed.

"*Christ*, Jess," Ellie pleaded.

A momentary silence ensued.

"Jesus, Liam," Jess continued. "What *is* the plan?"

"What else?" he said. "Find her boyfriend and get the ashes back."

"Find her boyfriend," Jess echoed dubiously, "who conscientiously impregnated and abandoned her."

Liam shrugged.

"That isn't a plan," she said. "That's a rosy scenario."

Tightly gripping Maria's twiggy shoulders, Ellie steered the teen into the kitchen. A peasant dress sheathed her tiny, swarthy frame. Her raven hair was pulled back in a neat ponytail cinched with a red barrette, and from a chain around her neck dangled a charm or talisman in the shape of what appeared to be the red claws of a cat.

In the kitchen's brighter light, Liam noticed Maria's delicate, distinctive native beauty for the first time, which resembled a cross between a Latina and a Native American. She resembled Selena Gomez, who had just appeared in the latest Marvel movie, with narrower, more angular features and a delicately arched nose.

And ink.

Lots of ink.

Jess also stared at the tattoos.

Liam stared at a round black-and-white one adorning her right shoulder.

Noting his interest, Jess said, "That's Hunab Ku, the Mayan symbol for peace, unity, and the universe."

"Reminds me of the yin-yang symbol."

"Yes," she said. "Balance. Harmony."

"Pretty woke."

"Yes," she repeated.

Shaking his head scornfully, Tate made a noise.

Clutching a mug of tea M had handed her, Maria wept softly, but her dark eyes were alert.

"Lamento haberme asustado."

"Anybody woulda been scared, chica," T said reassuringly.

T's grasp of Spanish was impressive, which made sense, as many Caminos appeared Latino.

"Quiero ayudarte to, uh, find Miguel," Maria said haltingly. "I need to see him."

Her English is evidently returning…

"Of course you do, mija," Ellie said. She brushed her fleshy lips tenderly against Maria's forehead and squeezed her.

"Mija?" Liam asked quizzically.

"Darling, daughter," Jess replied tersely. "Term of endearment." She shot a questioning glance at Ellie.

As Maria half-turned to meet Ellie's embrace, Liam saw with a start yet another picture, a familiar depiction of a snake swallowing its tail on her back just below her neck.

"*Ouroboros,*" M uttered.

"Yes," Jess responded yet again.

"Yes, suh…" T drawled, his head nodding knowingly.

Turning to Ellie's refrigerator, Liam scanned the contents before grabbing and twisting off the cap of a bottle of Dos Equis Amber.

Turning back to Maria, he took a swig. "Where's Miguel headed?"

"Yo creo he goes to Sandpoint," Maria said. "Or lo que sea is near the mill."

"Yo creo?" Jess echoed. "You *think*?"

"That's what he told me."

"So, you're in touch with him?" Jess pressed.

Maria frowned in concentration before nodding as though realizing something. She shook her head sadly. "He told me antes he go." *Before he left.*

M launched a holomap from her phone that hovered, glowing, above the table.

Tate's eyes widened anew at the effect.

"What's he driving?" M asked.

"A black SUV, I think."

"What time did he leave?"

"No estoy segura," she said. "Some tiempo después de medianoche, midnight, probablemente, después Maestro begins our slash session."

"Naturally," Jess chimed in. "Anybody with him?"

"Probablemente—probably una guardia."

"Are they armed?" M made a shooting motion with her hand.

"Probably."

"With Tasers?"

Maria nodded, frowning. "Y fantasmas."

Ghosts? Ghost guns!

Probably more of the type Liam had crammed into his tote bag, which remained in the van, crumpled among the pile of gear they'd stripped off.

"Jesus," T muttered.

"Where are the fires?" Jess asked.

"Good question. Show wildfires between Portland, Oregon, and Sandpoint, Idaho," M told her phone.

Several undulating red blots of varying sizes appeared on the map. According to the graphic, sporadic stretches of the densely forested mountains on either bank of the Columbia River Gorge were aflame.

"Christ," said T, who had limped over to the table for a closer look.

"What route do you think he'd take?" Liam asked.

"Is there any way to locate him?" M queried.

"Can you call him?" Jess asked.

"Maestro tomó mi teléfono antes… before our sesión," Maria replied.

Asshole took her phone. Naturally.

"I'm sure Ouroboros can block unwanted calls, anyway," M said.

"No doubt," Jess affirmed tartly.

"Ouro must be in touch with him," Liam ventured.

"Perfect," Jess replied. "We'll just call Ouroboros and have him patch us through."

"Just thinking out loud," Liam said. "Geez, Jess."

"What about the car?"

"What about it?"

"Anyone as paranoid and tech-savvy as Ouroboros probably put a tracker on it," M said.

"Transponder."

"Which means?"

"A sat signal."

"Which might be hackable?" Ellie noted.

Everyone looked at M.

Leaning back, she rubbed her chin thoughtfully. "I'll need to get in my office. And we're gonna need supplies."

"I can help with that!" Tate exclaimed with a grin.

> **DAILY NEWS**
>
> # BREAKING NEWS
>
> Texas governor proposes banning excessive use of LGBTQ language in official correspondence.

CHAPTER
TWENTY-FOUR

A receiver jutting from his right ear, Tate watched PNS on the dash when he wasn't scanning the surrounding pavement with his binoculars. He'd parked the cramped van amidst fuel pumps shielded by a canopy from the weather—and drones—at a Jubitz truck stop; they'd gassed up just off a heavily wooded Gresham freeway ramp onto I-84 East. A shamble of tents studded the tree line adjacent to the asphalt.

Freight rigs—sidelined by wildfires, soaring fuel prices, and the slumping economy—packed the expansive striped lot. The rumble of their idling engines filled the air, throwing off still more heat as they kept the vehicles' air conditioning blasting.

Resummoning her friend's AV, M had wriggled herself into

Liam's fades—his slang for Invisiwear—and set off for her office. She would rejoin them after finishing her business, which included feeding her and Liam's animals.

Occupying the van's passenger seat, Liam downed his evening meds with a swallow of tepid coffee. While M had abandoned T and him at the school, she at least had snagged his backpack, in which he'd prudently stowed a few days' worth of medication, from the vacant AV before sending it home to its garage.

Maria and T, clutching his phone, slouched wearily on the double bench behind him.

Ellie and Jess had detoured to procure a list of late pregnancy-related items Maria had texted them.

Yawning deeply, Liam gingerly swiveled his aching trunk in the seat and craned his neck to face Maria.

"So," he prompted, "tell me" —he paused, glancing at his companions— "tell *us* about Ouroboros and his... beliefs, his message."

"Sí, su mensaje," she said, nodding fervently as she absently rubbed her swollen belly.

Liam winced at the idea of this tiny girl, over whom even Ellie towered, squeezing out an infant.

"You mean like Freedom Lies Here," he persisted, picking at a scab on his arm. "And psilo, and slash?"

"Sí," she said. "Trascendencia."

Transcendence...

"Maestro says his destino is to guiarnos on nuestro viaje after we drink his tea, his poción," she intoned haltingly, evidently groping for more intelligible "Spanglish."

"Cuando soñamos mientras we're despiertos somos consiente of what has been and what can be."

Maria's "pretty good" English tested Liam's grasp of Spanish. From what he could gather, Ouroboros's destiny, roughly translated, was to guide his flock on their psilo and slash "journeys" while they dreamt of the past and the future.

T shook his head wearily.

"Maestro tiene—*has* muchos creyentes in Idaho," Maria said. Her wary gaze darted among her companions.

"Creyentes in English?" Liam asked his phone.

"Believers," it replied.

"He was there," Maria added.

"Who was *where*?" Liam asked.

"Maestro was at a campamento afuera de MillTown."

"A camp?"

"A migrant camp?" T ventured, his eyes closed.

"Sí," Maria confirmed. "Los soldados estaban arrasando our camps and rounding up immigrantes and other homeless people. They put us on buses se dirigió to the fires in the panhandle."

She blinked back tears as she continued, "They said the tribunales, the courts I think, gave them poderes de emergencia to make us fight fires o ser deportada."

Fight fires or be deported?

"We were scared," Maria said. "We didn't want to fight the fires but were desperate to stay en los Estados Unidos."

"Hell yeah," T snorted.

"As bad off as we are here," she added, "it's worse at home."

"If you came here legally," Tate clucked, "ya woulda been okay."

"*Cabrón*," Maria snapped at him, scowling.

"No shit," T concurred, glaring at his neighbor.

"Jus' sayin'," Tate muttered.

"Unos doscientos…"

"almost two hundred," T noted.

"Si, couple hundred of us camping out for the night next to the buses fuera de—outside of—MillTown," Maria continued, still glaring at Tate. "We were going to pass through the pueblo on the way to los incendios. The guards gave us one food paquete for every two or three personas."

Liam pursed his lips.

"Un negocio donated a truckload of bug food, but we ran out of water."

"Ground Bounty," T muttered.

"Yuck," Tate chimed in.

"Sí," she said. "Estaban haciendo videos secretos con sus teléfonos."

"They were making videos?" T asked.

"Sí," she replied. "They said, ah, that they los publicaban en línea."

"And posted them online," Liam said.

"Sí, of us, of nuestro situación…"

"And?"

"The next day, Maestro arrived towing a water buffalo."

"A *what*?" Liam asked.

"Portable water tank," Tate blurted like a know-it-all.

"I'm surprised they let him deliver it," Liam said.

"Les trajo the guards bottled water," she said. "Y cerveza."

"Hmm…"

"While we filled bottles," she explained in increasingly fluent English, "Maestro stood on top of the tank and talked to us in English and Spanish sobre El Camino and how he was, uh… potenciar a las personas…" She looked at T expectantly.

"Empowering people," he said.

"Gracious, tio," Maria continued, "empowering people to take control de sus vidas."

Their lives…

"He told us we deberíamos—*should*—organizar and take over an old nearby sawmill like he and his creyentes took over the school here in Portland."

Hmmm…

Liam tore open a Clif bar he'd ferreted out of the glove compartment.

"Then the guards told him to shut up," she said. "But a lot of people liked what he said and that he spoke good Spanish. No one could averiguar… uh… figure out how he got past the guards and drones and why they let him stay.

"Some people said he put a spell on the guards," she added in a near whisper.

"Rich fuck greased some palms," T muttered, nodding his head knowingly.

Jess had mentioned, Liam recalled, that Ouroboros had referred to himself as a trust-fund baby. Maybe he *was* a rich fuck, willing to spend to get his way.

"Did you talk to him?" he asked.

"He was… espeluznante," she said, frowning.

"Qué?" Liam's questioning glance drew a shrug from T.

Maria hunched over, bared her teeth, and clawed at the air with mock menace.

"He was creepy!" Tate exclaimed, mugging like a lecher.

Everybody laughed as Maria nodded fervently.

"He stared at me while I was filling bottles," she continued, "like he reconoció me from somewhere and asked me my name. Then he had Miguel start ordenar a la gente. It was like he knew somehow that Miguel was mandón."

T chuckled. "Bossy."

"And he said he really liked my tattoos."

Yuck!

"He told me I reminded him of some aldeanas he met in Guatemala." Noting their blank faces, she added, "Aldeanas… villagers. The women there son espléndidas, he said."

He told her, in so many words, that she was gorgeous—double yuck.

"Bogey at two o'clock," Tate muttered.

Following his neighbor's binocular gaze out over the van's hood, Liam thought he might have glimpsed a dark figure with a flashlight moving around the trucks across the parking lot.

He rubbed his weary, bleary eyes and looked again.

Nothing.

"He disappeared around a truck," Tate said as if sensing his companion's doubt. He massaged Ranger's ruff as the canine raised his blocky head to peer out the windshield. "See? He smells 'em."

Liam scanned the spot in question with the binocs Tate handed him.

Nothing.

"Or maybe you're freaking him out," Liam replied dismissively. He sighed. The longer they loitered there, the more likely they were to draw unwanted attention.

Where the hell is M?

DAILY NEWS

BREAKING NEWS

Texas governor signs budget slashing spending for dual language classrooms.

A spotlight exploded to life outside Liam's passenger door, blinding him as he was about to resume questioning Maria. An instant later, he started at a jarring *rat-a-tat-tat* on his window, closed against the heat and diesel exhaust beyond.

"Oww!" Liam yelped as Ranger, snarling at the intrusion, planted a huge front paw squarely on his crotch.

"Sorry, forgot to adjust the force," piped an R2-D2-ish bot a-blink with tiny lights and, presumably, cameras a few feet away. "You have to knock louder on those huge truck cabs or blow a horn to get their attention."

What the fuck?

Blinking vestigial motes from his stunned eyes, Liam gaped at the unwelcome visitor. Disappearing into its "torso" was a telescoping rod tipped with a hard rubber knob, evidently employed to startle the shit out of unsuspecting loiterers.

Seriously, what the fuck?

Glancing at the rearview mirror, Liam was relieved to see that Maria was out of sight.

A life-size holo of a middle-aged man with nondescript features, clad in rent-a-cop regalia, materialized from a lens peeping from the bot's abdomen.

Gen AI. Cheaper and more reliable, presumably, than a bored, screen-scrolling human.

Liam hesitantly rolled down the window.

"Good evening, folks," the holo intoned in a soothing register. "Hope I didn't startle you."

It's a chatty bot.

"Not at all," Liam lied. He tried to place the familiar, if synthetic, voice, which sounded East Coast.

"Name's Bart," Bart informed them, nodding amiably toward the other occupants.

Bart? Bot?

"And yours?"

"My what?"

"Your name, sir?"

"Ezekiel," Liam replied, ludicrously relieved that Bart at least pretended not to know his name. "Zeke for short."

Someone behind him snorted.

"Out kinda late, are you, Zeke?" Bart probed with a paper smile.

"We're waiting for someone," Liam replied.

"Ah," Bart replied in his flat voice. "I hope you don't have to wait *too* long…"

A veiled threat?

"I hate it when people keep me waiting," Bart shared.

"I'm making the rounds, as you may have noticed, checking on all the drivers," he continued, nodding toward the trucks yonder. "Some of 'em been stuck here for days, poor bastards."

Can a bot be bored, as Bart, indeed, sounds? Or is Bart a holo of a real bored person in real-time?

The conjecture taxed Liam's already overwhelmed mind.

"You folks look pretty harmless," Bart opined.

"We're not *that* harmless," Tate joshed.

Shut up!

"You folks look pretty harmless," Bart repeated jerkily. "Look pretty harmless."

A hiccupping bot.

"FYI," said Bart, apparently back on track. "I've had reliable reports that domestic terrorists kidnapped a pregnant teen from the El Camino homeless compound and shot the place up in the bargain. They're armed and considered extremely dangerous."

"Wow," Tate chimed in. "They could be anywhere."

Moron! Well, at least he didn't say "they…"

"Could be hiding in plain sight," Bart ventured before breaking into a tinny artificial laugh.

OMG!

"And these wildfires… damn!" Bart shook his translucent head.

Whatever generated this laughable AI-dude banter is ripe for an upgrade.

"So, when are you expecting your… acquaintance?" Bart inquired.

"Hard to say." Liam didn't want Bart around when M, Ellie, and Jess returned.

"FYI, there are prostitutes and drug dealers making the rounds of bored truckers out here," Bart droned. "And curb huggers." He jerked his bean in the direction of the tents.

"Don't know why they'd bother you since you look—"

"Pretty harmless?" Liam ventured.

"Pretty pretty, pretty harmless." The image jerked again as it repeated itself in the synthesized voice of, Liam suddenly recognized, Robert De Niro.

Surreal.

"You folks have a have a have a good night," the spasming avatar stuttered, "and keep your eyes eyes eyes open for those terrorists."

"Ask him what the terrorists look like," commanded Jess, suddenly within radio range as Ellie rolled her silent Tesla into shadows cast by the pump stanchions several yards behind the bot.

Liam drummed his right-hand fingers on the exterior of his door. "If we're to watch out for the *alleged* terrorists," he told Bart, "it would be helpful if you tell us what you know about them."

"Well played," Jess commented.

"That's logical," Bart said after a fleeting pause. "The most recent, reasonably reliable sources available report that the suspected terrorists are heavily armed and dangerous," Bart intoned.

"There are believed to be three kidnapping and terrorism suspects, for whom there are thus far no helpful physical descriptions available. The suspected hostage, a pregnant young Latina whose identity authorities have yet to confirm, is believed to be a member of the El Camino homeless cult in Portland, Oregon, where the incident occurred about 3 a.m. this morning.

"There are no reports yet," Bart added, "of a ransom note or demands. Authorities are withholding the names of three organizations, none of which are located in Portland, nor have any known connection with El Camino, who is claiming responsibility for the incident, which is trending on all prominent media platforms."

Wow…

"Any any any other questions?" Bart stuttered.

"Uhhh…"

Bart vanished as abruptly as he'd appeared.

Swiveling on its chassis, the ailing unit rolled off into the early morning haze.

"That was *so* fuckin' weird," T opined.

DAILY NEWS

BREAKING NEWS

North Korea secretly owns manufacturer of faulty security bots.

"So, Smart Bart," Liam said, "doesn't know who we are or what we look like. But we need to move soon."

"Smart Bart," Tate echoed, chuckling.

"Chat gets the benefit of the doubt," said Ellie, who joined them after Bart disappeared. She handed Maria a paper grocery bag. "More reliable than PNS."

"That ain't sayin' much," T noted.

"What's Jess doing?" Liam asked.

"Being Jess."

He grunted.

"This van smells like a locker room," Ellie sniffed. "Couldn't fit a shower in here?"

Wincing at the first inklings of a headache—exhaustion coupled with low blood sugar—Liam dug a second Clif Bar from the glove compartment.

He jumped when his phone buzzed with a text alert.

"M says leave without her if she's not here in ten minutes," he shared. "She's trying to get around roadblocks that cops and Caminos are setting up to—"

"Find us," Ellie finished.

"Surprised the pigs showed up," T commented.

"Well, you did, technically, kidnap her," Ellie observed.

"So," Liam said, "we head for Idunno in ten minutes."

Liam again turned back to Maria, who was methodically sorting through the bag's contents.

"So Miguel and Maestro were buddy-buddy?" Liam asked.

"Buddy-buddy," echoed Tate, chuckling. "You sound like Bart."

"Buddy-buddy?" Maria inquired. Twisting the cap off a bottled smoothie, she sniffed the contents before taking a big sip.

"Good friends," Ellie translated. "Buenos amigos."

"Oh, sí," Maria replied, wiping her mouth with a sleeve. "He spent a lot of time talking to Miguel alone. He told him our niños would be especial."

"Special, how?"

She shrugged.

"What else did he talk about?"

She shrugged again. "Miguel said Maestro le juró guardar el secreto," she said.

"Swore him to secrecy?" Liam ventured.

"It made me angry," Maria continued with a nod, "but he said I needed to understand that Maestro was a great leader who would help us, help our people."

He and T exchanged knowing nods. Factoring in the ebb and flow of unfamiliar words, her English skills were improving remarkably fast.

"Then Miguel started acting strange."

"What do you mean?"

"I think Maestro was giving him hongos de psilocibina and getting into his head," she said, tapping her right temple. "He convinced Miguel that we would have a son, Jesús, who was going to be a leader, a salvador, and that we needed to protect him and make sure his path is claro."

Jesús the savior?

"I thought you said Maestro swore Miguel to secrecy," Liam said.

"Mostly," she said with a sly smile. "But Miguel really likes sex."

"Imagine that," Ellie cracked.

T guffawed. Liam chuckled, and Tate's eyebrows arched.

"He told Miguel that Jesús's destino was" —she paused as if trying to recall something— "foreordained."

"He said he'd protect me and Jesús."

Maria. Jesús. Miguel?

"*Je*-sus." Shaking his head, Tate clucked his disdain.

"No le creo todo… I didn't believe all of it," Maria said, her head sagging. "But I fingida…"

"Feigned," T clarified. "Pretended."

"Sí," she said. "I pretended to believe because Miguel did and Maestro helped us."

Ah…

"Maestro told Miguel he could give him powers to protect Jesús," Maria whispered.

"*Powers*?" Liam recalled what Jess had told him about the ritual of ingesting ashes. He tried to imagine being convinced by some witch doctor while he was hallucinating that the ashes he'd ingested would give him new abilities. He'd read of primitive warriors convinced by a shaman or some such mystic before they charged into battle that they were bulletproof or otherwise immune to harm.

"Sí," she said. "Maestro told him he must nature them con cuidado."

Nurture.

"Miguel adora Maestro," she said irritably. "He told me tiene que obedecer las órdenes del Maestro."

Follow Maestro's orders?

"Then Miguel started going on and on about having a baby."

"Sounds like Ouroboros *convinced* him he wanted to be a daddy," Liam conjectured.

"Convencido, si," she replied, nodding thoughtfully as if she had considered the possibility.

"We were still having sex," —she looked at her feet shyly— "but I just went along to shut Miguel up. I made him keep wearing a condón."

Tate rolled his eyes.

"He was the only support I had, the only one I trusted," Maria said. "But I didn't want to have a bebé unless we were married and had algo de estabilidad. I wanted to go to college, maybe be a nurse or a médica."

"A nurse or doctor," Liam muttered.

A curandera.

"Maestro followed the buses to the panhandle, camped out with us, and talked Miguel's ear off."

"While he had him tripping?"

"I think so." She shook her head disapprovingly. "When we got closer to the fires, he said he had to return to El Camino."

More perfect English.

Liam tipped his travel mug high to drain it and wiped his lips on his sleeve.

"Then what?"

"Miguel talked his way into a job in the kitchen at the fire camp and then got me one, so we'd be más lejos—farther, I mean, from the fires," she explained. "We both cooked at the granjas—the, uh, farms we worked at."

T nodded at her translation.

"Strange they didn't send a big, strong guy like Miguel out to cut fire breaks," Liam noted.

"Sí."

"And then?"

"I got—" She dubiously patted her swollen belly. "Embarazada."

"You said he was using condoms," Tate noted.

"Condoms aren't foolproof," said Ellie.

"True dat," T muttered.

"I was scared," Maria said, swiping at fresh tears as she clutched the smoothie with her free hand.

"Of course you were, mija," Ellie purred.

Just as well Jess isn't here to hear that again.

"I didn't tell Miguel I was pregnant because, like I said, I wasn't ready."

Nodding fervently, Ellie held Maria's tiny hand.

"Then somebody else told him," she said. "He shocked me by suddenly agreeing we should wait and that it would be dangerous for me. He said he knew people in Portland that would help us."

"Ouroboros," Liam declared. He popped the remainder of the snack bar into his mouth.

Maria nodded. "I wondered why Miguel didn't just admit it," she said with a frown. "I started to wonder about him but had nowhere else to turn."

"So, you got away," Liam prompted curtly.

Ellie gave him a look.

"He noqueado…"

"Knocked out," Ellie clarified.

"Si, he knocked out the guards by putting a drug Maestro gave him in their food one night that put 'em to sleep."

T chuckled. "Sweet."

"He didn't tell me he was going to do it because he knew I'd tell him he was crazy, that they'd send us to the fires if they found out," she continued fluently. "But he said the drug would make them forget what happened. He and a friend robar a car, and the three of us headed for Portland with money they took off the guards."

"*Whoa,*" Tate exclaimed as he munched on peanut M&M's. "That's a lot of crime."

"Put yourself in their shoes," Ellie suggested.

"But when we got there," Maria continued, "Miguel's friend robbed us and took the car and most of the money, and we ended up in a homeless camp."

"Some friend," T noted.

"But Miguel must have told Ouroboros, or Maestro, that you were coming," Liam pressed her. "Why didn't he help you?"

"Miguel tried calling him, but no one answered," Maria replied. "His voicemail was full, so Miguel couldn't leave a message and didn't know anybody else at El Camino. Maestro kept showing up online, but Miguel said it was all fake."

"Naturally," T interjected.

"It was like Maestro disappeared, but somebody was trying to convince his followers he was still in charge."

Tate shook his head dismissively.

"They wouldn't let anybody new into El Camino without Maestro's aprobación," she said. "Miguel was really freaked out, and I was depressed and desperate. Then Miguel said someone told him about a clínica de aborto nearby."

"There's a couple of them," Ellie noted.

"We made an appointment and took a bus there the next day," Maria continued. "But the place felt extraño—weird. There was just a receptionist and a doctor. It looked more like somebody's house than a clinic."

Blinking back tears, she paused to take a long swig of her smoothie.

Squeezing the teen's thin, trembling shoulders, Ellie caught Liam's gaze. *Perfect English,* she mouthed with a trace of a smile, shaking her head in apparent wonder.

Freakishly fast learning. Could there be something to this slash bullshit? Could she have received some of Joan's ashes?

"I was the only patient," Maria continued. "They were masked, but I'm almost positive I recognized them afterward at El Camino."

Liam narrowed his eyes.

"Anyway, the doctor, she's asking me all these questions like she's trying to talk me out of the abortion without actually saying it," Maria recounted. "And she kept looking at her phone and holding it close to her face so I couldn't see the screen.

"I thought, what the fuck?"

"Uh-huh," Liam muttered.

"Then Maestro showed up."

Daily News

BREAKING NEWS

Idaho honors Sisterhood members who bulldozed clinic rumored to be promoting abortions.

Everybody stared wide-eyed at Maria except Ellie, who merely shook her head knowingly.

"Maestro walked into the office where the médica was talking to me," she said. "He looked awful like he was dazed. He was limping, and he had stitches on his forehead," she added, tapping hers with her index finger.

"Those meetings are supposed to be confidential!" Ellie exclaimed.

T snorted.

"Miguel was right behind him. I was shocked," Maria said. "The doctor made a big deal of acting like she was surprised."

"Yeah," T muttered. "I *bet* she was a doctor."

"Maestro apologized for missing Miguel's calls," she continued. "Said he'd had an accident and was in the hospital, but now he was fine."

"What kind of accident?" Ellie asked.

"He said he hurt his head," she said.

The looping PNS clip of Ouroboros's Onewheel face-plant flashed in Liam's mind. He and Ellie exchanged glances.

"He said there'd been a miscom—" Maria frowned, apparently trying to finish the word.

"Miscommunication," Ellie offered.

"Sí, gracias," she said. "He said we'd been sent to the wrong place. The doctor just played along with him.

"Then Maestro took Miguel and me to El Camino," she continued, "and put us in separate rooms in the school. He said he was going to treat me for depression."

Nearly invisible in her "fades" and clutching a briefcase, M yanked open the van's side door, startling them.

"So?" Liam queried.

"So what?"

"Did you feed my pals?"

"Of course, I fed your fucking pals," she said. "At considerable risk to myself."

He grunted a thanks.

"You're welcome."

"What about the transponder?"

"I found something better."

M paused dramatically as everyone stared at her.

"I think I can hack his chip."

His implant!

"Which carries a transponder," she continued. "Ouro can trace his movements using the chip. I think I can hack into that and pick up the sat trace, which means we can follow him."

"Wow!" Tate exclaimed.

"One caveat," she noted.

"Caviah…?" Maria muttered.

"Contingency."

Maria blinked.

"Whatever." M shrugged. "If he knows, or can figure out how, Ouro can detect the party unscrambling the signal from the chip."

"In which case *he* could find *you*," Liam muttered.

M nodded. "He has the capability to trace whoever is tracking the signal via his connection."

"Whaaaa?" Tate lamented.

"Shit," T said.

"The only way he could cut us off is to cut off his connection," she said, "but he'd know where we were when he did it."

"Only until he disconnects."

"What are you saying?" Liam asked.

"I put you at risk if I go with you," M explained, "but you don't have a chance in hell of finding Miguel if I don't."

"How do we know you ain't working for numbnuts?" T suddenly chimed in.

Everyone turned to look at him.

"She *ditched* us at the school!" he exclaimed.

"You did," Liam noted, fixing his gaze on M.

"I got you in there, didn't I?" she reminded them. "I bailed because you ignored me, and you fucked up. You lucked out finding Maria," she added frostily.

Maria opened her mouth but closed it again.

Lucked out?

<hr>

DAILY NEWS

BREAKING NEWS

More companies offering perks for microchipped employees, customers.

Tate methodically replaced carpet cleaning decals on the vehicle's chameleonic exterior with those of an appliance repair service, insisting that the time it took would be well worth it.

And it was, he reminded them, *his* vehicle.

T monitored the parking lot while Ellie aired out the restive canines.

After a few stretches, Liam resumed questioning Maria.

"So Maestro gave you slash for the depression."

"Just mushrooms the first time," Maria clarified. "At least that's what he *said*. It was kind of scary at first, but I felt so much better and safer afterward that I let him talk me into keeping the baby. I can't really explain it, but I felt like the baby would give me purpose. Maestro said Jesús would have special powers, be a healer, and spread Maestro's gospel of transcendence after he transitioned to the next realm."

"Powers?" Tate muttered. "Whaaa?"

"What about Miguel?"

"Miguel told Maestro he'd served in the National Guard, so Maestro made him chief of security."

"Security!" Liam exclaimed.

"From internal and external threats," T commented drily in his ear.

"That pissed off people who'd been there longer," Maria said.

"He pitted people against each other," Liam surmised. "Kept 'em off balance and fighting each other for Maestro's favor."

"A-*fuckin'*-men," T said admiringly. "You're one smart dude, bro, to figure that shit out."

Ellie nodded.

"That's a great story," Tate commented as he toiled, "that sounds like a load of shit."

Maria glared at him.

"How did the rest of the workers you were with get to MillTown?" Liam asked after a pause.

"They took the guards' guns while they were knocked out and stole the buses they brought the fire crews in on."

"I remember hearing about that," T said. "Numbnuts was going apeshit talking about the heroic farm workers turning the tables on their oppressors. The Idaho governor denied she knew anything about the whole shit show and shut it down. Said she'd launch an investigation," he continued, "then turned around and sent the militias to MillTown to end the occupation."

"So why did he send Miguel to MillTown?" Liam asked.

"I told you," she said, "Maestro wants him to start a new school there."

Right.

Liam fell silent for a moment as she sobbed.

"You mean a new El Camino," he said.

"Sí."

Motherfucker's franchising.

No one spoke for a moment.

"OMG!" exclaimed Tate. Having completed his detail, he had climbed back in the driver's seat and, to Liam's dismay, turned PNS back on. "We made the news!"

"What?" Liam snapped. "Keep your *voice* down!"

"There's a video of us raiding the school," Tate whispered. "Except you can't see us. It's crazy."

They all leaned in to view the images.

Blinking drones gyrated as Caminos chanted en masse.

Coyotes scavenged along the campus's margins and yipped on their haunches.

Ouroboros manically thumbed his phone and screamed as Goliath barked his rage and dashed in large circles beneath the dancing, flashing bots.

Uniformed sentries lurched and stumbled as the ground spasmed beneath them.

Other sentries and the giant dog scaled the fence in pursuit of the tiny, partially obscured body conveyed atop an amorphous blur.

Two bursts of fire and two drones exploded into shrapnel.

Doors opened and closed on the plateless black *(or was it?)* van —the very one in which they sat watching the video.

Long gun barrels poked from the backseat and rear door windows and spat fire at the fleeing Caminos, two of whom pitched forward on the pavement, apparently shot.

The van zoomed up the hill and out of sight.

"Domestic terror attack on Portland El Camino cult leaves three in critical condition: report," exclaimed the chyron snaking across the bottom of the screen.

As they stared, stunned, the loop began repeating as it inevitably would for hours.

"Oh, fuck!" Liam muttered. *What if the guard I tased died?*

"Holy shit!" Tate declared. "How cool was that? Maybe Doomsday or Mayhem will pick it up!"

"You want fake video of us machine-gunning people going viral?" Liam exclaimed.

"What the fuck?" T added. "We didn't shoot nobody. Well, we tased 'em, but..."

"That was inside the school," Liam noted.

"We didn't even *have* guns."

Liam looked at the tote containing the ghosts. "We sure as shit didn't have *those* guns," with a nod at the screen.

More silence.

"Somebody faked the shooting," Liam said. "Big surprise. Now we're well-armed domestic terrorists, according to the so-called 'report.' "

"Yeah, *whose* report?" T asked skeptically.

"PNS'," Tate replied.

"Penises?" Maria parroted quizzically, shaking her head. "No ent—"

T guffawed. "No es importante," he told her with a grin.

She frowned but said nothing.

"That footage could have come from anywhere," Liam noted, "and been manipulated by anyone."

"*I* know that," Tate snapped.

"And yet you watch Doomsday," Liam sniped. "Most of that shit is fake too."

"Anyway," Tate noted, "at least they don't know who we are."

"Not yet," T noted. "But they're on it now."

Dismissing any possibility of recourse regarding the fraudulent footage, Liam returned his attention to Maria. "Go on about Miguel."

"I got very depressed when I found out Miguel was leaving," she continued. "Maestro said I needed slash therapy."

"And the powers," Liam commented after a pause. "What kind of powers?"

"Powers the dead person might have had," Maria said. "Like

knowing what other people are thinking. Like making people think they can do things."

"Like a hypnotist?"

"Hippo?"

 "Manipulating them?"

"Man-*ipyoo*?"

"Like making impossible rifle shots?" T asked pointedly.

"Miguel wouldn't tell me about the powers," Maria said. "Teacher told him he might lose them if he talked about them."

It all reeks of bullshit. But she seems credible. Who could make all that up?

Liam turned to Tate. "You mentioned supplies?"

DAILY NEWS

BREAKING NEWS

Hospitals struggle to deal with the torrent of Onewheel injuries.

CHAPTER
TWENTY-NINE

On the way to his storage locker, Tate told his companions that the media drumbeat concerning possible civil war over many recent problems—race, water rights, abortion, gun rights, immigration, assassinations—had pushed him into survivalist mode.

"Once I got married," he explained, "I had to protect my family."

Upon arriving at the squat, sprawling complex, he instructed the others to stay in the vehicles.

Liam was watching Tate submit to an iris scan before disabling the alarm and a booby trap—the nature of which he was coy about—when Jess flung open the van's side door, jarring its occupants.

"What the *fuck*?" T exclaimed. "You scared the shit out of us!"

"May I see your tattoos again, Maria?" Jess asked. Her tone suggested it wasn't really a request.

They all looked at her as she thumbed on her phone's flashlight.

"Go ahead, mija," said Ellie, who appeared in the doorframe behind Jess.

"Mija, my ass," Jess muttered loud enough for Liam to hear.

Maria stared at both for a moment before shrugging wearily and thrusting out her arms.

On her neck appeared a word or name, Ix Chel, inked in what resembled an ancient, indigenous Mesoamerican tongue.

"Where and when did you get this tattoo?" Jess asked.

Maria cast her dark, wide eyes in search of Ellie's.

"I have to take photos to document this," Jess said.

"Chill, Jess," Ellie chided. "Can't you see she's terrified?"

"I don't tell you how to execute your tasks," Jess retorted, "and I'll apprise you if and when I require your assistance in this investigation."

"*Investigation?*" T muttered quizzically.

Ellie shrugged and rolled her eyes before nodding resignedly at Maria.

Jess returned her gaze to the girl.

Indicating the inked image with a nod, Maria said, "Ix Chel is my middle name. My mother took me to get the tattoo before my quinceañera."

"Are you Mayan?"

"Sí." She looked at Ellie, who said nothing.

"Your parents?"

"Mayan," she replied.

"Hmm," Jess commented.

"Why are you asking me all this?" Maria demanded. "Are you *fucking* ICE?" Sweeping her suspicious gaze over her companions, she settled it mistrustfully on Ellie.

"Ix Chel," Jess noted, "was the Mayan goddess of the moon,

love, gestation, medicine, and the textile arts. She was also the wife of the creation god Itzamná."

"Busy gal," T commented.

"Cómo sabes todo eso?" Maria demanded. Her eyes narrowed at her interrogator.

"I'm a cultural anthropologist."

"What's anthopol—"

"An-*thro*-pology," Ellie clarified gently. "Jess studies ancient societies, sociedades antiguas, como los Mayas y Incas."

"Oh," Maria said with a frown. "Entiendo."

"I wrote a paper on female Mayan deities," Jess noted. "Did su madre tienes el tattoo mismo?" She pointed to the depiction.

Maria stared for a moment before nodding pensively. "And my abuela."

"And the one with the rabbit head in the crescent moon?"

"Sí!" Maria exclaimed. "What does all this have to do with finding Miguel?"

"Good question," Liam chimed in.

"We should know as much as we can about how this guy thinks," Jess declared.

"By kibitzing about Mayan mythology?" Liam instantly rued the pointless jab.

"Fuck it!" Pursing her lips, Jess scowled at her brother and crawled back out of the van. "Have it your way!"

"*Jess*," Liam pleaded wearily.

"Never mind," she said, throwing up her hands. "No es importante." Turning heel, she stalked back to Ellie's Tesla.

They blinked in the sudden glare of fluorescent lights flickering to life as Tate directed the door to open. Liam eyed the alligatoring on the concrete floor and cracks in the wall.

"Quake damage," Tate noted glumly. "It's insured."

Neatly stacked jerry cans abutted cartons of MREs lining the spacious locker's white walls. Lanterns, batteries, bottled water, pre-loaded backpacks, sleeping bags, ammo belts, binoculars, handheld bionic ear, and first aid kits. Along one wall rested a small trailer, its hitch inviting quick coupling to a mount.

"Did you buy out a Costco?" Appraising the packaged meals, T laughed. "Hope those are better 'an Army issue."

"They're edible," Tate noted, "and they last forever."

"Yum," M opined. "Space grub."

"This stuff must have cost a fortune," Ellie said.

"I buy it in lots and sell it to a roster of clients at a big markup," Tate said with a grin. "Pays for itself."

"Well, I'll be damned," M said admiringly. "Tate, the wheeler-dealer."

"I'm ready when the shit comes down," Tate replied.

"What shit is that exactly?" asked Jess, who had returned to the group to help out.

"How about we get a fuckin' move on?" T suggested.

"Amen."

"My Filipino brother-in-law Pedro's a currency trader," Tate explained as they busied themselves loading the vehicles. "He got me into crypto and told me when to pull out before it collapsed."

"Collapsed which time?" Jess snarked.

Tate ignored her. "He's a fuckin' genius."

"Beats the shit out of selling Amway," T joshed.

"Now, *there's* a cult," Jess said.

"I *knew* this carpet cleaning van would come in handy," Tate gloated. "Now I want some of that stealth gear. That shit is savage."

Maria huddled with T briefly as they prepared to hit the road. Liam noted T's evident concern.

"What's up, man?"

T frowned. "She reminded me she's chipped, too."

"*Motherfucker!*"

"We all forgot," T said. "Numbnuts might have been tracking us since we left the school."

"Then where *is* he?" Tate asked.

"Maybe he's waiting to see where we go, what we do," M chimed in.

"Maybe he doesn't have another car," T said.

"Maybe we need to cut out that chip, stat," Jess declared.

Everyone turned to stare at her.

"Oh my God, Jess!" exclaimed Ellie, who was lugging a carton of MREs to her Tesla.

"This is already Mission Impossible," Jess replied, "thanks to all the unforced errors." She stared at Liam.

Scowling, Maria defiantly thrust out her left arm at Jess and pointed to a tiny scar, evidently where the implant had been inserted.

"Do it!" she demanded. "Corta esa puta cosa o lo haré yo mismo!" She mimed gouging out the bug with a phantom knife.

"Whoa," T exclaimed, unconsciously rubbing his own scar. "No, you ain't doin' it yourself, chica."

"You have medic training, Ellie," Liam noted.

Ellie stowed the carton she was carrying in the back of the van and turned to face them. "Where's that first aid kit?"

Tate considered Maria with a new admiration. "You've got guts, kid."

"Amen," Ellie muttered.

"Can't you just say, 'You *have* guts?' " Jess carped.

"Jess," Liam pleaded.

Tugging on latex gloves, Ellie laid out on a clean towel a foil-wrapped alcohol pad, a sterilized Swiss Army Knife, tweezers, gauze pads, medical tape, and an ACE bandage.

Frowning in concentration, Ellie rubbed the scarred area with alcohol after probing the tiny chip's outline with her meaty thumb.

"I'm gonna make the smallest incision I can," she explained to Maria, whose eyes were squeezed shut and turned away from the knife's target. "T will grab and extract the implant with the tweezers."

M gripped Maria's arm at the shoulder and elbow, and Liam trained a flashlight beam on the target area.

Ellie nodded at T, who rested the grip end of the tweezers next to the opened knife blade with one hand and held a wad of gauze in the other. She nodded at Liam, who exclaimed, "Miguel!"

Ellie incised Maria's pectoral as her patient's eyes flew open and fixed on Liam. With her other hand, she folded back the tiny skin flap with another pair of tweezers while, squinting, T slid his implement into the cut and probed for a grip on the implant.

Maria cursed and groaned in pain, straining against M's grip on her limb.

In a few dicey seconds, T found a grip on the chip and delicately wiggled the tiny, bloody capsule free of the wound.

"Jesus," Tate muttered, wincing.

"Madre de Dios!" Maria moaned. "Eso duele!"

"I'll *bet* it fuckin' hurt!" T replied.

"Brave girl," M muttered, nodding her esteem while maintaining her grip on the girl's arm. Ellie gently swabbed alcohol on the wound before taping a pile of gauze on it and wrapping it all in the bandage.

"Amen," T muttered.

"Everything loaded?" Jess asked.

"Looks like it," Tate said. "We got enough supplies for several days, depending on events on the ground."

"Tate, I gotta hand it to you," Liam said, surveying the packed van with his hands on his hips, "this is amazing. I am eternally grateful."

"Amen," T repeated. "Now let's get the hell outta Dodge!"

DAILY NEWS

BREAKING NEWS

Black market for arms remaining from Russia-Ukraine war expands in U.S.

Wildfire smoke fouling the windy Columbia River Gorge thickened as they drove east on I-84; save for Jess, whose sense of smell remained lost to Covid, they could all taste it, smell it, or both. T passed out respirators from one of Nate's bins in the back.

The pall obscured the huge river—a series of massive reservoirs punctuated by hydroelectric dams—flowing sluggishly toward the Pacific. They got intermittent glimpses of flames racing across distant, thickly forested hills and huge copters skimming low over the surface, filling their giant buckets with water to douse the fires.

Sitting yogi style on the folding cot, M mumbled unintelligibly to her phone mic as her fingers danced over her notebook keyboard, the screen of which was blocked into several different windows. Liam wondered how she made any sense of it all.

"So far, so good," she declared. "Don't see any sign that Ouro's made me. Looks like Miguel's a few miles outside of Spokane."

Liam rubbed his temples as he answered the call from Jess, who rode shotgun in Ellie's Tesla pickup.

"Do you think Ouroboros is just going to"—he heard a finger snap—"hand over the ashes?" Jess inquired. "You heard Maria. He believes he's on a mission and that he has some kind of powers."

"I know all that," he snapped. "Why do you think I'm trying to get more information?"

He hung up and turned back to Maria. "The *word*, you said?"

"Sí, El Mensaje," she replied. Nodding fervently, she absently rubbed her round belly. "His teachings."

"His teachings?" Liam questioned. "You mean like Freedom Lies Here. And psilo, and slash?"

"Sí," she said. "Transcendence."

"Transcendence?"

"When he guides us on our journeys after we drink his tea," she intoned. "When we dream, we're aware of what has been and what can be."

Robotic recital.

"Nutjob," Tate said, chuckling.

Eyes still sealed, T shook his head slowly at the words.

"Why does Ouroboros trust Miguel so much?"

As if in search of guidance, she looked at T, who shrugged.

"Just tell him what you know," he counseled. "He's okay."

She wept.

"Miguel and I sneaked out of Idaho so I could…" She rubbed her belly again.

Get an abortion.

"But like I told you, Maestro found us and talked me into keeping mi bebé," she said. "He kept saying mi bebé is going to spread his gospel of peace and transcendence after Maestro enters the next realm.

"My son will show people the way to transition, he said."

"OMG!" Tate chortled.

"Fuck you, gringo," Maria snapped before continuing. "He convinced Miguel that Jesús was going to be a great man and that we needed to make sure his path was clear."

Make sure his path is clear… By raising him as a cult leader?

"He told Miguel it was"—she paused as if trying to recall something—"foreordained, and he would *never* ask him to do anything else.

"Maestro knew Miguel would do whatever he asked him to."

She fell silent.

"Why did you name your baby Jesús?" M asked.

"It was Maestro's idea."

"*Naturally!*" Jess chimed in.

Everyone jumped as Tate cranked up the dash screen audio.

"What the fuck?" Liam carped.

"Listen!" Tate exclaimed.

Everyone stopped talking, leaving auburn-tressed PNS co-host Ginger Preenz's prattling on the I-Dash to fill the void.

"I understand," she addressed Ouroboros's avatar, "that they fired on you with automatic weapons?"

"You saw the video," the avatar replied. "I'm fortunate to be speaking with you right now."

"But some of your followers weren't so fortunate?" Preenz prompted.

"The shooters critically wounded three of my assets and nearly killed Goliath."

"Goliath?"

"My fearless, heroic mastiff." A holo of the enormous canine thrashing at a trainer's padded arm appeared fleetingly in its master's place.

"Oooh!" Preenz exclaimed.

The avatar beamed proudly.

"So we've been unable to confirm either the casualties shown in your video," Preenz pressed on, expression grave once more, "or that the terrorists fired assault weapons at you."

"Is there a question in there somewhere, Ginger?"

"People are raising the possibility that someone—possibly yourself—" she persisted, "tampered with security video showing the shooting to exaggerate the violence."

"So now you're promoting conspiracy theories?"

"I'm just—"

"You're just carrying water for the haters," Ouroboros opined with a thin smile. "You know, Ginger, I've been very nice to you, but I lost three followers to a terrorist attack and had a fourth kidnapped, for God's sake, and all you want to talk about is conspiracies."

Visibly flustered, Preenz tacked. "You maintain you're persecuted—"

"That's a fact." The avatar vanished abruptly.

Preenz stared agape for a moment at the now empty spot just occupied by the avatar before recovering.

"And there's your takeaway, Jared." She turned to the camera with a grave shake of her glowing, flowing auburn tresses. "Straight from the dear leader's mouth–virtually. Stay tuned for more coverage of this fast-breaking story."

"So now we're fugitives," T muttered.

"Amazing interview, as always," her co-host Jared Jeberische remarked, "from comely gal Friday Ginger Preenz.

"Aces, Ginge," he concluded. "Catch you on the flip flop. Savage dress, by the way,

BREAKING NEWS

'Invisiwear' stock price soars after video of users evading capture goes viral.

THIRTY-ONE

"We have breaking news from the daffy El Camino cult in Portland, *Bloregon*, tonight!" declared PNS host Jared Jeberische, better known as JJ to the circle of scripted, smirking "fundits" to which he played host. A goofy, dated image of Ouroboros appeared behind him, dreadlocks wildly askew as he slo-mo tumbled from his seatless Onewheel into a brutal faceplant.

"Jesus!" exclaimed Liam, who had taken the wheel after Tate's incident with an elk. He couldn't tell at a glance, particularly on the small screen, how authentic the footage appeared. He veered away, just in time, from a honking pickup he nearly hit while distracted.

The driver playfully waved a handgun—who knew if it was real or not?—in his direction as, eyes wide, Liam sheepishly shrugged an apology.

Riding shotgun was T; Ranger lazed on the floor next to Tate, who was stretched out on the folding cot. The party, including the threesome of Jess, Ellie, and Maria trailing them, was nearing a Walmart near the Washington/Idaho border, from which M had traced the signal from Miguel's implant. The source hadn't budged for more than an hour.

What is he doing at Walmart?

Everyone was exhausted and edgy, a circumstance that the encounter with the elk, a way south of Ritzville on Washington 395, had only aggravated. Maria had awoken in the back seat of Jess's sedan shrieking about an elk in the road that Tate, who'd evidently nodded off at the wheel, was about to T-bone. Jolted alert from a drowsy reverie, Liam had seized and yanked the wheel to the left just in time, miraculously dodging the huge beast as Ellie and Tate slammed on their brakes.

Shaken, the posse pulled off the road for a reset as the elk, appearing dazed, wandered off toward the river. A light, steady rain slopped the windshield with an ashy soup; the wipers swoosh, swooshed it away as fast as they could.

How the fuck could Maria have possibly known—in her sleep—that there was a huge elk in the road in the smoky dark, with the van in front of her blocking any possible view?

She had no explanation other than, "I just saw it like in a dream."

"My bad," Tate whimpered. "I'm sorry I burned everybody.".

"Forget it, man," Liam replied, climbing back in the driver's seat. "Let's go."

"Amen," said T.

"My wife read my mind sometimes," Liam said. "It freaked me out, so she stopped."

"She stopped reading your mind?" T asked curiously.

"She stopped saying anything if she did," he replied drily.

"That's why Ouroboros wants her back, Liam," Jess declared in his ear. "He's convinced she's telepathic. Like Joan."

Liam stared at the dark, soggy road before him.

Joan knew things, predicted things she simply couldn't have known nor predicted.

"I think Maria's trying to come to grips with a transformative experience she had with the slash," Jess said.

"Si," Maria, who was sitting right behind her, replied tersely, "transformadora."

Being spoken about as if I weren't there would annoy me. No one ever accused Jess of being a people person.

They stopped long enough at a truck stop at the junction of I-90 and Washington 395 near tiny, comically named Ritzville to hit the restrooms, get coffee, and stock up on NoDoz and Mocca Shots gummies before getting back on the road.

The governor had ordered another evacuation of residents and businesses along a forest corridor east of the Walmart toward which they were headed. Westbound traffic thickened as they drew closer to the Walmart, now a staging area for firefighters and refugees. Swarms of grim, haggard, Latino farm workers plodded on foot and huddled shoulder to shoulder in the sagging beds of weathered pickups.

Panhandling families lined the withered grass strip as Liam steered the van down the exit ramp to the access road and into the Walmart parking lot.

"Need gas/food. Anything helps. God bless you," one scrawled sign read.

They waved and smiled with false optimism as the vehicles streamed past them, unseeing or refusing to see. Some waved American flags. A woman rinsed out bandanas in a weathered, plastic bowl of water before handing them to the children, who pressed them to their faces against the air, foul with smoke and exhaust.

A sign in the side window of a truck read: "Go back to your shithoal countries."

Smog tinted the dawn roseate.

"Respirators on, everybody," Ellie texted.

"Patriotic viewers may recall that El Camino's leader, Ouroboros"—JJ smirked as the faceplant looped repeatedly in slo-mo— "also known to his followers as Maestro, has appeared on PNS previously to discuss his controversial views on treating homeless alkies and druggies with"—*wait for* it (punctuated by a rimshot)— *"more* drugs, namely psilocybin, alias magic mushrooms, alias fantastic fungi, alias powerful hallucinogen. Blokes just can't seem to handle reality." He took a long swig from a water bottle.

"And this just in from a reasonably reliable source that Ouroboros's real name is—get this—Ignatius Adler. You heard it here first, Patriots!"

Pulsing, kaleidoscopic images of mushrooms dissolved into sixties-inspired psychedelic imagery swirling in the background punctuated by gyrating, bell-bottomed silhouettes.

"PNS has been unable, so far, to confirm persistent rumors that Maestro also has patients ingest" —the image bled into a fresh one of an open, fancy cremation urn that morphed into the remains of a Hindu funeral pyre— "human ashes.

"You heard me right," he said. "They swallow human ashes, *reportedly."*

"Asshole," T muttered.

"Our most recent Patriot implant poll," JJ continued, "shows seventy-nine percent of implanted respondents think Ouroboros is, in fact, having his followers consume human ashes. There's *something* goin' on. Remember, Patriots, you heard it here first—*or else!"* Waving his revolver around insouciantly, he chuckled and shot off a blank round after his companions had donned the provided red, white, and blue earmuffs.

"You're *insane,* JJ," a fundit sounded off.

"But I have fun."

"Someone's getting a silencer in their stocking."

They all removed their encumbrances.

"While *Maestro* declined to speak on camera," JJ noted to the camera, close-up, "he did respond by phone."

Liam prepared to turn into the Walmart parking lot, which, choked with smoke and traffic, covered about four acres of scorching, quake-riddled blacktop. Heat waves undulating from the pavement distorted the carnival they were about to join.

"Looks like hell," T opined.

"Christ on a crutch," Jess muttered over the radio before breaking into a coughing fit.

Making the turn, Liam maximized the tracking display on the dash, shrinking PNS to the size of a candy bar. An aud-sim replication of Ouroboros's face jerkily parroted his apparently authentic words.

"Domestic terrorists wearing cutting-edge, light-bending fabric —making them very hard to see—broke into El Camino headquarters early this morning and stole sacred cremains of those who have entered the next realm," Ouroboros's avatar announced. "As the ashes' humble guardian, I have to say this is an act of shocking disrespect and inhumanity. Consequently, I am employing all possible means to recover these cremains, which I plan to appropriately transition."

"And does 'all possible means' include violence?" JJ inquired.

"They have left me no choice, Jared. Sad to say, I can't rule out anything."

"There you have it, Patriots," JJ said. "Better stock up on body armor if you piss off Ouroboros."

The panelists hooted and guffawed.

"We have to take a break, friends," JJ said, waving the business end of his signature vintage Colt .45 toward the camera. He warned, "Don't you *dare* go away."

On a hot mic, he muttered, "Mofo's quotable."

DAILY NEWS

BREAKING NEWS

Portland cult leader denounces terrorists'
'shocking inhumanity'.

Liam rolled to a stop at the rear of a listless line of dusty pickups, most of whose beds and windows sported Stars and Stripes, Confederate flags, or both. RVs, ATVs, and Humvees idled in search of parking spaces. Patriot flags jutted from the rear of many, snapping in the fire-whipping wind.

"If this *ain't* hell," T muttered, "it must be in shoutin' distance."

The megastore itself was a football field away, spectral in the haze to which the idling vehicle exhaust contributed. License plates were a mix of Idaho and Washington with a scattering of Oregon plates.

High above the gridlock roared tanker planes. Choppers, like colossal dragonflies, hefted 300-gallon drop buckets of lake water in an attempt to dampen the encroaching blaze. The din was apocalyptic.

Expanding red circles on the computer tracer display emanated, apparently, from the far northeastern corner of the massive aluminum and polymer jungle, a good eighth of a mile from the group's present position.

Liam leaned wearily on the wheel, accidentally honking the horn and drawing scowls from neighboring drivers.

"Shit!"

A gaunt man sporting a flowing white beard and soiled robes trudged between vehicles, schlepping a huge white crucifix over his shoulder; he drew vitriol from drivers whose vehicles his burden inadvertently bumped or scraped.

"Jesus!" someone bellowed. "Watch where you're goin'."

"That ain't Christian, brother," scolded an older, spike-haired woman in another pickup towing a horse trailer. A slim cigar clamped in her maw, she offered the cross-bearer a bottle of water. A black mask sporting a cartoon smile dangled from her left ear.

"Neither's blockin' traffic in an emergency!" the man hollered. "Whose side you *on*, bitch?"

"Nobody's gettin' nowhere fast, bro," she noted.

Adding to the bedlam, religious and political orators perched on streetlight stanchions preached through mics and megaphones.

"Ditto on finding hell," Liam told T, who slumped disconcertingly in his seat and didn't respond.

I hope this isn't a goose chase.

JJ crowed breaking news: "PNS just received an update on the developing domestic terrorism story out of *Pot*-land from an inside source, although he may be out in the cold, or should I say, *hot*, following this report."

His unblinking eyes fixed on the camera, JJ sipped from his mug.

"Another MillTown worm," he said, "has turned in the unfolding terrorist kidnapping, Patriots."

His panelists shifted expectantly in their lush swivelers.

"One of Ouroboros's top lieutenants is reportedly on his way to northern Idaho to reconnoiter with other followers occupying an abandoned sawmill. Word is he has a boatload of magic mushrooms and human ashes with him."

"Oh, my God," Liam uttered with a sigh.

"Par-*tay!*" a fundit joshed.

"How the *fuck* did they know that?" Liam mused resignedly.

"It gets better," JJ added, beaming. "I'm told that while said lieutenant goes by the spinach moniker Miguel—oh, I can already hear the blokes (that's blue wokes for the underinformed) on their way to cancel me."

"Cut to the chase, JJ!" a fundit exclaimed.

"Yeah, yeah," JJ snapped. "Anyway, Miguel's actual first name is José. You know these spinach-speakers have foot-long names. Desi Valdez, my chic mocha chica, José is Joseph in English, no?"

A lavishly tressed fundit sheathed in a bosomy red minidress and heels rolled her smoky eyes at the host. "Duhhh!" She made a show to the camera of scratching her temple with an extended, scarlet-tipped middle finger.

The audience and her co-panelists howled.

"According to my source," JJ continued, "our odds-on illegal amigo José knocked up his Guatemalan squeeze, Maria, back at the ranch.

"Apparently, Latino non-doms no use condoms."

"Have you no sense of decency, sir?" implored another fundit, dabbing at his eyes with a tissue.

"Well, I could act like I host an elitist talking heads punditocracy," he said, to nods of exaggerated assent, "but what fun would that be?"

Jesus H.

"Are you with me so far?" Jeberische queried his viewers. "Joseph and Maria—Mary in good, old native English—plan to name their bouncing, anchor-baby boy—she just *knows* somehow, it's a ninny—I mean niño—*yes, you guessed it*—Jesus. 'Course, *they* pronounce it *Hay-zoos*. The schools down there just don't, y'know, get it. So, Jesus, Joseph and Mary!" he declared. "Anyone see a pattern here? And they have *powers* beyond making anchor babies!"

"Is sucking Uncle Sam's mams so they don't have to work a superpower?" a panelist queried.

"Are the terrorists—or as I've decided to call them, the Jesus Squad—here illegally, Patriots?" Jeberische posed to viewers. A colorful graphic burst onto the other half of the screen.

The Jesus Squad?

"Merciful heavens," he heard Jess mutter.

"Now we're *really* famous," Tate gloated.

"You heard it here, Patriots!" he crowed. "Now, let *us* hear from *you* on the latest Insta-Poll, made from the best questions on earth. Don't go away." He planted the gun's business end against his left temple and winked. "Remember, if you switch channels, I'll shoot myself.

"And I'm *way* too pretty to die."

"So don't go away." He planted the gun's business end against his left temple and winked. "Remember, if you switch channels, I'll shoot myself.

"And I'm *way* too pretty to die."

"Why are you still listening to that garbage?" Jess inquired testily in their ears.

"Because it's my fuckin' van, lady," Tate parried. "I could switch to country music."

"Oh, good God!"

"That's what I thought."

Liam surprised himself by snickering.

Now on screen were a bickering man and woman peering through the blinds of a living room window as the sounds of an angry mob issued from the speaker.

The image gave way to a pajamaed little girl standing behind them clutching a teddy bear to her chest. A tear slid down her cheek in a close-up.

"Daddy, I'm scared."

"All right," the man said, looking at her. "We'll get one."

The next scene showed them stockpiling survival gear with a bank of GearUPPrint 3-D printers in the background.

"Man enough to stand your ground?" a male basso challenged.

"Fuckin' A," Tate muttered.

"Woman enough to protect your family?" a stentorian woman's voice questioned.

"GearUPPrint is your first and last line of home security," the male narrator opined.

Ghost gun parts flew out of a cartoon printer before assembling themselves into actual firearms in a gun case as a cartoon Minuteman, brandishing a flintlock, nodded his head approvingly.

"That's Ted Nugent's voice," Tate announced.

Thought he was asleep.

"That figures," T chimed in.

"Thought he was dead," M commented.

"It's AI," Jess said flatly.

"Love that ad!" JJ crowed.

DAILY **N**EWS

BREAKING NEWS

Fears of urban violence drive 3-D printer sales.

Liam inched the van forward. Vehicles flanked him on every side with no obvious way out. He mopped the sweat oozing down his face with his shorn tanktop.

"This is gonna take all fuckin' day," T muttered, his eyes still closed, his face ashy and damp.

"Welcome back, Patriots," JJ beckoned from the dash. "Here's more video of the El Camino mayhem from last night, including the sudden jolt from an aftershock of the Election Day Quake.

"Remember that shitshow?"

Liam shook his head wearily as the exact same footage they'd seen repeatedly rolled across the screen. Suddenly, a huge, pixelated message, IGNORANCE IS STRENGTH, knocked PNS from the screen for a few seconds before the network broadcast recovered.

With a weary shake of his head, JJ smirked at the camera. "Those low-IQ MFs," he uttered. "Give a knucklehead an inch, and she'll take a mile. Third time this week," he informed his guests. He craned his head around as if he were addressing someone offstage.

"What the Hillary?"

After inching forward for a few minutes, further into the crush of flesh and metal, Liam steeled himself for action.

"I can't stand this," he told M, who was still hunched over, scrutinizing Maria's disabled implant under a pocket microscope.

"What's the punchline?" she asked.

"I'm going on foot to the signal," he said with resignation.

"Good idea," Jess chimed in over the radio. "Be careful."

"Duh," Liam replied, before turning back to M. "Wake up Tate. I need him to drive."

"I can drive," M said.

"I need you to focus on the signal."

"Copy that."

M reached over to rouse Tate, whose bulk faced the van wall.

"Hey, wake up."

Voicing a low growl, Ranger raised his imposing muzzle to stare menacingly at M.

"Easy, fella," she cooed to the dog. He settled back on his belly after a moment but kept his eyes fixed on her.

"Tate!" M exclaimed, leaning over his prone, blanketed form. *"What the fuck?"*

Liam twisted around to see M snatch Tate's phone from his fumbling hands.

"Gimme that!" roared Tate, whose earbud was visible. Ranger snarled. M lurched backward nimbly, yanking a stool between her and the angry dog. Jerking himself upright, he lunged for the device.

Liam gaped in turn at his two companions.

"He wasn't sleeping!" M cried. "He was texting!"

Liam looked at her, the phone, and finally, Tate; falling ominously silent, he looked like a whipped puppy.

"Texting who?" he asked, even as it hit him. "You texted PNS?"

"Hate to say I told you so," M chimed in.

"Why would you *do* that?" Liam cried. "They probably traced the call."

"It wasn't a call," Tate bleated.

"Don't split hairs, damn it!" Liam snapped. "Like they *can't* trace texts."

"Of course they can," M confirmed.

"I told you not to trust that Trumpie bastard," Jess exclaimed.

"Not helpful," he said with a sigh.

"Way to fuckin' go," he snapped at Tate. "Now we really *do* have to move."

"I *got* you here," Tate parried. "And you fuckin' libs shit all over me while I did it.

"That's fuckin' gratitude!"

"I see your point," Liam said, "but you probably fucked up my chance to get those ashes back! I thought you wanted to *help*."

"They're gonna find out anyway," Tate replied, "so I figured I could get out ahead of it."

"Oh, now he's a spin doctor," Jess cut in.

"Fuck you, *lezzie*," Tate said, settling his chunky rear on the cot as he calmed Ranger.

"Enough!" Liam declared. "Tate, you're driving."

"Now you're talkin'," Tate exclaimed, apparently buoyed by the prospect of redemption.

"No more texting!"

"I *know*."

"Say it!" M demanded.

Tate looked from one to the other.

"All right," he said testily, "no more texting. Promise." The others turned away as he made a zipping motion across his mouth.

"I need someone to go with me," Liam said. He slipped a

loaded ghost into his waistband and reluctantly tugged off his respirator, thinking it might attract eyeballs among the largely unmasked crowd.

"What about T?" Ellie inquired over the radio.

"T ain't lookin' good," Liam replied.

"Roger that," M said.

"I'm going with you," Jess said.

"You're sick," Liam replied. "You shouldn't even be here."

"I have to do *something*."

"I'll go," said Ellie, a former cop. "And Jess can drive."

"Bring the ghost gun I gave you.," Liam replied. "What's Maria doing?"

"She's in one of her sleep trances or something," Jess said.

"I don't want her to go," he said. "She might attract attention."

"Not many Mayans around these parts."

"Roger that," M interjected.

"No respirators," he said. "Too conspicuous."

"You're paranoid."

"You don't know the half of it," he replied. "Bring Magnus with you."

"No way!" Jess howled.

"He's trained," Liam noted. "He'll be a huge help and he'll get a charge out of it."

"It's too dangerous," Jess protested.

"He *is* trained, Jess," Ellie noted. "And he needs something to do."

"Okay," Jess said after a moment.

"Keep an eye on Maria," Liam said.

"Worry about your end," Jess snapped. "And for god's sake, be careful."

With an iron grip on Magnus's leash, Ellie joined Liam by the van.

"Let's go."

DAILY NEWS

BREAKING NEWS

PNS' "Jeberische" rocks cable ratings.

THIRTY-FOUR

On the way to the beacon's source, the three passed cars that had run out of gas as they got caught up in traffic trying to exit the parking lot after learning the pumps were dry. Other cars tried to edge around them as they waved cardboard signs begging or offering cash for gas.

Yet others, stupefyingly, waited stubbornly for cars to leave spaces close to the store. Those disabled, or feigning it, tried to weave their scooters through the snarl.

Drivers glued to their phones or jawing with passengers missed cues from other drivers.

Random, hobbled cart rollers with spent batteries were added to the bottlenecks while luring curious kids to play on them. People pressed napkins and towels to their faces.

Someone hurled a water bottle from a car at a blue-vested store associate trying to direct traffic. She promptly vanished back into the store, to the dismay of those who appreciated her efforts. Many threw debris at the offending driver.

Scary fucking circus.

Virtually everyone, teens and older, was openly armed. Liam and Ellie reflexively fingered the ghosts jammed in their waistbands. People pushed or pursued scarce shopping carts. Litter spilled from garbage cans awash in a heap of plastic cups, discarded masks, and fast-food wrappers.

Petrified dog turds dotted a strip of scorched grass abutting the sidewalk. A metal pole bearing an empty poop bag dispenser lay toppled on the ground.

Liam felt a chill despite the heat and paused fleetingly at the sight of a blanket veiling a corpse-like shape. It reminded him of a promo he'd seen for *Fear the Walking Dead* way back when.

"Just keep moving, Liam," Ellie murmured, her eyes forward.

"Oo-*rah*," M concurred in their ears. "This shit's nasty. There may be more."

Magnus's nose wrinkled at the smoky air before he set it to the ground. He pulled toward the veiled figure before giving in to Ellie's counter tug. She gave him a big whiff of Miguel's T-shirt that Maria had given her for the purpose and stuffed it back in her pack.

"Lowd Boyz DROOL!" was scrawled in red bubble lettering across a section of the exterior near the entry, a makeshift *D* added to the "ROOL" by an apparent prankster.

"Ignorints is strength."

"Ah," M snarked in their ears, "an Orwell fan."

"I'm sure he'd be flattered."

"And we're still in Washington," Ellie marveled.

"Roger that," said M, viewing the video feed from Ellie's I-Ware on her iPad.

Cruising through the haze overhead, a fleet of quads wove every which way, no doubt recording everything.

"Just as well Jess isn't here," Ellie commented. "She'd be ranting about facial recog."

A burly, bandanaed man in rhinestone cowboy regalia, including a red, white, and blue Stetson, galloped recklessly on horseback through the narrow lanes between cars. Waving a Don't Tread on Me flag bearing the iconic coiled serpent, he tossed leaflets into the gusty air. Similarly clad deputies deposited the fliers—abridged and annotated copies of the Constitution—on dusty windshields and handed them to passersby, most of whom dropped them on the ground.

The horseman had his steed leap over the hood of an occasional subcompact where there was room to land "safely." Some captive spectators hooted and applauded the antics while others bellowed profanities and charges of animal abuse. The horse reared at the sound of a siren, almost knocking over an old woman schlepping a battered suitcase.

"Asshole," someone yelled.

"String 'im up," a second bellowed.

The horseman flipped them off and cranked up his jam, "The Angry American."

The music trailed off as he yawed his mount toward a fresh audience in the next tier.

Liam scurried to catch up with Ellie and Magnus.

Another horse was tethered to a bike rack on the sidewalk outside the megastore's sliding doors, a reflective emergency blanket shielding its flanks. A shirtless man in ragged cutoffs and duct-taped sandals filled bowls of water set out for dogs and horses from a gallon jug.

Hand-scrawled signs, as well as digital messages mounted on stanchions, announced that gas pumps were dry. People yelled and honked their horns. Customers threatened each other.

Not a single blue-vested employee or rent-a-cop was in sight.

Apparently standing in as security, however, were armed

militiamen in military garb, who must, Liam thought, be sweating buckets. Jutting from their pockets were what looked like industrial zip ties and vials of some kind of spray.

Jesus, fuck.

"FYI," M noted, "don't look up, but there's a sniper at either front corner of the roof."

"Thanks for sharing," Liam replied drily.

Most customers seemed to take little notice of the armed sidewalk posse. He'd read that citizens still voting in person acclimated quickly to the presence of armed poll watchers.

"Unbelievable!" a bald, burly, ZZ Top-bearded man stationed just outside the sliding doors raged at customers, who generally ignored him. A hunting rifle was slung across his chest.

"Do you believe this shit?" the man shouted in Liam's direction. "They're outta fuckin' gas! They're outta fuckin' ammo! They're outta fuckin' shit paper!"

"They're outta fuckin' weed, too!" a passing man chimed in.

"Fuck you, faggot," the man shouted. He fingered the butt of his weapon.

Liam gave them all a wide berth. The party, after Magnus lapped greedily at the tepid water, threaded its way to the right side of the building.

"Dead ahead," M said. "I'm getting an aerial shot of tarps or blankets spread out in what little shade there is, but the canopies are obscuring the view.

"Looks like a homeless camp."

DAILY NEWS

BREAKING NEWS

Toby Keith's "The Angry American" roars back up the country charts.

Magnus whined and strained at his leash as they neared the site.

"Looks like Deputy Dawg is onto something," M murmured.

"Maybe Miguel stopped here to evangelize," Jess chimed in.

"Or maybe he was meeting someone."

"Or both," Liam ventured. "Wonder if Ouroboros *told* him to stop here?"

"Good question."

Liam found himself slowing once more as they approached the figure of a leathery, black-haired man sprawled on his stomach in the withered grass. Below his left knee sprouted a weathered-looking prosthetic leg.

A veteran?

His face was turned to the wretched turf. He appeared to have lain down in the shade, which had moved on as he napped. A tattered knapsack and an empty water bottle lay near his head.

He stank of stale piss and BO.

Liam and Ellie exchanged nervous glances.

"He looks bad," M commented over the radio. "Be careful. Is he breathing?"

Hard to tell.

Magnus sniffed the man gingerly, then licked his exposed cheek. The man's eyelids flickered, blinked tentatively, and closed again.

Liam took a deep breath.

"Is T watching this?" Liam asked. "He might've run into him at El Camino."

"T's checked out," M replied. "He looks ashy, but his breath and pulse are steady, for now. But hurry the fuck up."

"You all right, man?" Liam asked the prone figure on the ground. "You're burnin' up."

"Went to sleep inna shade," the man rasped. "Dunno how long I've been out."

"You're dehydrated," Liam said. "Here."

The man rolled over with an effort and looked directly at Liam, who handed him his water bottle. "Just sip it," he cautioned, "gulping will—" Liam was about to protest as the man chugged the liquid, but Ellie's look stopped him. What was the point? Hoisting himself to all fours, the man hacked and retched, coughing up water.

"Ah, fuck," he groaned. He warily eyed Magnus, who answered with a low growl.

"He won't hurt you," Ellie said, stroking the dog's head. "Just checkin' you out."

Grabbing his pack, the man crawled into some nearby shade and collapsed on his back, his eyes closed.

"You can't stay here, man," Liam said. "Fire's comin'."

"Fuck da fire," he said. He squinted at Liam. "*Fuck* are you?"

"Name's Jasper," Liam replied.

Ellie smirked.

"Call me concerned," Liam continued. "You need to get outta here."

The man shrugged feebly, "Got nowhere to go, Jazper. No family. No dinero."

The man eyed Ellie as if only now noticing her, "Who's he?"

"Swine," M remarked.

"Name's Elvis," Ellie replied.

Jess and M burst out laughing in their ears.

The man grunted as if assuaged.

"You can't just stay here and die," Liam declared.

"Your name God?"

Liam shook his head.

The man shrugged as if he'd settled the matter.

"We're looking for someone," Ellie said. "Have you seen this man, by any chance?" She held a photo of Miguel on her phone to the man's furrowed, stubbled features, which defied racial categorization.

"Mexican, huh?" the man commented after a pause. "Lotta Mexicans here."

"Jerk," M muttered in their ears.

Liam pulled a twenty from his wallet and held the man's eyes with his own while he fingered the bill.

"What's your name, man?"

"Soli."

"Sully?"

"Soli," the man repeated slowly as if it were habitual. "*S-O-L-I*." Liam thought he detected a West Indian lilt.

"Okay, Soli, so we're looking for *this* Mexican in particular," Ellie continued. "Driving a black SUV, maybe.

Another guy with him, maybe Mexican, probably the same clothes."

"Like a uniform," Liam added. A gust of hot wind blew and pressed a long slip of paper against his shin. Absently peeling it off, he stuffed the receipt in his pocket.

"You cops?" Soli squinted at them dubiously.

Ellie rolled her eyes. "Do you think cops would be chasing someone in the path of a forest fire?"

"Why'd anybody be out chasin' anybody in the path of a forest fire?" Soli posed.

"The man we're looking for has something important of mine," Liam interjected.

Helping himself to the twenty Liam proffered, Soli held it up to the sun as if checking its authenticity; apparently satisfied, he stuffed it in the pocket of his grimy khaki shorts.

Liam chuckled. Ellie winced.

"You know," Soli said, as if the bill had jogged his memory, "some weird shit went down earlier."

Liam and Ellie stared expectantly.

"Can't say it was your Mexican," Soli began, "cuz he 'as all masked up and shit and wearin' those weird smart glasses, like yours"—he nodded pointedly at Ellie—"but he was inked, and he had a ghost, and he's wearin' a tanktop."

"Inked?"

Inked? Tattooed.

"What kind of ink?"

"Big one on his arm of a snake eating itself."

Liam and Ellie eyed each other.

"Aha," M chimed in.

Miguel was almost certainly here. Which leaves us where exactly?

Panting heavily, Magnus flopped on his side in the scant shade. Ellie stooped to let him slurp from a water bottle.

"Nice dog," Soli said. "I used to have a dog."

Liam grunted. "Remember anything else?" he asked. "It's important."

"I can see that," Soli's eyelids drooped.

Liam pulled another bill from his wallet and snapped it between his index fingers in Soli's face.

Liam withdrew the bill a bit when Soli's eyes fluttered open again.

"*Anything else?*" Liam growled.

"Easy, Liam," Ellie admonished.

"I woulda started with a ten," M joshed. "*Hurry up.*"

"Guy was weird," Soli offered. "Had one of them," —he groped for the right word— "not a skateboard or a scooter, it just had, oh, there's un right there," he said, pointing over their shoulders.

They turned to see Ouroboros's giant image on the digital billboard doing yet another faceplant. This time, however, a lingerie-clad, presumably DF'd image of a writhing, Blue state veep America Orinda Sanchez cushioned his landing.

"Douchebag," Soli muttered.

"A Onewheel," Ellie noted.

"Bingo," M uttered.

"Yeah, a Onewheel," Soli affirmed. "I can *not* figure out how they get on and off those fuckin' things."

JJ and Flash—a.k.a. Flash 'N' Da Kash, JJ's resident hip-hop maven—sprang from their seats and boogied around each other gleefully before the looping image. The remaining fundits rose as one and clapped along in unison.

Liam returned his gaze to Soli. "Did you talk to him?"

"He was handing out cards and spoutin' garbage about freedom and some place called Fort Mill and transcendence." He shook his head in apparent bemusement.

"Mmm," M said.

"Anyone with him?"

"Another guy dressed like him," Soli said. "He didn't say nothin'. He was on foot."

"*Uh-huh,*" Ellie coaxed.

"And then he got drilled."

Daily News

BREAKING NEWS

Agencies slammed for stalled efforts to evacuate ag workers from wildfire's path.

Liam gawked at Soli. "What do you mean, he got drilled?"

"When the shootin' started, numbnuts," Soli replied.

"The *shooting*?"

"Some morons started arguing on the sidewalk over there and opened up on each other," he said. "Poor fuck took a single shot to his head. Dropped like a rock. Wrong place, wrong time." He shrugged.

"Oh, my God!" Jess cried over the radio.

"Sorry to give you the bad news," Soli said, absently snapping the fresh twenty between his soiled digits.

"Is Maria listening to this?" Ellie asked in a whisper.

"She's still in her trance," Jess replied, "but she's thrashing around like she's having a nightmare."

"What happened to Miguel?" Liam demanded.

"Who's Miguel?" Soli asked.

"The *Mexican!*" Liam snapped. "The Onewheel guy!"

Soli scowled. "How the fuck would I know his name, asshole?"

Liam realized they hadn't mentioned it. "*Sorry.*"

"Anyway," Soli continued, "I think three guys went down."

"Were *killed*?"

"Far as I know," Soli replied breezily. "A few more got hurt."

"And Miguel?"

"Oh, yeah, the Mexican," Soli said. "I guess he was just lucky. He dragged his dead buddy into some shade and laid him out all nice like a corpse. 'Course he *was* a corpse,"—he chuckled at his own words—"and then…"

"And then *what*, for Christ's sake?"

Soli's eyelids drooped.

Struggling to preserve what remained of his composure, Liam made a show of pulling yet another twenty from his wallet.

Soli eyed the twenty. "Got anything bigger?"

Ellie laid a hand on Liam's wrist.

"We'll see," she said. "What happened to Miguel?"

"Couple of those militia guys are checking you out," M whispered.

Shit.

"From where I was sitting," Soli said, "looked like he pulled a knife from a bag he was carrying, and this blew my mind, he dug the blade into his upper arm like this." He aped the motion. "And then it looked like he dug something out, out of his f'ing arm, man, wrapped it in somethin', and tucked it in one of the other dead guy's pockets."

He took a sip of water.

"Then he did the same thing with his dead buddy's arm."

"Are you sure they were dead?" Ellie asked.

"Saw their eyes, man," he said. "I patrolled in Kabul. I know dead eyes."

"And then?"

"Then he came back to his dead buddy, and there were two guys in ICE jackets standin' by the body."

"*ICE!*"

"I think they were fake," he said. "They didn't act like ICE."

"What do you mean?"

"They helped him lug off his friend's corpse."

"To where?"

"I dunno," Soli shrugged.

Liam's mind reeled.

"So where are the other corpses now?" he asked. "Did the coroner or the cops get them?"

Soli laughed bitterly. "*Cops*," he spat, shaking his head.

"No cops responded to a mass shooting?"

"No cops," he repeated. "No coroner. No priest. No medics. There were bodies here already," Soli elaborated. "People been dyin' out here for weeks from heat, sickness, dehydration, all kinds uh shit."

Jesus.

"A deputy showed up the day after the shooting last week."

"There was a shooting last *week*?" Liam exclaimed.

"Told us there was nobody could pick up the bodies," Soli continued. "He told the store manager to put 'em in the coolest spot they could find. And to find more security. Didn't ask questions."

He chugged the remaining water in his bottle, coughed, and wiped his lips with the back of his hand. "An old school bus with some guys in hazmat suits pulled up a couple of days later and took away the bodies and gimps and left some body bags. Just in case, dude said."

"*Whoa...*" M muttered.

"So where are *today's* shooting victims?" Liam asked.

"Over there, behind the fence." Soli pointed to the access alley that disappeared behind the store. "They put the corpses in an old, refrigerated truck that somebody managed to fire up. But I heard the refrigerants ran out a couple of days ago, and they can't get more." He shook his head ponderously. "Must be gettin' ripe in there."

"And that's where the corpse with the chip in his pocket is?"

"What chip?"

"Implant," Liam clarified, instantly regretting it.

"Way to go, Inspector Clouseau," M said.

"Oh," Soli mused. "So *that's* what it was."

Liam and Ellie said nothing.

"Who the hell *are* you guys?"

"Do they keep it locked?" Ellie asked.

"Keep what locked?"

"The truck, for Christ's sake," Liam snapped.

"Fuck if I know."

"Did they strip the bodies?"

"What am I, Sherlock Holmes?" Soli asked. "Go see for yourself."

Liam looked at Ellie helplessly. Miguel might have left a message for them or Maria in particular.

"There's no time to look, Liam," M warned. "I have Tate trying to turn around and get us the fuck outta here. Things have opened up a hair."

"I have to see that note," Liam insisted. "Otherwise, why did we stop here at all?"

"All right," M said. *"Haul ass!"*

Jess cut in, "Maria's awake and wants to know what's going on."

"Jesus," Ellie said. "Tell her we think Miguel's okay."

"Think?"

"Miguel esta bien," Maria cut in. "Lo sé."

To Liam's surprise, he and the others seemed to simply accept her conclusion, absent any evidence that Miguel was all right.

Weirder and weirder. Do they have some kind of psychic connection?

"I'm taking Magnus to check out that truck and sniff out the right corpse," he announced after a moment. "Poor bastard must have Miguel's scent on him."

"I'm going with you," Ellie declared. Digging an MRE and a bottle of water from her backpack, she handed them to Soli.

"All I got, bro," she said. "You know how it works?" She wiggled the MRE.

"Like I said, I fought in Afghanistan," he replied. "*You* all right, Elvin."

"Vaya con Dios, Soli," she said. "Now get the hell outta here."

DAILY NEWS

BREAKING NEWS

U.S. Chamber of Commerce backs House bill to subsidize armed security at retail businesses.

CHAPTER
THIRTY-SEVEN

They walked by trashed and apparently abandoned RVs, campers, and cars on their way to the twenty-foot refrigerator truck. Security cams jutting from the store's exterior were smashed, spray-painted over, or both.

"Lowd Boiz dRool," proclaimed bubble-lettered graffiti spray-painted on the wall below the cams, with the *d* in "dRool" evidently tacked the R to the rest by some wiseass.

An unlocked padlock dangled from a latch on the truck's roll-up cargo door.

"So much for security," Liam muttered.

"Who'd want to steal rotting corpses?" M queried.

"Somebody who wants to incinerate their assets into ashes," Liam cracked.

"Or vice versa," Jess chimed in.

Ellie snorted.

Seeing no one else around, they raised the door and grimaced at a mild odor of decomposing flesh; sunlight fell on corpse-like shapes in the body bags Soli had mentioned.

Magnus issued a low growl and tugged at his leash.

"Easy, fella," Liam cooed doubtfully.

After giving Magnus a fresh whiff of Miguel's T-shirt, Ellie stood sentry, ghost in hand. Liam seized a strap with which to hoist himself into the truck before summoning Magnus to follow him. The dog hesitated, whining to Ellie.

"Go on, baby," she pleaded.

Magnus momentarily gathered himself before suddenly leaping into the vehicle, almost knocking Liam off his feet.

"Show me the money, Mags," Liam pleaded.

Pressing his muzzle to the floor, Magnus made straight for the body bag to the far left and sniffed intently at what Liam guessed was the torso. Steeling himself for the task at hand, he pulled from his pocket and slipped on a pair of latex gloves; he realized as he did it that he should have done it before he opened the truck.

Oh, well.

"Floor it!" Ellie exclaimed.

Holding his breath, he nudged Magnus aside and unzipped the bag. Avoiding the occupant's face, he trained his eyes on the man's heart area and slipped his right hand through the slit, probing gingerly in a shirt pocket.

He felt nothing.

"Fuck!"

"Move it!" M commanded. "Something's going down up front!"

Unzipping a few more inches of the bag, Liam felt for pants pockets. His digits slid over something like paper beneath the fabric that formed a small auxiliary pocket.

He heard something unintelligible over the store's PA system.

"They're closing the store!" M exclaimed. "Get back here!"

He slid two fingers into the tiny space and pinched the paper between his fingertips; he tugged it out into the light just as what sounded like a gunshot rang out.

"Oh, shit!" Stuffing the find in his pocket, Liam leaped from the rear of the truck in time to see Ellie fire her ghost toward the building's roof.

"Over here, Zeke!" an armed man on the roof yelled to an unseen companion. "We got grave robbers!"

Another shot whistled by Liam's ear. Magnus barked like mad at the snipers firing down on them.

"Run!" Ellie screamed, taking another wild shot as she trailed him, zigzagging.

One of the men screamed and jerked backward and out of sight.

Did Ellie manage to hit him? With a cheap ghost like that?

Even as he dashed, gasping, toward the parking lot, he recalled Tate's miraculous drone shots.

It has to be more than luck.

The traffic was budging, even as the chaos scaled up. People fled the store with whatever they could carry in carts and in their arms. Shots rang out across the lot: people fell to the pavement, bleeding and shrieking in pain.

A woman's shaky voice rang eerily across the sea of vehicles.

"Take whatever you want. Our associates have left the building. Just please stop shooting. People are dying." She sobbed audibly.

"Run toward the gas pumps in the northeast corner," M barked over the radio. "Tate's headed there with Jess right behind us. 'Bout a hundred yards."

Liam fleetingly wondered how Tate could have extracted the van from the automotive chaos as he staggered forward, spurred on by gunshots. Zigzagging blindly, he stumbled into a dish-sized pothole and tripped, plunging headfirst to the ground. He threw his arms out before him, partially breaking the fall as he careened past a car to his right. He heard a car door swing open right behind him, followed by an explosion. Turning his head, he saw a man eyeing the fresh, jagged hole in his door, the density of which had probably saved Liam's life. The man dove back inside the vehicle after shrugging helplessly at Liam.

His hands and knees lacerated, blood-smeared, and stinging viciously, Liam scrambled behind parked cars; stooping, he scuttled after Ellie and Magnus, who were closing in on the slow-moving van. Losing his bearings as he stayed low, he felt a rising panic.

It has to be the fucking snipers firing on us.

"You hit?" M inquired.

"Scraped up." He sheepishly thanked God for the sound of her voice.

"Keep your head down," she said. "Move toward ten o'clock. I'll steer you in."

Continuous gunshots punctuated her words.

"It's snipers," he yelled over the staccato racket. "They'll shoot you or shoot out your tires."

"Move!" she hollered. "We're shooting back at 'em!"

As he scrambled to his left, his eyes happened upon the Jumbotron. He was astonished to see a moving, aerial shot of what appeared to be himself, crouching between cars, moving toward the van, maybe fifty feet away, and watching the screen. He saw gun barrels poking from the rear windows of the vehicle and a figure that must be Ellie somehow carrying a huge dog in her arms before disappearing around the side.

The other half of the split screen displayed two snipers firing away from the roof of the Walmart. A chyron announcing breaking news of the unfolding mass shooting crawled across the bottom of the picture.

The snipers could track them on the Jumbotron!

He stared, perversely fascinated, momentarily before a familiar voice summoned him back to his senses.

"Move it, bro!" T yelled.

How could T, who'd looked like a goner, bounce back so fast?

Gulping one huge breath, Liam forced his legs, near collapse, to propel him by cars and across a small gap to the rear and around the side of the van, as Ellie had done. M and T squeezed off semiautomatic rounds in the direction of the roof.

Jess sat in her car, shielded by the van from the gunfire. They exchanged fleeting glances of profound relief to see each other before he flung himself through the van's side door; Ellie slammed it shut behind him after pulling his legs inside. He lay gasping next to Magnus, around whose bleeding front leg Maria was wrapping a gauze bandage over some kind of smelly application.

Completing the task wordlessly, she slipped a sleep mask over her eyes and noise-canceling headphones over her ears and propped herself against the side of the van, still as a statue.

Is she putting herself in another trance?

"Mayhem is streaming this shit show live!" Tate exclaimed from behind the wheel. "We're viral!"

"Surprise, surprise!" M yelled from the back.

Jared Jeberische's mugging countenance suddenly appeared on the Jumbotron under a breaking news banner.

"This just in!" he declared, snickering. "We've just learned that Mary—pardon, *Maria*—the preggers Mexican kidnapped by the El Camino terrorists, actually left Idaho to *abort* her baby boy but *changed her mind*. Say what you want about the invaders to the south, but this one at least has her priorities straight."

"Oh, my God," Jess muttered.

"It'd be awesome, wouldn't it," he posed, "if some baby-loving patriots tracked her down and got her to talk about her awesome decision to squeeze out her little brown anchor niño. I don't think anyone could argue that we don't need more of that kind of moral fiber in our Ameri Chicano communities. Be great if he speaks Inglés, eh?"

He sipped something from a mug sporting a photo of himself.

"Your wokeness is bringing us to tears over here, JJ." Flash made a show of tugging tissues from a box the identical fire-engine red of the backdrop.

Eyes still closed, Maria suddenly thrashed against her confining seatbelt.

A deep male voice boomed across the expanse.

Heeding amplified commands from the fire trucks to abandon the vehicles in their path, terrified customers ran, walked, limped, and pushed wheelchairs with whatever they could carry toward the far end of the parking lot.

"How do we get outta here?" T asked.

A terrifying sound of metal crashing into metal put an exclamation point on his question.

"Holy shit!" T cried as he peered up at the giant display.

"Oh, my God!" Tate cried.

Too exhausted to scrape himself off the floor, Liam looked to his colleagues for intel.

Staring through the sliding door window, M shook her head in disbelief.

"What?!" Liam screamed.

Lifting his trunk carefully, M propped him up and pointed to the giant display.

On it was an aerial shot of two forest-green fire engines fitted with cow catchers ramming presumably abandoned vehicles to clear, by way of brute force, a route through the gridlock.

Beyond stood the gas pumps and the road back to the freeway.

The shot of the engines receded into one of four screens, another of which showed armed, camo-clad men resembling those working security, directing traffic to the cheers of onlookers. A third screen captured huge military choppers that had been dowsing the fires ominously approaching the parking lot; dangling from their bellies on cable were giant grappling claws.

"Holy shit…" Tate muttered in awe.

The crack of gunshots dimmed. The lumbering Chinooks grew larger on the screen as they descended on the parking lot with a deafening roar; grappling hooks seized and hoisted abandoned vehicles up and out of the packed lot, dropping them in nearby fields to clear space, adding to the firetrucks' efforts.

"I saw a video like this when New Orleans washed out last year. Governor just told 'em do what you gotta do. Never thought I'd be in the middle of it. Shee-*it*," Tate gloated with a grin. "PNS says they're bringing in buses to pick up people on foot."

Encouraged by the opening avenue to the road, volunteers jumped out to direct traffic. A young woman in medical scrubs waved at Tate to proceed into the line of traffic falling in behind the engines.

Drivers cooperated and behaved themselves…

Within minutes, the lines of cars were moving smoothly, if not rapidly.

Liam's posse was back on the road, which also had been cleared, within ten minutes and headed for Fort Mill, Idaho.

Daily News

Breaking News

New law shields government from liability for damage to vehicles incurred when clearing traffic jams.

Tate nosed the van onto a narrow dirt road, stopping at a spot under a screen of scorched firs along the all but deserted I-90, just outside State Line. Hopping out, he busied himself swapping the large, magnetic exterminating business decals adorning the truck for those of a locksmith firm and switching the Oregon tags out for Idaho plates on both vehicles.

His companions gathered tree boughs to camouflage the vehicle from curious aircraft.

Liam carefully handed over the tiny implant to M, who set to work disabling and then examining it. He waited for Maria to resurface from whatever mystical, psychotropic realm she was adrift in to give her Miguel's cryptic message.

It might be dangerous, Jess noted, to rouse her before she was ready.

Liam didn't venture to ask her what she meant. He struggled to process the insanity at the Walmart from which he'd somehow escaped. He wasn't certain he'd have been more astonished had aliens beamed down amid it all.

I could have fucking died. Ellie could have died, and it would have been on me.

Burying his face in a towel, he sobbed.

Miraculous as it was, she somehow managed, on the run, to hit one of those trigger-happy fascists on the Walmart roof and sprint several yards carrying a dog almost as big as her.

Jess, who'd had him text a photo of Miguel's scribbling to her, was positive it was Mayan pictographs. "I'm confident he's telling her to meet him somewhere."

And there was the matter of T.

M said Maria had gotten some foul-smelling herbal tea into him that she'd brewed with the contents of the little leather bag that dangled and swayed from her neck; she also appeared to have whispered unintelligibly in his ear for several minutes and made certain he didn't vomit up her potion.

"As I noted," Jess said, not quite gloating, "she's a curandera, a Mayan priestess or something akin from a long line of them. I believe she's coming into her powers amidst all this craziness and maybe her slash sessions."

"We interrupted her first slash session when we broke into the school," Liam noted. "Maybe Ouro was jealous and was trying to control or even appropriate her powers."

Tate stared at them incredulously, "Are you brainiacs actually buying this voodoo shit?"

"All I know," T said, "is I thought I was dyin', and now I feel pretty fuckin' good. If that's voodoo, I'll take it."

"Amen," M chimed in.

Their attention turned to Maria as her eyes suddenly fluttered open. Grabbing a bottle of water at her side, she drained it and rubbed her belly absently.

She looked at each of them in turn, reserving a scowl for Tate. They glanced at each other and back to her.

"Miguel is here," she declared.

"Here as in—"

"Nearby," she replied. "I can sense him. We *communicate*." She returned their bemused looks a little sheepishly.

No one questioned her.

"Did you find his message?" she implored.

Liam exchanged glances with the others.

"What message?" Tate interjected. "Are you guys freezing me out again?"

"You ratted us out to PNS," M declared, not troubling herself to turn away from her delicate task. "Now we have mobs of kooks and morons and thugs after us because you had to get your nut going viral."

"Ouch," T chimed in with a chuckle and grimace.

"Why *would* we trust you?" M asked.

Tate sulked.

"We haven't time for this!" Jess exclaimed. "Give her the communication, Liam."

"Amen," T concurred.

Nodding, Maria absently but vigorously rubbed her shoulder, evidently still painful from the incision. She accepted the message eagerly.

She held it in her trembling hand for a moment, her eyes closed; she sniffed it, then pressed it, still folded, to her forehead for another. After a few minutes, she unfolded and peered at the cryptic pictograph.

They watched her with a mix of expressions.

"He's here," she said with a knowing nod. "He's waiting for me."

"For you?"

She looked at Ellie. "For *us*," she stressed.

"This is bullshit," Tate cried. "Why should we trust her—or him, for that matter? We don't know anything about this *guy*.

"How do we know what that fucking note really says?" He crossed his arms across his chest petulantly. "We're just takin' her word for it?"

Maria scowled at him.

"Does he have the ashes?" Liam asked.

"He doesn't mention them, señor," she said, shaking her head and shrugging apologetically.

Jesus.

"He wants us to meet him?" Ellie asked.

"Sí."

"Where, exactly?"

"At the border."

"Where at the border?"

"State Line."

"The state line *is* the border!" Tate said triumphantly.

Maria ignored him. "State Line *Village*, cabrón. It's right *on* the border."

"It's pretty remote," Ellie remarked.

"Aren't militias shooting at each other there?" M asked.

"I heard there's been a recent truce so the firefighters, or what's left of them, can get in there," Ellie said. "Who knows if it's real or if it'll last?"

"Sounds like a trap," T noted.

"*Perfect*," Tate declared.

<u>DAILY NEWS</u>

BREAKING NEWS

Idaho National Guard scrambles to staff checkpoints on its Washington border.

Liam chased Daisy and Vonnegut through a forest fire with Goliath close on his heels. Bullets splintered trees and the air overhead.

"You fucked up, asshole!" Ouroboros taunted him from somewhere ahead in the smoky haze. "You abandoned her, just like you're going to abandon Maria."

Goliath's hot, panting breath was on Liam's back when he awoke, thrashing and drooling. He blinked and stared at the ink-black night outside the car.

Assaying the weather with wide, blinking eyes, Liam was silent.

"Yup," Tate commented as if reading his mind, "freak thunderstorms tampin' down the fire."

"Freak," Liam echoed absently. "Where ?"

"We're coming up on State Line," Tate said brightly. "There's a checkpoint ahead."

They rolled past the scorched remnants of non-dom squats, human and animal corpses, and burnt hulks barely recognizable among the campers and cars that littered the sites.

Liam closed his eyes.

"Jesus, God," T muttered, crossing himself.

"What were these people doing out here?" Liam asked no one in particular.

"Nobody fucks with 'em out here," T said.

"Out here where they got burned alive?" Liam shuddered.

"Freedom's a fundamental human desire," Jess chimed in from her trailing vehicle.

"A lot of 'em don't like the rules in shelters," T added, "and they're afraid of being mugged, or worse, or catching something."

"And not all shelters take animals," Ellie noted in their receivers, "and nobody wants to give up their animals."

"Never thought about all that," Tate muttered.

"*That* I believe," Jess snarked.

"Numbnuts don't take animals," T noted. "'Cept his hound of the Baskervilles."

Shaking his head, Liam chuckled as he recalled their recent close encounter with the great beast.

M prepared an MRE for Liam, the same oleaginous beef stroganoff entrée he'd eaten for his last three meals. He winced at the now overly familiar aroma, but his stomach grumbled its demands. There *were* the brownies, which weren't bad.

They fell silent as Liam poked at his noodles with a bamboo fork.

A bullet-riddled road sign warned drivers to prepare to stop at the checkpoint within a half mile and to be searched, as circumstances warranted, by the authority of the state of Idaho's

Department of Border Security. The bottom of the sign, bearing what Liam guessed was a Spanish translation, was spray-painted over.

"We need to pull off the road and make a plan," Liam announced.

"We formulated a plan while you were reenergizing," Jess said. "Google Earth shows an old logging road just ahead where we'll reconnoiter out of view of the checkpoint."

"We should scout the checkpoint on foot," Liam said testily.

"T and Ellie are putting on Invisiwear and NightEyes," M noted. Gesturing toward the ashen air outside the van, she added, "Ideal for this monochromatic palette."

"*And*?"

"Maria is 'resting'" —M made air quotes— "under a blanket on Jess's back seat."

"Great plan," Liam pouted. "Glad I thought of it."

"Affirmative," Jess replied.

Liam hung an abrupt left onto what seemed to be the rutted, washboarded logging road in question, jouncing to a stop on a small, crescent-shaped clearing about two hundred feet in. The opening was screened to the west by a stand of ponderosa pine singed, but not destroyed, by the recent inferno.

Liam flung open the driver's door. The rain had cooled and cleansed the air a bit.

"Should be invisible to anyone on the road," Tate said.

"It'll do for now," M muttered. "We need to camo again, stat."

"*Stat?*" Jess snarked. "Are we on a hospital show?"

"We're viral," Tate reminded them gleefully.

A shattering report of a high-powered rifle went off like a bomb in the direction of the border.

Liam flung himself to the ground and lay there, trembling. "Are they shooting at us?"

"Nah," T said calmly. "Too far away."

"How can you *tell*?"

No one answered.

"*I* should go," Liam muttered without moving. "I should be taking the risks."

"We're all taking risks right now," Jess said flatly. "You need rest."

"So, *you* can call the shots?"

"*Liam*," she chided, adding, "Relax," as M thrust a semiautomatic rifle toward him.

"*That's* gonna happen," M commented. Liam nervously fingered the assault weapon; he nodded his readiness as firmly as he could as she watched him questioningly.

"Okay," she said. "Remember what we practiced and keep your eyes open."

He nodded again, struck by the relative seamlessness of their teamwork. *God bless Tate, whatever his fucked-up politics.*

Moving quickly but cautiously on either side of the road to the checkpoint, T and Ellie melted into the gloom.

Liam flinched at the sound of more rifle shots.

All of them, save for Maria, stood flanking the vehicles, armed and alert; nervous glances swiveled in all directions—more staccato gunshots.

"Are they shooting at you?" Liam asked, covering his ears with his hands.

"Welcome back from the dead, Liam," Ellie said. "I think they're shooting dead soldiers."

"Dead soldiers!"

"Empties."

"*Empties*?" Liam asked in apparent disbelief. "They're shooting at beer cans?"

M snorted. "Drunk, bored, or both," she conjectured. "Surprise."

"And wasting ammo," T noted.

"*Oorah*," Ellie said.

"Cut the chatter," M hissed. "They could be listening."

"Over that racket?"

"Got a visual," Ellie said. "What about you, T?"

"Copy that."

"There's five, maybe six of 'em," Ellie said.

"Maybe more in the woods," Jess cut in. "And odds are they have flies."

"Flies?" Liam asked.

"Drones, boomer."

"Flies," he echoed appreciatively, savoring the jargon.

"Any sign of Miguel?"

"Negative," T cut in. "Can't really see their faces, but Miguel's too big to be any of these guys."

"Good to know."

"Could just be out of sight."

"Visibility sucks," Tate said. Sitting on a camp chair next to the van, he guided his quad over the trees, torched, scorched, or otherwise. "I can't see shit."

"Then ground it," Jess snapped, "before someone else does."

"*Make* me!"

"She's right, Tate," M interjected.

Liam's weary mind reeled.

"What are they doing?" M asked the scouts.

"Beating their meat," T said with a chuckle. "Drinkin', and I swear I smell weed."

"Nick Fury and his howling commandos,"

"Nick *who* and his *whats*?" Tate queried.

"Can the chatter," M growled. "Are you getting any audio from that ear?"

"You'll hear it when I do," Ellie said. "I'm gonna get closer."

"Be careful, El," Jess pleaded.

Liam smiled; it was the first time Liam had heard Jess call her estranged wife by her nickname since they'd separated.

"We're invisible."

"Famous last words."

"I'm fine," she said. "This would be fun if it weren't so iffy."

There was silence for a long moment.

"I'm about twenty-five yards out," Ellie said. "They're using a beat-up four-by-four, as a kind of depot, to block the road. They're all armed."

"Surprise," M said.

"You should be close to getting audio," M said.

They suddenly heard faint, if strident, voices.

"They're arguing," Jess whispered.

"Shut it!" M commanded.

"There's a mob out there," a man said.

"They're camping," said another.

"Nobody's gettin' through our perimeter," a woman said.

"They're gonna kite our asses."

"Eyes out for ganks."

"I'm tellin' ya."

"Ain't gonna happen."

"Mob at two o'clock!" a man shouted.

A barrage of automatic rifle fire.

"Oh my God!" Liam screamed. "They're gonna kill 'em!"

The gunfire stopped as if on cue.

DAILY NEWS

BREAKING NEWS

Reports of 'problems' at state border checkpoints soaring.

Liam held his breath. Could the posse possibly have heard him?

"What the fuck?" T muttered.

"*What*?" Liam demanded, unable to contain himself. "What do you see?"

"Three of the people we're watching just vanished like smoke."

"Holos," Ellie said. "High-end."

"I think they're playing EndDaze," T added.

"Whoa!" Tate exclaimed. "So they *weren't* shooting at T and Ellie. Crazy fucks are LARPing."

"In wildfire country," T noted.

"Larping?" Liam mused.

"Live action role playing," T clarified.

"They're bored," Jess chimed in. "Who knows how long they've been out here?"

"Keeping Idunno safe for idiocracy," Liam added.

"I hear something else," T whispered.

They fell silent as a vehicle crunched over gravel before skidding to a stop. A heavy car door opened and slammed shut. Someone approached the guards.

A deep male voice shouted unintelligibly.

"I'm moving closer," T whispered.

"I ordered you useless fucks to patrol while I was gone!" a man bellowed.

"About fuckin' time you got back, Dutch," declared the woman, who sounded young. "I hope to Christ you got water and some real eats."

"Copy that," said another male. "We're down to cricket chips."

"I told you idiots to stay alert, and here you're fuckin' veering," the apparent leader scolded.

Veering, Liam considered. *VR'ing*.

"Not to mention wasting ammo and batteries," Dutch added. "Somebody could be shooting at you, and you wouldn't even hear it over that racket."

"Patrols are a joke," the woman spat. "This heat's killin' us, we're eating bugs, and we ain't seen any tourists for hours."

"She gotta point," the second man ventured. "You said we were gonna clean up on bribes."

Bribes.

"You shut your mouth," Dutch warned.

"I didn't sign up for settin' fires," the woman said. "We might've killed people!"

"Just some non-doms," the second man chimed in, laughing.

"Fuck you, Jelly!" she snapped.

Jelly?

"You shut it, Marley," Dutch exclaimed. "We followed orders.

That's how we get paid. You're gonna bring the wolves down on us, bitch!"

"The wolves are pinned down at the mill," she countered. "Losers can't handle a few non-doms."

"*Armed* non-doms."

"Whatever."

Liam's posse exchanged excited glances at the first real news—assuming it was accurate—they'd received about their destination.

"You're lucky I haven't dragged your knocked-up ass back to the Coeur d'Alene cooler," Dutch declared. "I never shoulda sprung you to work on this crew, and that after you tried to kill your kid."

"Shut your filthy mouth, Dutch."

"You'd rob my ma, your own kin, of a grandkid, the only fucking thing she ever talks about."

"Andy got himself killed, all over that Patriot bullshit," she snapped. "I don't want his kid. He raped me."

"You fucked him for a fix."

"*Fuck. You. Asshole.*"

Jess guffawed, triggering a harsh cough that brought her to her knees.

"Shut up and do your job, or you'll be back inside with that baby killer you went to," Dutch exclaimed. "See how those bull dykes with batons treat runaways."

The men laughed.

"You'll have that kid, one way or another, bitch."

"So, what *are* we doing here, Dutch?" another man asked plaintively. "*Seriously?*"

"If you were on your shit," Dutch said, "you'd know these terrorists, the ones who kidnapped Poca-fuckin-hontas or whatever and shot up Walmart, are headed this way."

Jesus, what garbage.

"Says *who*?" Marley snorted.

"They're armed and dangerous," Dutch announced. "They killed five people in a shootout, according to PNS."

Liam and his companions shook their heads in concert.

"So here's the deal, *Patriots*," Dutch spat. "Chatter is there's a stiff bounty on 'em or at least Pocahontas. I want that fuckin' cash, and so do y'all. We took an oath," he continued. "We got mouths to feed. Pick up your popguns and patrol!"

"Nobody's out there," Jelly protested. "Wokes hightailed it west and left us here, waiting for ghosts."

A loud rifle shot pierced the air.

"Jesus' *fuck*!" Jelly shrieked.

"Next one'll be closer," Dutch said with a bitter laugh. "Now go get me some terrorists."

DAILY NEWS

BREAKING NEWS

Texas sues feds for cost of landmines it planted along Mexico border to keep out migrants.

"I told you to ground that fucking thing!" M snapped at Tate just as Ellie and T, tugging off their headgear, made themselves visible at the edge of the clearing.

"I did," Tate murmured, looking mystified. He stared at the device, hovering about twelve feet above them. "I'm not operating it."

"Then somebody hacked it," she said in a lowered voice. "Great."

"No way!" Tate declared.

Bursting from the drone's belly, a flickering holo of a swarthy young bear of a man materialized before them, appearing to stand on the ground. He wore a gray tank top and I-Ware.

Liam gaped at the apparition. "Everybody seeing this?"

His companions voiced their affirmation.

"Where's Maria?" the avatar inquired in a tinny, accented voice.

"Estoy aquí, Miguel."

They turned as one to find Maria standing behind them with a hard look.

"Pero dónde estás, mi amor?" She stared, unsmiling and unblinking, at the avatar.

"I couldn't be there in person, Maria," the avatar intoned. "I'm being watched."

"Join the club," T replied.

"¿Dónde estás, Miguel?" Maria repeated.

She still hasn't blinked.

"I need to talk to you privately," Miguel's avatar said.

"That's not going to happen," Jess declared.

"That's not Miguel," Maria declared. "It's a fake."

The avatar smiled condescendingly. "They said you'd say that."

"How do you know he's fake?"

"Show us your keister, Miguel," Maria said mockingly.

"*Whaa?*" Tate muttered.

Everyone stared at her, but no one spoke.

"He has a picture of Ouroboros tattooed on his butt," Maria said. "Prove it's you, mi amor."

"They said you'd say that."

"They *who*, exactly?" Jess inquired.

"¡Quítate los pantalones!" Maria commanded flatly, still unblinking.

The image vanished as suddenly as it had appeared. Amazingly, T managed to catch the suddenly disabled quad before it crashed to the ground.

"I'll take that, thanks," said M, grabbing it from T before Tate could stir. She dropped the device on the ground.

"What the fuck?" Tate protested.

"I didn't realize this thing could be hacked," she said. Wielding a tire iron she'd apparently scrounged from the van, she smashed it to bits.

"Whoa!" Liam managed.

"*What* the *fuck*!" Tate protested.

"It was compromised," M said flatly.

"Obviously," Jess affirmed.

Tate glanced from M to the wreck on the ground, sulking.

"That tattoo business was inspired," Jess told Maria.

"There was no tattoo," Maria said, unsmiling. "I wanted to see how he'd react."

"Wow," T commented.

Jess nodded admiringly.

"Everybody shut up," M said. "I have an idea about how to get past those trigger-happy yokels."

DAILY NEWS

BREAKING NEWS

Reports of armed civilian drones on the rise.

Five guards, rifles trained on the approaching "tourists," fanned out behind a makeshift checkpoint: a battered, mud-caked Dodge Ram pickup blocking both lanes of the rural highway.

"Guess they're not gettin' much traffic," T ventured.

Towering, fire-ravaged conifers, or what remained of them, flanked either end of the extended-cab model, blocking a prospective end run.

Liam slowed the ash-coated van to a stop about twenty feet from the barrier. Tate rode shotgun. M leaned over the front seat between them, binoculars pinned to her face. Jess pulled up a few yards behind them.

"Flies," M muttered, her neck craned to the sky. "Troop trainers. How the hell did these yokels get their hands on 'em?"

"Can you tell if any of those wingnuts are holos?"

"I don't think so."

"Thought they were out of batteries."

Tate filmed it all, his mouth agape.

"It's like we're in an action movie," he marveled.

"At least one," M muttered.

"Don't even think about uploading this," Jess growled.

"Put that fucking phone away," Liam snapped. "We don't want them to see us filming."

Tate complied, grumbling.

M shook her head scornfully.

"Keep your cool," Liam said. "And stick to the plan."

A lanky, balding man with a wispy, reddish-white beard and ponytail broke from the center of the security line and approached the driver's side of the van; he waved his gun up and down.

Rolling down his window, Liam caught a pungent whiff of pot smoke.

A fat, bearded comrade with tape-wrapped glasses secured with a strap stationed himself near the passenger side, trying to appear menacing.

"Good afternoon, sir!" Liam trilled.

"Throw *all* your weapons on the ground," commanded a voice Liam recognized as Dutch's. "Then hands on your head and everybody out of the van, nice and slow."

"No funny business," the man on Tate's side added. His round belly pushed up the bottom of his camo shirt, exposing a hairy abdomen.

"Shut up, Jelly," barked Dutch, his eyes still fixed on Liam. "We find any contraband in either vehicle once you're out, you're toast."

Contraband?

"Got it?"

"Copy that," Liam said.

"Copy that," Jelly mocked in a girly voice.

"You losers chipped?"

"Negative," Liam replied. He glanced at Tate and M, one of whose mannish hands was poised on the sliding door handle.

"Hah!" Marley spat. "Scanner's dead, anyway."

"Shut it, Marley."

"Jus' sayin'."

"You're *allus* jus' sayin'," he mocked.

"She's opening the side door," Liam called to Dutch. "Don't shoot."

"Move it," Dutch barked.

Three ghosts flew out of the van's windows and sliding door, along with screwdrivers and a Taser.

"That *it?*" Dutch queried suspiciously.

"That's it," Liam replied evenly.

"Copy that," Tate said.

"Shut it, midget," Jelly snapped.

"Shut your maw, Jelly," Dutch growled. He scowled at Tate. "Marley, scoop up the hardware."

"Why me?" the freckled redhead protested. "I'm carrying more than guns, remember? Don't want me damaging ma's grandbrat, do you?"

"Jesus', fuck!" he roared. "All right, *be* a bitch!"

"You have no idea, shit-for-brains."

"Rabbit!" he beckoned.

"Make *her* fuckin' do it, Dutch," a third, jug-eared man interjected. "Or you too *whipped?*"

Everyone flinched as Dutch fired a round at the man's feet; the bullet tore loose a bit of asphalt that caromed off Rabbit's shin.

"Fuck me!" Rabbit wailed. Bending down, he rubbed the reddening point of contact vigorously. "Are you crazy?!"

"Jelly," Dutch growled, *"please* collect the weapons."

Jelly set to work, scowling at comrades and tourists alike as he scuttled about, picking up the scattered "contraband."

Dutch watched M as she stepped from the van, her hands on her head. "Check out Cousin Itt here."

His comrades chuckled.

Liam held his breath as, scowling, M opened her mouth. To his relief, she closed it and merely glared at Dutch.

Following her cue, Liam and Tate slowly exited the van, fingers entwined atop their heads.

"Respies and masks off," Dutch ordered.

After exchanging glances, they complied.

Dutch and his comrades gawked. "What the *fuck's* wrong with your faces?" Dutch asked.

"We all have prairie pox," Liam replied. He glanced around at his comrades' flaming features. They had tried not to overdo it with Tate's makeup kit.

Tate evidently is prepared for anything.

"Say *what*?"

"I think we're past the contagious stage."

"Never heard of it," Dutch declared skeptically.

"It's like a mild flu, but it makes your face break out," Liam said. "Sometimes the skin flakes off."

"It's a bitch," M chimed in. "Like shingles."

"Shingles?"

"Jesus!" Jelly exclaimed. "My brother had shingles!" He stared in evident horror at the ghosts in his bare hands before dropping them like hot coals; he examined his palms as though searching for germs. "It's not that flesh-eating shit, is it?"

"I don't *think* so," Liam replied.

"Can't you see he's full of shit, numbnuts?" Dutch exclaimed, shaking his head. "You're so stupid. He's *fucking* with you! And where are your latex fucking gloves, by the way?"

"We're out, remember?" Marley chimed in. "You were gonna get more."

Dutch's jaw stiffened, but he said nothing.

"I heard about that virus," Rabbit chimed in.

"You heard squat," Dutch exclaimed, fingering his beard. "And you wouldn't know Covid from cow shit."

"I ain't worried 'bout Covid," Rabbit countered. "I'm worried about whatever they said."

"Prairie pox," Liam repeated.

"Yeah, that perry pox shit," he said, running a meaty hand over his pasty features.

"I ain't touching anything they touched," a fourth man piped up.

His face flushing, Dutch shook his head in apparent exasperation.

"I bet *they* got gloves," Marley ventured, nodding toward the tourists. "They look smart."

She blew a gum bubble until it burst. "Maybe they should be doing our jobs."

"I swear to God," Dutch snarled, "you little whore." He wagged his gun toward her.

"If it'll speed things up," Liam replied, "you're welcome to some of our gloves."

"We'll *take* whatever we fuckin' need, fuckwad," Dutch snapped. His hands shook as he clutched his weapon.

Is he tweaking?

"Excuse me, Mr. Dutch," ventured Jess. Leaning precipitously on her walker, she'd schlepped herself up to join the rest, a bandaged, muzzled Magnus alongside her, trying to hide his limp. Watching the armed strangers, the dog growled, his robust ears pointing at two o'clock.

"Dead dyke walking," Dutch announced. He examined Magnus appraisingly. "Nice dog."

"Rumors of my death have been greatly exaggerated," Jess announced gravely. "For your information, Mr. Dutch, I'm coping with the indignities of long Covid on top of the prairie plague."

"Long Covid is bullshit," Dutch replied. "You're just genetically inferior."

Oh my God.

"I understand it's rampant in Idaho," Jess replied.

"Long Covid or genetic inferiority?" M snarked.

The guards exchanged glances.

Dutch studied Ellie's pickup curiously before returning his attention to Liam.

"Why y'all need two rides for the four uh ya?" he asked, cocking his head like a puzzled pooch.

Jess suddenly broke into a nasty fit of coughing; a scarlet mist spewed from her mouth. Convulsing, she collapsed to her hands and knees.

Daily News

Breaking News

Ten Idaho inmates freed to fight wildfires found dead in inferno.

CHAPTER
FORTY-THREE

"Nobody move!" Dutch warned, as M and Liam reflexively pivoted in Jess's direction.

"Jesus fuck!" Jelly exclaimed as he backed away from her hastily, his comrades following suit. "She's spitting blood!"

Stage blood.

"You gonna live, butch?" Dutch inquired nervously. He scowled at his timorous colleagues.

Still on her hands and knees, Jess cleared her throat and made a show of sipping some water. Gripping her walker for support with a grimace, she groped her way up to shakily regain her feet.

"Under whose authority," she asked after catching her breath, "are you contriving to search our vehicles?"

"By authority of the armor-piercing choppers we're aiming at your woke coconuts, butch," Dutch informed her with a sneer. "Them and the great state of Idaho, who deputized us."

Marley rolled her wide blue eyes as the men laughed.

Keeping his eyes on Jess, Dutch nodded pointedly toward the van and barked, "Toss 'em."

His comrades shuffled forward hesitantly, weapons raised, giving the detainees, and Jess in particular, as wide a berth as the cramped space allowed.

"Is this really necessary?" Liam inquired mildly. "You have our weapons, and surely you don't want your faces peeling off. This virus is airborne, you know."

Holding a fist to his mouth, he coughed heartily, as did Tate.

Plucking something from a breast pocket, Dutch planted it in his mouth and held a lighter to it with his gun-free arm. He took a robust drag on what appeared to be a joint.

"What do you know," he inquired, squinting through the smoke, "about those terrorist kidnappers who shot up the Walmart?"

"Where'd you hear *that*?" M asked skeptically.

"I'm talkin' to *him*, bitch."

"Sounds like fake news."

"Fake news, hell!" Jelly exclaimed. "PNS showed it *live*."

Marley laughed. "*Penis*."

"If they can fake a Mars mission and Trump's death," Jess chimed in, "they can fake a Walmart shootout."

"Or a kidnapping."

"But *why* would they?" Dutch began.

"There's a laptop in here, Dutch," a man interrupted from inside the van.

"*There's a laptop in here*," he echoed mockingly. "So, grab it, numbnuts," he commanded. "Marley, would it be askin' too much of you to check out the computer?"

"Bring it on," she said with a smirk.

An unlikely techie, used to getting her way, evidently.

"If you're tourists," Dutch asked, "where you gotta get to drivin' through a forest fire?"

"Never said we were tourists," Liam noted. "We're trying to catch up with my brother. He's on his way to blow up Fort Mill; we're trying to stop him before he hurts anybody."

Dutch narrowed his eyes and took another hit off the joint.

"Fort Mill?"

"Yeah."

"Your brother have a name?"

"You don't know him," Liam said.

"*That's* a funny name."

"It's Jasper," Liam said with a shrug. "He's schizo."

"Schizo?" Dutch mused.

"Schizophrenic," Jess said.

"I know what the fuck schizo means, lady!"

"I beg your pardon," she intoned.

He scowled at the group, and Jess in particular.

"You people, you come over here to the east side," Dutch ranted. "you think you're so much better and smarter than us. I bet you're retired, with all kinds a fuckin' pensions and shit, so that you can afford seven-dollar-a-fuckin'gallon gas or Teslas."

"My brother's off his meds," Liam said. "He thinks aliens are taking over the bodies of non-doms."

"Holy shit," Jelly said. "I *heard* about that."

"Hell, *yeah*, ya did!" Tate exclaimed.

"If your bro's from Bloregon," Dutch noted, still bogarting the joint, which his compatriots watched covetously, "why not blow up El Camino? Lot less drivin'."

Still suspicious.

"He says the crazy cult fuck that runs the place has an arsenal," Liam replied breezily. "And that Fort Mill is short on weapons and organization. It's ripe for a siege."

"So, your *brother's* a terrorist?" Dutch asked suspiciously. "And why you keep lookin' off into the woods over there?"

M glanced furtively at Liam even as he turned his attention back to Dutch.

"This scenery brings up some stuff for me," he said somberly. "I lost someone in a forest fire a while back."

Dutch narrowed his eyes at Liam again, but said nothing for a moment.

"Sorry to hear that," he muttered.

"My brother's an ex-Army Ranger gone rogue," Liam replied. "PTSD, drugs, the whole nine yards. His wife dumped him. He's into conspiracy theories. He recruited some armed service buddies for the mission."

"They smoked ten people at the Walmart!" Jelly declared.

Everyone flinched as Dutch fired a shot in the air. "Last warning, numbnuts. Shut it and search the woods."

"Now, who's wasting ammo?" Marley cracked as her fingers danced over the keys on M's antique Powerbook, perched on the Escape's filthy hood.

"What's with the ghosts?" Dutch queried, indicating the weapons Jelly had arranged on the vehicle's capacious hood. Stubbing out the joint on his rifle, he stuck the big roach in his breast pocket.

"Ask the border guard, pointing street sweepers at us," M muttered.

"Fair enough," chimed in Marley, who was typing rapidly.

"Please be careful with that," M pleaded. "It's personal stuff."

Marley looked at her thoughtfully for a moment. "C'mere and show me."

Dutch watched but said nothing as M crossed cautiously to join Marley.

"Are they paying you guys?" Liam asked lightly. "I heard Idaho is broke."

The guards exchanged nervous looks.

"You heard shit," Dutch declared, glancing at his comrades. "He's messin' with you."

Marley suddenly craned her head toward the woods. "Shut up," she hissed, loud enough for everyone to hear.

"There's somethin' moving over there," she uttered in a low voice, indicating a scorched copse of firs a few yards away.

With a finger to his lips, Dutch motioned his armed charges toward the indicated direction. They scurried to distance themselves from the infected tourists.

"We're in position," Ellie whispered into Liam's earbud. Dutch gave no sign of having heard anything.

Reciting one of the agreed-upon phrases, Liam whispered to Dutch. "What do you want?"

"I don't know what you wokes are really up to," Dutch addressed Liam in a low voice, "but if you know anything about Pocahontas, let's talk."

"Pocahontas?"

"The knocked-up Mexican," Dutch replied. "Don't try playing me, smartass."

"I wish I did," Liam said. "I'd turn her in myself for the reward."

"Gimme your wallet."

Liam shook his head dolefully, but tossed it over.

Satisfying himself with a glance to ensure his charges were busy tracking down the phantom noise, Dutch thumbed through Liam's meaty billfold, removing and stuffing bills into his pocket before suddenly glancing at the ground at Liam's feet.

"What's that?" he asked, his eyes narrowed.

Fatigued as he was, Liam still caught his breath when he noticed the crumpled Walmart receipt, which must have tumbled from his pocket unnoticed when he removed his wallet.

"Nothin'," he replied as casually as he could muster.

"Pick it up and hand it to me," Dutch said menacingly. "Nice and slow."

Dutch held up the receipt, growing soggy in the rain.

Fuck!

Liam saw a pair of drones rising in the air behind his tormentor. On the far side of the truck, he saw M and Marley working the controls.

"You lying cocksucker!" Dutch raged. "You *were* at the Walmart."

No sooner had he said it than EndDaze holos sprang to life beneath the flies, firing virtual assault weapons. Dutch whirled around in a rage to see Marley scrambling away in a crouch from the controllers into the woods. M dove under the SUV.

"What the fuck?" Dutch bellowed.

After stuffing Liam's wallet in his pocket, he raised his AK and aimed it at Liam's head. "We're getting ambushed from the woods," he screamed. "Kill 'em."

He turned back to Liam.

"Adiós, motherfucker."

Liam pissed his pants.

Before Dutch could pull the trigger, half his skull exploded, showering Liam's closed eyelids, makeup, and shirt with blood, flesh, and bone.

Liam screamed as more shooting broke out. He was on his knees, shaking and vomiting when Tate seized his shoulder; Tate pulled him to his feet with his arm around his shoulder.

Screams and more shots.

"Liam!" Tate ordered. "Get under the van."

A few seconds later, the shots stopped.

"Clear," Ellie yelled.

"Copy that," T declared as they entered the clearing, brandishing AKs and Tasers and schlepping through the ashes with canvas sacks containing the rest of the guns.

Tate and Liam emerged from under the van. M rolled out from under the 4x4.

Rabbit lay thrashing and moaning as his partners stood gawking, their mouths agape, hands up, and weapons at their feet.

"He's fine," Ellie said. "I got close enough to tase him."

Gaping at Dutch's corpse, Liam said, "What the fuck just happened?"

M grimly draped a towel over what was left of Dutch's head.

"He got fragged," T said, looking at Jelly, who stared at the corpse in apparent shock, a lowered rifle in his hands.

Marley had vanished, leaving the laptop on the Escape's hood.

Liam was dimly aware of T, who handed him his wallet and led him back to the van as Jess, who'd abandoned her walker, addressed the terrified survivors.

"It's over, people," Jess said. "You're done here."

T and Tate, along with Maria, who appeared after a moment, collected the surrendered weapons.

"We're leaving you some MREs."

Defeated, the disarmed guards nodded mutely.

"Now, we need to move the truck so we can get by," she said. "Where are the keys?"

"Where's Marley?"

"We have no business with Marley," Jess said.

"Keys are in the truck," Jelly bleated.

"Dutch took my money while you all were distracted," Liam said shakily. "The wad in his pocket is yours, along with the MREs and the ghosts."

After reloading the vehicles and climbing back in, the posse awaited T, who shot one tire out on each of their foes' vehicles.

"Sorry," he said, "but the drones will find you. They find everybody."

The surviving border guards were visible in the rear mirror, arguing as the posse drove out of sight, jouncing down the muddy road.

Daily News
Breaking News

False reports of new pandemics on the rise.

"Now we have an exclusive report," Jared Jeberische announced from his cavernous lounger, "from our VR man, Lance Rancette, on the ground—*so to speak*—at MillTown."

Half the split screen displayed a high-end holo of a reporter resplendent in crisp fatigues and an Army helmet.

"Fill us in, Lance, on the scene in MillTown, where we hear all hell is breaking loose."

Liam, riding shotgun, scrutinized the dash screen in vain for any sign of said hell breaking loose.

The camera swept over a swarm of people—non-doms, Liam supposed—cooking and eating at makeshift dining tables cobbled together from sawhorses and plywood in what appeared to be an industrial warehouse.

"This is where the insurgents prepare and take their meals," Rancette informed his viewers in a deep voice.

Thank you, Captain Obvious, but insurgents?

Rancette's avatar roamed past the diners into an even larger adjacent compartment of the squat industrial complex, noting points of supposed interest to viewers. Occasionally, he walked right through one person or another, all of whom were busy emptying bags and cartons and sorting the food and clothing they removed from them.

Donations? How?

Laborers raised a din of hammering as they boarded up broken windows with sheets of plywood. Some replaced lights, brightening the gloom. Others were creating posters and tagging walls and support beams with bubble-lettered resistance slogans.

Fuck Idaho fascists!

Freedom lies here! Here lies home!

And, of course, renderings of Ouroboros, the tail-swallowing serpent.

Ever helpful, Tate had informed Liam on the way that Ouroboros, psilocybin, and Inviswear were the most-searched words on GChat at the moment.

A few workers vacantly watched Rancette's avatar and, a few feet overhead, the quad projecting it and employing its several cameras before returning to their tasks.

Liam conjectured that the fly, an airborne blur, was wrapped in some kind of invisifabric.

M had informed him in private that she'd read on an arcane military stealth tech site that the fabric's makers were suddenly talking IPO, garnering a tsunami of biz press as news of the prototype went viral. A marginal insider apparently leaked the patent application to WikiSpex, where it stirred enormous, instant demand among militants, survivalists, and weekend warriors.

Reading between the lines, he assumed she was giving him a

killer stock tip in exchange for giving her, albeit inadvertently, the opportunity to demo the product for the entire world.

Rancette's avatar questioned workers, clad in a patchwork of donated garments, about the nature of the massive machines and conveyances dominating the space.

Most ignored the intrusive apparition. One man's animated reply was bleeped beyond meaningful comprehension.

On the other half of the screen, Jeberische guffawed at the outburst. "I want to interview *that* guy!"

Liam shook his head.

"There you have it, Jared," Rancette said. "These determined, unhoused men and women are too busy fortifying this creaky old sawmill to talk to a reporter."

Exiting the plant through a huge portal at the far end, Rancette continued his narrative in the gloom outside.

"Here," —he gestured unnecessarily— "is where the vintage Huey army copter crash-landed inside the Mill Town perimeter yesterday after being winged by militiamen on the ground."

"And I assumed that was fake news," Jeberische marveled. "My bad."

The school-bus-sized aircraft lay listing on the ground like a huge, crumpled insect, its mangled tail rotor thrust skyward. It was already scrawled with graffiti echoing the messaging on display in the building.

"The crew miraculously survived with a few scrapes," the avatar noted, "and helped the MillTown occupants unload its cargo of assault weapons, RPGs, and other military hardware.

"The crew has been tightlipped regarding who paid for and sent the chopper."

"Holy shit!" Tate gawked at the screen. "Where did they get all that stuff?"

"Watch the road!" Liam snapped, seizing and straightening the wheel for a second.

JJ, too, gawked at the scene. "Jesus God, Lance, are they prepping for Armageddon?"

"Responding to reports of a large number of vets among the non-doms," Rancette said, "veterans' organizations have leaped into action, calling for support of the insurgents, including providing defensive weaponry. JJ, some of the more wild-eyed denizens have dubbed this mill the Alamo."

"Defensive weaponry," Jeberische mused. "Has anyone claimed responsibility for the attack on the Huey, Lance?"

Raising the phantom mic to his phantom lips with his phantom hand, Rancette's phantom replied, "Jared, the Lowd Boyz, a white nationalist, Christian, anti-woke paramilitary, bragged on Gabbel about downing the chopper, but we've been unable to confirm that claim."

"Unable to confirm that claim," JJ echoed, chuckling.

"If somebody can take out a big Army bird like that," he mused, "why don't they just blast their way into the place?"

"Another great question, JJ," Rancette replied. "We're looking into that as we speak."

"I'm confident," Jess chimed in sarcastically, "that this is immaterial to the topic at hand, but a deputized militia group shot up a non-dom camp a while ago on a bad tip they got that the occupants were plotting to take over some buildings."

"That went viral on Mayhem," Tate observed.

"No doubt," she replied. "Whatever cognitively impaired foundlings organized that slaughter probably want to avoid another PR disaster."

"I think I heard about that," Liam said. "Figured it was fake news."

"Fake news seems to be in the eye of the beholder."

"It's possible," Rancette ventured after a pause, "that the shooters wanted to make an example of the would-be occupiers. Then somebody close to the governor decided it wasn't a good look and told them to stand down and stand by or forfeit their pay."

"Better and better," Jared Jeberische declared with satisfaction.

DAILY NEWS

BREAKING NEWS

Leaked internal memo indicates PNS plans to phase out human reporters.

CHAPTER
FORTY-FIVE

A pop-up roadside carnival had sprouted along the approach to Fort Mill; RVs, food carts, and bicycle-propelled smoothie vendors dotted the roadside, neighboring pastures, and parking lots.

"Place is *happenin'*," T commented as Tate inched the van along.

"Place is *a* happening," Jess edited crisply.

T muttered something unintelligible.

"We could push this thing faster than I can drive it," Tate muttered.

A huge tent was being staked down for what appeared to be a revival meeting.

"COME HOME AT LAST!!!!" said a banner boasting a

conventional likeness of the adult Jesus, albeit with his iconic, flowing locks piled into a man bun and a spliff dangling from his lips.

A small, neighboring army of bearded hipsters was erecting a Burning Man-lite featuring what was advertised as a homelessness theme. Doubtlessly lured by a slew of Fort Mill memes and a collective FOMO, so-called slashists (distinct from slashers) sculpted a spectacle atop the ashes of a sprawling pasture.

Talk about a rabble magnet.

A scrum of scrawny cows watched the madness absently as they nosed the earth for scarce forage.

Among the wide-eyed onlookers were women in long-sleeved pastel dresses and skirts that fell below their ankles; they herded a gaggle of children as they navigated the carnival, their heads bowed. A few armed young men in dark hats, pants, and shirts flanked them; they scowled at the artists, yelling "whores" and "harlots" as they passed.

"Fuckin' Saints," sniped Marley, who'd hidden herself in the bed of Ellie's pickup under cover of the melee. She'd waited until a few minutes after they'd left the checkpoint behind to announce herself by popping up from beneath the tarp. Given that she'd helped them escape and that she, like Maria, was pregnant, they let her join the party.

"They aren't Mormons," Jess countered. "A lot of women here are dressing like that now in exchange for some freedoms."

"Fuck you know about marmots, lady? I grew up here."

"For starters," Jess informed her, "Jesus reportedly is going to return in a red-colored robe, so that's off limits. Dark colors are banned because they're associated with Satan."

"The hell you say," M joshed.

"How do *you* know?" Marley inquired.

"I'm a cultural anthropologist," Jess answered. "I study subcultures."

OMG.

"Whatever," Marley conceded sulkily, "but I still think they're Saints. Lookit those poor little shits in their potato sacks."

"For the nth fucking time," M snapped, *"everybody shut up!"*

Graffiti was everywhere.

SLASH = TRANSCENDENCE

SLASH SAVES

MAKE SHROOM FOR ENLIGHTENMENT

SLASHHOLES NOT WELCOME

Slashholes?

Flimsy kiosks advertised FDA "Authorized" magic mushrooms for sale. Liam saw no sign of anyone—*yet*—shilling cremains. He marveled at the speed at which this performative, mobile zeitgeist had arisen in the middle of Buttfuck, Idunno.

During construction of the transcontinental railroad, he'd read, the mobile manufacturing towns required to complete that massive engineering feat had acquired their own camp following: rolling red-light districts catering to laborers stuck in the middle of Buttfuck, Utah, as it were, craving some release from their toil.

A gold rush on rails. Imagine the lawless conditions those camp followers must have endured, not to mention the immigrant laborers themselves.

The vendors here peddled assault rifles, ammo, ghost guns, machetes, MREs, bottled water, and what they at least touted as Invisiwear, at exorbitant prices from the backs of pickups and vans.

Jesus, how long will this little gold rush last?

Merch-toting drones choked the damp, smoky skies.

"Wow," Tate marveled as he peered upward. "They're everywhere."

Turning, he scowled at M, who shrugged her indifference.

"Your fly was compromised, Tate," she said. "Assuming we ever get back, I'm good for a new one."

Everyone, masked or otherwise, appeared to be coughing.

"Prairie pox," M deadpanned.

"Perry pox," T corrected her.

They all snickered.

Vehicles of all descriptions choked the two-lane road to MillTown, situated near the Sandpoint city limits and the air above, including military and those bearing logos of various media outlets.

Who is piloting all these drones, anyway? Some probably pilot themselves.

The flies and all manner of small planes somehow found ways around each other under the low, hulking cloud cover. If any of them had made the van or the pickup as those belonging to the so-called Jesus Squad, they had yet to show any cards.

On the I-Dash appeared an ostensibly live feed of what their flight gear suggested was the Huey crew. They seemed to be training quizzical-looking "insurgent" non-doms in the use of the downed aircraft's deadly cargo. They examined their weapons, some more adroitly than others.

"Excuse me," the phantom reporter interrupted a man issuing instructions, "Lance Rancette, PNS. First off, thank you, sir, for your service."

The tall, masked man turned to the source of the voice. "What the *fuck* are you supposed to be?"

"Again, thanks for your service, sir," the avatar replied nervously. "Who's in charge here?"

"Fuck off is in charge here!" He pointed to his helmet, across the front of which the epithet was scrawled in red ink, which producers belatedly pixelated.

The instructor's charges laughed.

The gunman turned his gaze upward, staring directly into the drone's camera.

"Who let that flying fuck in here?" he roared. "You're showing our position, asshole."

"I'm sorry, sir," Rancette persisted, "but I didn't get your name." He thrust his phantom mic at the gunman, who pointed, again, to the now-pixilated epithet on his helmet.

"Okay, sir, I get it," the avatar added hurriedly. "But what about all the other drones up there?"

Swiveling, the drone directed another of its cameras to capture the scene of an eerie constellation of similar devices; like so many jellyfish swaying with the tide, they dangled objects of all sizes and shapes from cables attached to their bellies.

"They're *workin'*," the man growled. "*You're* spyin'." Aiming with his rifle, he fired; the half screen went blank with a resounding crack.

Jeberische chuckled. "Well, *that* was informative. They'll probably take that fly outta my next paycheck."

"They *pay* you to do this, JJ?"

"I work for tips."

"You mean news tips."

"You mean *rumors*."

More laughter from the panel.

Tate picked his nose absently. "How much do you think that guy makes?" he asked no one in particular.

"Whatever it is, it's *way* too much," T chimed in.

"And yet, we watch," M muttered.

Liam shook his head wearily and yawned.

"Lance is back with us by phone," Jeberische announced with a resigned sigh. A still image of Rancette's holo appeared above the closed captioning.

"So, Lance," Jeberische began, "if the militias outside Fort Mill can take out a Huey, why don't they just shoot down those drones supplying the rebels?"

Rebels?

"Like fuckin' Star Wars," Tate muttered in awe.

"Savage question, JJ," Rancette replied. "I've learned on background that the drone industry, in general, is upset over janky PR about their product; they think the video of militia members blasting flies from the skies gives them a black eye."

"Savage how he sneaked that 'janky' in there," Kash noted.

Frowning, Jeberische rubbed his forehead in cartoonish

puzzlement. "Lance, there's chatter that it's actually tourists downing rebel aircraft to smear local Patriots."

"Not to mention, JJ," Rancette replied, left eyebrow cocked, "chatter that the videos themselves are fake."

"Down the rabbit hole we go." Pink CGI bunny ears sprouted on Jeberische's head.

"We hear the big makers promised the Patriot militias their advanced drones," Rancette added, "if they stop shooting down the other ones."

"*Ahhh*, so long as they're not sanctioning more mischief."

"Whoever thought of that should be in the White House," opined Desi Valdez.

"Probably for the best that Rancette's not really there," a neighboring panelist commented.

"*Whatever*," Jeberische replied, slumping in his chair.

Inanity or insanity?

DAILY NEWS

BREAKING NEWS

MillTown militant takes out PNS 'reporter'.

At a near standstill, the traffic stretched as far as they could see.

"What's the play here, Liam?" Jess inquired.

"I guess we park somewhere and head to the mill on foot and hope to hell we hear from Miguel."

"A plan par excellence," she sniped.

"You have a better idea?"

"Turn around?"

"Be my guest," he countered. "You invited yourself."

"Stop it, you two," Ellie pleaded. "Not helpful."

"We are in profound need of Americanos back here," Jess said.

"*Americanos?*" Maria asked with puzzlement.

"Fancy java," Marley replied glibly.

"Java?"

"Coffee," Ellie said.

"Ohhh," Marley replied with exaggerated understanding. *"Whyn't you just say so?"*

Liam smirked.

Because she can't help herself.

"Now," Jared Jeberische declared from the dash, "from a suddenly viral old sawmill to the ever-churning rumor mill. As PNS viewers are aware, it's our official policy to neither endorse nor condemn conspiracies; we also believe, however, that it's critical to your understanding of current events to be alert to what chief influencers are thinking and saying about the world hour by hour."

Game show music issued from the dash speakers as a caricature of Jeberische depicted as a Minuteman sporting a tricorn hat and firing a musket, burst onto the screen; the gun's barrel blasted flame and a cloud of smoke that morphed and spun out into words—conspiracy theories, to be exact—to the revolutionary lilt of electrified fife and drum.

Oh, my fucking God.

"Oh, that'll be hilarious," Tate trilled.

"You, our patriotic viewers," Jeberische announced, "get to vote for the best rumor. The winner gets to post a personal video of three minutes or less that will air and afterward be posted on our website. They'll also earn the chance to vie for the title of official PNS influencer."

Jeberische clicked through a series of tweets and video clips that flashed on the alternate half-screen. The panelists took turns reading the tweets.

"Do favor us, Flash, with your stentorian delivery."

Flash delivered dutifully: "Rumor No. 1: Telepathic Mayan curandera Maria what's-her-name revived two clinically dead men." A blurry picture appeared of a woman vaguely resembling

Maria, her facial outlines prominently pixelated, tending to the image of a prone man.

"Pathetic," Jeberische lamented. "Again, we don't endorse these images, folks; we leave it to you, the informed patriot, to draw your own conclusions."

The next panelist read: "Rumor No. 2: Maria's fiancé, Miguel Joseph Sanchez (unconfirmed), father of her unborn baby—*Jesús*, remember?—is being manipulated by agents of a privately funded black op aimed at obtaining access to Maria to see if she can somehow rejuvenate a crazy, dying trillionaire—at least depending on how you counted."

"That's a mouthful," Jeberische commented drily. "You heard it here first, Patriots."

"You're gonna need a 'Guess the right crazy, dying trillionaire' segment for the show, JJ."

"Rumor number three: The great Ouroboros, emperor of El Camino and purveyor of so-called slash therapy, mashing up magic mushrooms and human cremains, is on his way to take over Fort Mill and spread his woke, groovy gospel."

"Rumor number four: people are breaking into funeral homes, crematoriums, and tombs to steal cremains to sell underground or use them in DIY slash therapy in hopes of acquiring superpowers."

"Gotta say I'm relieved," Jeberische noted, "that our patriotic followers aren't overly suggestible, else they'd all be out there doing crazy shit."

"Rumor number five: Cremains are scarce because green burials have soared in popularity at the same time the cost of fuel to incinerate corpses has driven rapid price increases."

"Last but not leastest, Rumor No. 6: people are literally fighting over supplies of magic mushrooms, which suddenly, if not surprisingly, are in viral demand. Noobie 'shroomers' are trampling delicate woodlands looking for a quick buck. ERs nationwide are reeling from a tsunami of slashists ingesting poisonous fungi."

"Another mouthful…"

Of shit.

"And finally, there's a prize for the first person to correctly guess which—*if any*—of the aforementioned rumors have been confirmed."

"Wadda ya think?" Tate asked with a collegial glance at Liam.

Liam gave him a *look.*

"Once the timer starts, you have thirty seconds to vote for the most savage rumor submitted," Jeberische soldiered on. "Chipped viewers can vote simply by extending the designated finger at the embedded camera of the device in use."

"Wow," Tate marveled.

A huge sign advertising parking spaces in a huge pasture siphoned a steady stream of vehicles from the road.

"We'll take our chances in there," Liam told Tate, who nodded.

"Lightning round!" JJ trilled. "There's fresh chatter that the ashes Maria swallowed are from the 'cremains'" —he made flamboyant air quotes— "of someone who was a test subject in a secret government experiment."

"You need new writers, JJ."

Stiffening, Liam took a long, deliberate sip of water.

Where the fuck did PNS dig up that ESP study? It certainly wasn't from Tate.

"Government researchers in the Cold War '70s," Jeberische continued, "in their infinite, eggheaded, allegedly scientific wisdom, experimented on children who exhibited unusually strong indications of psychic abilities such as ESP—extra-sensory perception—like mind reading and clairvoyance."

"Clara?" Maria uttered questioningly.

"Clairvoyance," Jess said. "Predicting the future."

"I dream sometimes," Marley joined in, "about stuff that actually ends up happening."

"The researchers," JJ continued, "allegedly appealed to the subjects' moms' and dads' patriotism during the Cold War plus a little sugar, like subsidized home loans."

"What's a cold war?" Liam heard Marley ask.

"It's complicated," Ellie replied.

"Well, *excuse* me for livin' and breathin'," Marley snapped.

Ellie shrugged.

"Where's Miguel and those fucking ashes?" Liam muttered. He pointed out a relatively isolated parking spot near a brick wall large enough for two cars. Tate jounced the van to a bumpy halt and dashed for a stand of torched trees to take a well-deserved piss.

Could Maria be playing us? Anything seems possible at this point.

"This story broke two days ago, Patriots," Jeberische jokingly chided the camera. "And this is all ya got?

"Send us some *real* fake news!"

DAILY NEWS

Breaking News

PNS 'Jesus Squad' coverage notches record ratings.

They parked the vehicles in a scorched, muddied pasture whose gates the owner had opened to camp followers and tourists in exchange for exorbitant fees or barter. Bored-looking teens in fluorescent vests wielding glow sticks guided drivers to tight openings.

Tate once again swapped out business decals and license plates as the growing posse gathered around him to shield his activity.

Drones towed digital banners promising rewards to anyone who claimed to have information regarding the Walmart terrorists.

The display included a crawl of blurry photos of Liam and his companions snatched, or simply faked, from God knew where.

Insanity.

Backpacks, machetes, masks, guns. Even man-bunned hipsters were carrying.

People unloaded merch and display tables from the swelling sea of vehicles. Many sported decals boasting that they were fueled by everything from vegetable oil to garbage to hydrogen to "green" batteries.

Green batteries? Gratteries?

Liam spied a man he was almost certain was the same, white-robed Jesus freak he'd seen at Walmart schlepping the huge white cross.

Angry they hadn't heard from Miguel, the party was about to set off for MillTown in separate twosomes in hopes of discretion.

T's phone suddenly chimed.

"Incoming text from unidentified sender," a woman's silky voice announced.

T checked the message with a curious expression. "What the fuck?"

"What is it?" Liam snapped.

"It's a bunch of coded characters," T said. "Looks like the message Miguel scribbled for Maria."

Liam peered at the screen over T's shoulder. As T noted, the characters resembled those on the note he'd removed from the corpse the day before, which now seemed like an eternity ago.

Finally!

Still wriggling into and distributing their various burdens for the least discomfort, everyone turned their attention to the phone. Liam gestured at them to gather in a small clearing on the far side of a crumbling stone wall adjacent to their vehicles, in which a huge dent had been punched.

"Everyone hold hands and bow your heads like we're praying," Liam said.

Everyone complied.

"Looks like we finally heard from Miguel in code," he informed them. Catching Maria's eye, he handed her the phone.

She accepted it, wide-eyed, and looked at the screen.

"Translate that out loud for us," Liam directed.

She nodded gravely.

"Are you certain it's from Miguel?" Jess asked.

"These pictographs are our secret code," Maria replied with a curt nod.

"He wants me to meet him," she continued, "in a secret tunnel that runs from outside the fence on the east side of the complex to a utility building behind the main building."

"A secret tunnel," Tate muttered in awe.

He has a real hard-on for this cloak-and-dagger stuff.

"Oh my God!" Marley gasped.

What was that about?

T whistled softly.

"You said he wants to meet *you*," Liam noted pointedly.

"He means all of us," she countered emphatically.

"*Does* he now?" Jess snarked.

"And we find this tunnel, *how*?" Liam asked.

"I'll show you!" Marley declared.

All eyes turned to her.

"I *know* that tunnel!" she exclaimed, glancing dramatically at each of them in turn.

"Why should we believe you?" Jess asked dismissively. "We don't even know you."

"I helped you take down those losers, didn't I?" Marley declared. "And you helped me escape."

"I'm listening," Liam replied.

"My grandfather ran that sawmill," she declared. "My brother and I used to play outside there when we were kids. I found the tunnel when I was looking for my dog."

No one spoke.

"*No* lie," she insisted.

"Miguel says his assets want us to follow her," said Maria, eyes fixed on the phone's screen. "I need you, Maria," Miguel texted her —*if it was, in fact, Miguel.* "You and Jesús."

She glared at the phone.

"Everybody thinks we're terrorists," the translation app lamented as Maria thumbed with dizzying speed.

"That's why you need to get here as fast as possible," she translated his reply. "You can tell your story—our story—in safety."

Our story?

"And give birth to him."

Liam groaned.

"All I want are my wife's ashes, Miguel," Liam dictated tearfully to Maria. "How do I get them?"

"The ashes are safe," the correspondent replied blithely. "My assets have secured them."

"Who *exactly* are these assets?" M inquired. "And that could be *anybody* texting."

Silence.

"And why don't they meet us out here," Liam demanded, "instead of forcing us to sneak in?"

"Good question," M chimed in as Maria thumbed away.

"Because," she said momentarily, continuing her translation, "*they—we*—control the environment at the sawmill."

"Why should we trust him—*or* her?" Tate protested, turning his suspicious gaze to Marley. "The whole shit show back there at the border could have been a trick."

"A *trick*?" T asked. "That racist prick got his head blown off!"

"They coulda faked that," Tate insisted. "Maybe that fat fuck Jelly was shooting blanks. Maybe *they* had makeup, too."

"Fuck Dutch," Marley sneered.

"Shut up," Liam pleaded.

"*Move!*"

Maria's startling urgency drew her companions' renewed attention.

"Miguel said that and hung up," she explained sheepishly.

DAILY NEWS

BREAKING NEWS

Jesus Squad breaks the Internet.

FORTY-EIGHT

Flanked by Liam, who informed her that he had a ghost in his pocket trained on her, Marley led her new companions through the soggy, twilit, cacophonous carnival. He had no clue if he could spur himself to use the gun, if necessary, nor if she believed he could.

The latter seemed doubtful, at best. How evident was his mounting trauma to the others? He tried to banish the sight of Dutch's face exploding.

Marley seemed content for the moment to go along with the intrigue.

Several yards behind them came Jess with her cane, on which she at least appeared to lean heavily, and Ellie. Liam was pleased to get no argument when he paired them up, possibly because he charged them with flanking tiny Maria. Ellie kept a tight grip on Magnus.

Maria lurched along as if hampered by palsy; passersby offered her—in addition to Jess's hammy hobbling—pitying looks and a wide berth.

A ploy worthy of Joan.

M and Tate, Ranger at his heel, brought up the rear another several yards behind the threesome.

Exhausted as he was, Liam struggled to make sense of a raft of unanswered questions concerning his remarkable recent circumstances. *How is everyone recovering so quickly from their various pains and ailments? Does Maria, who has attended to most of them in one way or another, have some kind of healing powers?*

Did Ouroboros give her a dose of Joan's ashes?

What do Miguel's "assets" know about Maria?

What do they know about Joan?

About me?

For whom, moreover, do they work? Assuming Miguel's so-called assets, if they exist, have, in fact, rescued him, they haven't done it out of altruism.

How did they know where Miguel was?

Does Miguel even exist?

How fucking tired am I that the thought even crossed my mind?

Likely scanning the pilgrims for familiar faces, quads jockeyed for sightlines and sprouted rotating spotlights, rendering the scene even more eerie. As dank darkness fell, generator-powered lights burst to life on the ground. It reminded Liam of a Who concert during which strobe floodlights swept over the ecstatic, dancing crowd.

Sporadic fireworks and flares evoked the incendiary cinematography of *Apocalypse Now*.

The posse kept their covered heads bowed as best they could, trying to avoid unwanted attention from the overhead traffic.

"I thought Idaho was full-a rednecks," T commented. "This looks like fuckin' Portland."

"Maybe the rednecks are disguised as hipsters," Tate ventured.

"Everybody shut up," M muttered yet again.

A smiling, bearded Uncle Sam ambled by on stilts, locking eyes with Liam for an uncomfortably long moment; he juggled glowing bowling pins with a woman perched on his shoulders whose attire consisted of an intricate rainbow mesh of glow sticks.

Nearby was a b-boying demonstration.

Encircling a blazing brazier fire, Coeur d'Alene tribal members drummed and chanted.

Distracted by the sideshows, Liam walked right through Lance Rancette's holo; to his relief, it appeared to take little notice of him beyond a curious glance.

A shower of slimy button mushrooms rained down from somewhere onto the crowds.

Are people supposed to think they're magical?

Vendors hawked Ground Bounty insect snacks and merch, including tees and hats sporting a contented mealworm patting its sated belly.

A truck with a flashing light, bearing a cargo of portable toilets, inched its way through the crowd, blasting its air horn.

"If I remember right," Marley informed her companions via their earbuds, "about fifty yards ahead, there's a brick post office or something with a parking lot around back."

"You're not sure?" M asked sharply.

"*I'm* sure."

"Go on," Liam said wearily, shooting M a look and fruitlessly stifling a huge yawn.

Dead on my feet.

"There's an old gravel road that starts back there and narrows to a path a little way in. That'll take us to the tunnel."

"Who dug the tunnel?" Jess asked over the radio.

"Gramps said it was left over from a strike a long time ago when workers took over the mill," Marley said authoritatively, grateful perhaps for the chance to show off some knowledge. "It runs under the east side of the sawmill to about fifty yards outside the cyclone fence."

"Like Miguel said."

"Yup."

"Well, at least we know *something* he said holds water."

"How long since you've been there?" M probed.

"A while," Marley conceded, "but I spent half my time there when I was a kid. My grandparents raised me and my bro."

"Where's he?"

"He's a homeless tweaker," she said. "For all I know, he's in MillTown."

"Hmm."

Liam noticed Marley filling her baggy overalls' pockets with merch plucked from gabbing vendors' tables as they passed.

"Cut the shit," he whispered to her. "Or forget about that ride to Spokane."

"Force of habit," she replied with a shrug, unsheathing a freshly nicked Bug Bar in her hand. "*You ever* been broke? You *ever* go hungry?"

"I don't care if you steal," Liam informed her. "I do care if you get caught and they make us."

She nodded knowingly.

In front of the post office Marley had mentioned was a gaggle of anti-abortion demonstrators, garbed in ankle-length dresses, not unlike the women they'd seen earlier; reciting the Ave Maria, the women pivoted to Liam and Marley, brandishing signs and glowing phone screens against the dark, as the pair tried to skirt them.

JESUS IS LOVE

JESUS HATES BABY KILLERS

UNBORN LIVES ARE LIVES!!

IDAHO WELCOMES MARY/Maria AND JESUS.

Animated holos of Madonna and Child hovered in the air above the group.

"God bless you and the fruit of your womb, child," a woman wearing an EyeRIS called to Marley.

To Liam's horror, Marley stopped in her tracks and turned to the woman.

"*What* treasure, *lady*?" she replied with a sneer.

"Why, your precious cargo," the woman said with a smile, indicating Marley's midsection.

"I'm aborting this little rape ape—*sister*!" Marley yelled, indicating her abdomen with both index fingers pointed.

"Not in Idaho, child," the smiling woman replied matter-of-factly.

"No shit, Sherlock," Marley replied. "That's why I'm going to Spokane."

"They'll catch you, Marley," the woman said, her tone hardening slightly. "Don't force the child to be born behind bars."

"They already caught me, and here I am anyway!" Marley exclaimed, evidencing no surprise that the woman knew her name. "So, fuck off!"

"Have you ever seen a murdered fetus, sister Marley?" the woman asked. She touched something in her hand, and a blurry holo of a dismembered fetus appeared; its scrunched, obviously photoshopped, countenance bore an expression of agony.

"Leave her, Sister Sadie," a nearby woman called, "we have larger concerns."

Larger concerns?

Sister Sadie fell back as the pair strode away from the group and across the pavement toward the opening to the gravel road, around which tents were sprouting, before hiking down the empty gravel road.

"It's not too late, Marley," she called. "The sisterhood saves."

"Self-righteous fuckin' assholes!" Marley screamed, flipping them off again.

"I *said*, cut the *shit*!" Liam said, tugging on her arm.

"*Ow!* *Yanking it away, she* thrust her index finger in his face. "Don't you *ever* do that again, mister."

"Sorry, but you can't let them get in your head," Liam noted. "We can't afford any more hitches."

"What's going on up there?" Jess asked.

"Witch convention!" Marley snapped.

"Which what?"

"Watch out for the Hail Mary's," Liam warned.

"Hail Mary's?"

"Ave Maria's, actually," he replied. "They're chanting in Spanish, which means they're probably—"

"On the lookout for Maria."

"You'll know when you see 'em," he said, "in front of the library."

"They somehow picked up that Marley's pregnant."

"Maybe they recognized her," M ventured, "and already knew she was pregnant."

"They knew Marley's name," Liam said. "And she had an EyeRIS."

DAILY NEWS

BREAKING NEWS

Pope condemns media coverage of Jesus Squad.

Liam and Marley paused on the muddy path after a couple of minutes to allow the others—*hopefully*—to catch up. The woods were black beyond the reach of Liam's flashlight beam, which was trained on the overgrown trail beneath their feet.

Trembling with fatigue, Liam thought he saw figures dashing among the trees in front of him.

Hallucinations? Exhaustion? Stress? Thank God the dogs are coming.

Marley's noisy chewing notched up his nerves.

"Could you possibly lose the gum?"

Marley stared at him dubiously. "Gum?" She popped a bubble.

"*Pretty* please?"

Spitting it out, she jammed her hands into her overall's pockets.

Liam suddenly ached for Daisy and Vonnegut, whose quirky charms and demands had helped keep him grounded while Joan wasted away before his eyes. It occurred to him that he hadn't touched base with his pet sitter since he'd left.

He swiped and blinked at tears. His earbud feed continued carrying the ambient din of the carnival, through which the remainder of the posse was winding its way. His ears pricked up when he heard again the distinct chanting of the so-called sisterhood.

Suddenly, the chorus broke into a commotion. Magnus barked shrilly.

"Sisters," he heard a familiar voice plead, "let us assist you with the fruit of the child's womb."

"We have no need of your assistance!" Jess snapped.

"Pride goeth before a fall, sister."

"*You're* not my—"

"Back off!" Ellie exclaimed.

"Ellie," Liam cried, "what's going on?"

"She's got a Taser," yelled another woman.

Magnus snarled viciously.

"The dog!" another woman screamed. "Get the *fucking* dog off me!"

"Language, sister."

"Run, Maria!" Ellie yelled.

"Magnus!" Jess shrieked.

"*Jess!*" Ellie shrieked.

"Fucking cunts!" Jess exclaimed.

Liam's weary mind reeled. Jess *never* used such language.

"They tased Ellie and Magnus and got away with Maria."

"I'm coming," he heard himself croak.

"Stay where you are," Jess replied more calmly. "There's nothing you can do."

"*But—*"

"We'll be there in a minute, Jess," M cut in, panting.

"Ellie and Magnus will be okay shortly," Jess assured them.

"*They just got tased!*" Liam exclaimed.

"They're stunned, not injured," she replied. "You haven't spent much time with Maria," Jess replied. "I can't tell you, Liam, how much better I feel since I've been with her. Kind of scary.

"She's a genuine healer."

"A *healer*," he muttered. "But she ain't there."

"She's close," she said. "Believe it, but don't ask me how she does it."

His heart racing, Liam slumped against a tree.

"Drink some water, dude!" Marley commanded. Shining a light on his face, she proffered his water bottle. "You look like my grandpa when he kicked it."

"Thanks," he replied drily before guzzling the contents of the half-full bottle.

After what seemed like an hour of heart-pounding silence, during which he struggled to keep his eyes open, he heard stirrings on the path; he was relieved to spot a pencil beam of light as Jess approached with a brisk gait.

"Maria?"

"Those anti-aunties engaged us and hustled her off while we were distracted," Jess said ruefully.

"How did they recognize Maria?" Liam asked.

"So-called Sister Sadie had an EyeRis," Jess said. "It seemed like they knew she was coming and how she'd look."

"Meaning *what*?"

"They mean her no harm," she asserted. "Maria has huge propaganda value."

"Or ransom value," Tate ventured.

"Because she decided to have the baby," Jess continued. "Those sanctimonious twits are staking a claim to the alleged Second Coming."

"The Second Coming," Marley echoed, awestruck, as she noisily worked a fresh wad of gum.

Liam cringed.

"Whoa," she said. "We're gonna be famous."

"We already are," Tate corrected her.

"Are famous people rich?"

"Jesus."

"You said it."

"But Miguel wants *Maria*," Liam insisted.

"Maria and Ellie can handle themselves," Jess replied breezily. "They'll talk their way out of it and be here before you know it."

"Out of *it?*"

"Whatever it is they want Maria for."

Always that certainty.

Hearing footsteps on the path, Liam greeted M and T with relief.

"Ellie and Magnus will catch up," Jess declared. "Let's go."

Marley led them over a modest rise when Liam, brandishing his SOUNdR, an eavesdropping device, stopped short.

He held up a hand, "Shh."

Marley nodded and, to his relief, worked her fresh gum behind closed lips.

Maybe twenty feet in front of them, Liam saw through his NiteEyes what appeared to be two men wrestling and grunting on the ground.

"OMG," Marley whispered. She squelched a giggle with a palm over her mouth. "They're fucking."

Sure looks that way.

"On the down-low from moron duty," M whispered.

"Naturally."

"Fags," Tate muttered. "I thought they'd all moved to Portland."

"Watch your homophobic mouth," M snapped.

"Tate."

Tate grunted.

"Let's wait for them to finish," Liam said. "Be easier than trying to sneak around them."

They stood in silence, watching, listening, or both for a few minutes.

So much for a quickie.

"Takin' their sweet fucking time," M whispered, breaking the excruciating silence. "We can't stand here forever, Liam."

"Amen," T said.

"Might get noisy."

"We'll have to risk it," M said.

To his surprise, Jess nodded.

"All right," Liam whispered. "Tasers ready. We need to get within fifteen feet. Tase and gag 'em. Where's the duct tape? Ties?"

Grinning, Marley pulled zip ties from her pocket and tape from her backpack.

"Good work," he said. "Remember, if they raise an alarm, we're fucked."

"Amen," whispered T, his camo drenched with sweat.

Hands trembling, Liam took a deep breath and shook his head briskly. Brandishing the Taser, he forced himself to advance as stealthily as possible toward the grunting men. He was mere steps from Taser range when a footfall snapped a scorched twig.

The grappling men froze.

"You hear sumpin'?"

Ranger barked sharply.

"Shit!"

DAILY NEWS

BREAKING NEWS

Supreme Court punts on hearing challenge to 'don't ask, don't tell' laws governing LGBTQ civil servants.

CHAPTER
FIFTY

Rolling apart, the men were lunging for their weapons when one of them jerked onto his back, groaning, followed by the other an instant later.

"Sorry, brothers," a woman's voice issued from the shadows, "break's over."

What the fuck?

Two penlights snapped on, capturing a blur of motion as what appeared to be three women in long, baggy dresses pulled something from somewhere in the ample folds of their attire. With efficient motions, they slapped duct tape over the mouths and zip-tied the hands of the two writhing men, pants around their knees.

Tasers.

The tallest of the three turned to Liam and his companions.

"I'm Sister Sadie, brothers and sisters," she said. "We're friends of Maria, mother of Jesús."

"Are you fuckin' kiddin' me?" Marley squawked.

Maria appeared solemnly behind the other woman; her features appeared inscrutable in the scarce light.

"How do you know about Maria?" Liam asked.

The women exchanged glances.

"Are you serious, elder?" the woman asked in apparent surprise. "The world awaits her holiness and dear Jesús."

"Someone's been swilling Kool-Aid," M replied.

"This is a miracle beyond your understanding," Sadie informed them. "We promised Maria that Jesús would have a safe birth with us. It's all part of the plan."

"Plan?" Jess exclaimed. "This is a self-fulfilling prophecy in the making, sister. That millions or billions of halfwits are seeing and hearing exactly what they want or need to see and hear on their devices doesn't a miracle make."

"The girl has remarkable abilities, but the mother of God she isn't."

Is anyone recording this stunning dialog?

"This is a transcendent moment in human history," Sadie replied. "We are all merely His servants."

"Again, with the transcendence," Jess countered. "This girl, whose name just happens to be Maria, needs a safe place to deliver her baby, who just happens to be named Jesús.

"Two of the most common Hispanic names in the world," she noted.

"Are you unaware," Sadie offered with an indulgent smile, "that millions of souls worldwide are channeling what blessings they can spare, and perhaps beyond, to His welfare?

"What more proof do you require?" she asked.

"Blessings?" T muttered.

"North of ten million and counting."

"Ten million dollars?" Marley gasped. "Holy shit!"

"I *know*, right?" Sadie trilled as though not quite believing it herself.

"Unbelievable," Tate muttered.

"I just want my wife's ashes back," implored Liam, fighting back tears.

"Your wife's ashes aren't really our concern," Sadie said sympathetically. "But we'll pray for them."

"*Not your con—*" Liam began.

"We need to move," Sadie cut him off. "His time is near."

"You mean his birth?"

"Naturally."

"How close?"

"Hours."

Caressing her bulging belly, Maria shrugged solemnly.

"And you know this *how*?" Jess inquired.

"I'm a midwife," she replied.

"How convenient," Jess opined.

"Sister," the woman replied, "midwife is one of the few honorable professions that welcomes women in these parts."

"No one held a gun to your head," M chimed in, "to stay when you could have left."

Sadie shook her head slowly with a sad, tolerant expression. "We have families, just like you."

Everyone turned to the sound of a stirring on the path: Ellie and Magnus, creaky but intact, limped up to join the gathering. Ranger greeted his comrade with collegial sniffing.

"Sorry we tased you back there," Sadie offered, "but you gave us no choice. We had them on the lowest setting just to buy us a minute."

"I get it," Ellie replied icily.

Sadie turned to the prisoners.

"Your perversity, brothers," Sadie informed them, "is between you and the shepherd you forsake. If you try to escape, incel brothers, we'll upload your bestial act."

One of the men sobbed. "He forced me."

"Shut up, pussy," his companion snarled. Turning to the others, he pleaded, "They'll kill us if they find out."

"So, find some righteousness, brothers."

"Who the fuck are you to judge them?" Ellie demanded. "You condemn gay men, you condemn lesbians, too."

"And trans," M chimed in.

"Amen!" Jess declared.

Despite everything, Liam chuckled to himself.

"Mere labels, sisters, for the errant and misguided," Sadie replied. "Make time to read your Leviticus and Romans."

"Which can mean whatever you want them to," Jess noted.

"We're all but flawed servants striving to carry on His ministry," Sadie replied blithely.

"What bullshit!" Ellie exclaimed.

Whoa.

Sadie swigged some water. "I'd love to continue this conversation," she said, "but time's a wastin'."

"You damn us," Ellie noted, "yet you're helping us."

"Like you, we're helping Maria and her unborn holiness," she said. "And the enemy of my enemy is my friend."

"Fuck me," Tate muttered.

"Fuckin' Mormons," Marley concluded, her hand ruffling her ginger curls.

The rest of them shook their heads resignedly as the anti-aunties wrangled the blindfolded men out of hearing range, plugging their ears for good measure.

"And I thought *I* was a hard-ass," M muttered.

A sudden gust of wind stirred airborne ash and the remnants of the torched brush surrounding them.

"Where's the tunnel, Marley?" Maria asked in a steely voice that cut through the chatter like a laser etching glass.

BREAKING NEWS

Hispanic pols, clerics call for boycott of PNS.

Visibly startled, Marley collected herself and pointed to an area a few steps from where the anti-aunties stood. "Should be underfoot right around there."

Sister Sadie took a couple of light steps and, to Liam's surprise, performed a graceful jeté with both feet, landing with a thud on what sounded like wood.

"I thought I ran over something hollow," she said.

"T and Tate, keep an eye out, will ya?" Liam asked.

"Copy that."

"I wanna see the tunnel," Tate protested.

"You showed off your shootin' eye on those drones at the school; you and Ranger will be a lot more valuable out here than crawling through a wormhole that might collapse on you," M said. "Somebody's gonna come looking for Bert and Ernie there."

Liam was too exhausted to snicker.

Penlights combined to illuminate a rectangle of muddy, debris-covered earth. Bending for a closer look, Marley nodded her head excitedly and stomped on it, eliciting thuds.

"This is it," she said. "They laid a door across it."

After whisking away the soup of ash and mud, they probed with their fingers for the outline of the makeshift lid, using pocket knives to scrape away debris from the crack. After digging a pry bar out of her backpack, M worked the chisel end into the gap and wiggled it, budging the door.

"I'll try to lift it high enough for you guys to get your fingers under it."

A stale, musty draft met them as they pushed the door aside. Magnus sniffed eagerly at the large opening.

Penlights illuminated the aperture and a weathered, though solid-looking, wooden ladder.

Jess turned to Marley. "Ever been down there?"

"I went in a little way," she said, "but I got scared."

"Scared of what?"

"It's really narrow, at least in the beginning," she said. "You have to crawl. I chickened out. I had nightmares about getting stuck in there afterward."

Fuck.

"That crawling is gonna kill our knees."

"We can tape some cloth around 'em," Ellie said.

"I'm going," Maria said. "I need to see Miguel before I have the baby."

"Lest anyone forget," Jess noted, "Miguel was *supposed* to meet us here."

"Maybe he got sidelined."

"Maybe we're walking into a trap."

"Maybe," M snarked, "we should get our asses in gear."

Liam planted a foot gingerly on the ladder's second-highest

rung, testing its strength. "Seems solid," he said dubiously. "What are we taking with us?"

"No backpacks," M said. "Anything bulky could snag."

"Snag on what?"

"I don't know," she said. "The quake might have weakened the walls."

"It might be boobytrapped," Tate chimed in from the woods.

"Shh."

"Either go, señor," Maria demanded, "or get out of my way, por favor."

"Do as she'll have you, brother," Sadie said, pointing a ghost at Liam. "Or suffer the consequences."

What the fuck?

"You don't have to do this, Liam," Jess said.

Liam was astonished to see more armed women materialize from the surrounding woods—evidently undetected by T and Tate—arms trained on his companions.

"Yes, I do."

He paused for a moment to shrug off his backpack; from it, he retrieved a water bottle, a larger flashlight, extra batteries, which he stuffed in his pockets, and his headlamp, which he affixed anew to his head and switched on.

The activity left him lightheaded; he took a moment to steady himself.

Jess caught his bleary eyes with a worried expression. "Liam, I don't thi—"

"Hide the pack for me," he interrupted her as he gingerly stepped onto the third step of the ladder, followed by Maria. At the bottom, there was barely enough space for the two of them to stand.

Falling to her knees, the tiny mother-to-be poked her head into the passageway.

"Give me your headlamp," she ordered.

Liam removed it and handed it over without a word.

Tightening it to fit, she promptly set off, the bobbing headlight stabbing into the horizontal well of darkness.

Liam broke into a sweat, which seeped into and stung his fatigued eyes.

Jesus' fuck, would Joan think her ashes were worth this insanity?

He heard others come behind him, but his exhaustion overwhelmed any curiosity as to who followed him or any concern for them.

They were all smart enough to understand the possible consequences.

At intervals, they passed what appeared to be rudimentary attempts at fortifying the excavation with two-by-fours. They were pushed aside or wormed by piles of claylike earth that appeared to have fallen from the ceiling, possibly shaken loose by the quake.

He tried not to consider the possibility of being buried alive.

He employed every ounce of willpower he could summon to blindly keep following the indomitable girl in front of him who risked having to deliver a baby and possibly perishing in the process in this rabbit run.

Maria scuttled ahead of him as though born to the task.

"Slow down, Maria," he gasped, straining to maintain his grip on his flashlight. "I can't—"

Everything went black.

Moments that to Liam might have been hours later, he was vaguely aware of Maria whispering rhythmically and unintelligibly into his ear.

"Wha' happ—"

She held a vial to his lips. "Drink this."

"What is—"

"He's having some kind of breakdown," a familiar voice said.

What appeared to be a laser drilled into each of his eyes in turn, the glare veiling the face peering down at him. He'd been buried alive, he recalled, and they'd dragged him into a warren and were going to sacrifice him.

No, I was dreaming.

"Drink it, gringo!" she hissed.

"Drink it," another voice echoed from the ether in which he was suspended.

Hesitantly imbibing the bottle's bitter contents, he fought the urge to vomit.

"Keep it down," Maria said. "That's all I have left."

"What?"

"It'll relax you."

Whatever he'd ingested hit him like a Valium he'd popped once at a college party, except this was nearly instantaneous. Closing his eyes, he relaxed. In a waking trance, he became aware of the sensation of being pulled along the passage on his back, although it felt like he was gliding in the air. Trying to move, he found himself bound up in a large coat or tarp, his limbs bound to his sides.

Grunting, Maria tugged his bulk behind her through the tunnel with that tiny frame of hers. It was a virtually impossible feat of physics, and yet she was doing it on her knees.

In another minute, the tunnel ceiling opened to where they could stoop; a few more yards brought them to another old ladder and the tunnel's terminus.

As Maria hefted the trapdoor and pushed it aside, blinding lights flooded the scene. Liam felt himself jerked upright in his restraints. Then his feet left the ground. He felt himself rise toward the ceiling as his feet pushed against nothing as if he were taken skyward in the Rapture.

A warm fluid that smelled faintly of pee dribbled off his head, into his gasping mouth, and onto his neck and shoulders as Maria hauled him up, hand over hand, through the hole in the floor above; he spat in revulsion, quickly closing, and reopening his eyes. He absently thought he smelled pot smoke.

Is she pissing on me?

"If you just joined us, we're streaming live from MillTown, Idaho," a man's accented voice announced, "as Maria, mother of

Jesús, destined to be the greatest influencer of all time, emerges from a secret tunnel with her colorful entourage."

"Miguel?" the girl cried, holding a hand up to her face and blinking at the shadowy figures behind the blinding lights.

"Ahora me llamo Joseph, mi amor," the voice said. "They said it would make things simpler."

"*They*?"

Liam was dimly aware of Maria being engulfed by a swarm of bodies.

"Get the hell away from her," a male voice bellowed. "You're blockin' the cameras! Fuck, if I have to *reshoot* all this."

"He's coming," Maria bleated. "Jesús is coming. I need to lie down."

"Liam," a nearby voice called.

Something lightly smacked his face. Then again, a bit harder. Then, a third time. Ellie was slapping him.

"Are you with us?" She suddenly stopped and sniffed her hand. "Your sweat smells like pee!"

He tried to focus as she shone a penlight on his pupils.

He groaned.

"Liam?"

"What happened?"

"I think you had a psychotic break from all the stress and exhaustion," she replied calmly. "Maria is going to give you slash therapy. She said it will—"

"How is he?" Sister Sadie interrupted, kneeling beside Ellie.

"He's conscious," Ellie said, adding quizzically, "and his head smells like piss."

"Piss?" Sadie echoed. She turned to peer at the group of men apparently ministering delicately to Maria, breathing shallowly. Her features, stripped of her mask, had taken on an ashy pallor.

"Didn't she just pull him up behind her?" Sadie asked.

"Yeah," Ellie said. "So?"

They locked eyes for a moment.

"Yup," Sadie said with what sounded like grim satisfaction, "her water broke."

Liam groggily followed Sadie with his eyes as she shouldered her way through the scrum surrounding Maria and started barking orders at those assembled.

Beginning to regain his faculties, Liam was astonished to survey life-size, internally illuminated statues of the nativity, including animals, surrounding the hatch through which they'd come.

"Where *are* we?"

"We're in a storage shed where we're supposed to meet Miguel," she said. "Except he ain't here."

Dᴀɪʟʏ Nᴇᴡs

BREAKING NEWS

New Trump video mocking Jesus Squad deemed a deep fake.

L iam came to alone and gasping for breath; he lay in near total darkness on a padded surface to which his wrists and ankles were strapped. His scalp felt oddly cool.

He struggled to recall how to get air into his lungs.

How could I forget to breathe?

He flashed back to an acid trip he'd taken during a hike up to Lower Yosemite Falls; he'd suddenly had to remind himself to respire as he bedded down for the night near a burbling stream.

Now, his heart racing, his flesh slick with sweat, he forced himself to take some deep breaths, a useful remnant from his meditation days.

I'm tripping.

This revelation at once soothed and terrified him in the blackness.

At least I know it.

As his pupils dilated, he found himself captive in a room the size of a walk-in closet. A desperate need to check his pockets for his keys, wallet, and other trinkets seized him; he pulled madly against his restraints until he exhausted himself.

Primitive, haunting, eerily mystical flute strains, akin to Mesoamerican musicians he'd heard at a street fair, startled and then enthralled him, brushing his auditory cilia and resonating in his temporal lobe. A whiff of a smoldering herb met his heightened senses.

The mystical notes transformed into sparks arcing between two electrodes that morphed into exquisite fractals, undulating colors, and pulsing waves.

Overcome, he wept.

What the fuck?

Buried alive?

Or have I already died?

I'm tripping.

He clung to a certainty in the back of his altered consciousness that his companions, for whom he suddenly found himself consumed with tenderness, had to be nearby. He recalled, as if from the tatters of a dream, the spectacle of Sister Sadie, the self-proclaimed midwife, deftly wiggling a squalling, bloody Jesús from between tiny Maria's bloody legs; cameras, airborne and stationary alike, relayed the event to anyone who had an interest and a device or a chip. An accented male voice narrated the action; panting, the girl had lain on her back on a blanketed mattress on the floor amidst the illuminated nativity figures and straw from the crèche.

He'd been dimly aware of Ellie wandering off to join Maria after making sure he was okay. Clutching her newborn in her arms, Maria appeared to be arguing, within minutes after delivering, with a man who resembled the pictures he'd seen of Miguel.

In Ellie's absence, a masked, robed figure bent over him, gesturing at him wordlessly to drink from the glass of cloudy liquid he proffered; too drained to protest, Liam allowed the stranger to pour the foul-tasting concoction down his throat.

He retched, and everything went black.

It might all have been a dream.

Yet here he was, a prisoner. Unless this also was a dream, one from which there appeared to be no waking.

Auditory vibrations morphed into protean, elastic light sculptures; they flailed and gyrated against the confines of the cramped space, pushing against the walls before exploding into shards at the peak of a run of high notes.

Liam screamed but heard nothing. His labored breath vaporized, rising into a cascade of neon rainbows.

He sobbed, taking gasping breaths, as he had when Joan's face went slack after her last shallow breath.

The mystical flute tootled to a stop.

"You've no doubt grasped by now that I dosed you, Liam," noted a familiar voice. Ouroboros appeared on his right side. His masked countenance morphed fluidly somehow into a great, fanged maw of a serpent, not unlike the tattoo that adorned the maestro's flesh.

Liam gaped as a swarm of tiny drones, red recording lights a-blink, streamed from the beast's gaping mouth and into the room.

"My apologies, my friend," continued the serpent, seemingly oblivious to the bizarre spectacle he was the source of. "But I had to prevent you from further shitting on the party."

The beast's head swayed above him like a cobra weighing the optimal nanosecond to strike.

Confront, rather than shrink from the boogeymen conjured by the magic mushrooms, counseled the experienced therapists he'd read about.

"*Fuck you!*" Liam roared as a warm flow dampened his pants.

"So, here's the thing, Liam," said the serpent. From its right side emerged Ouro's intricate bionic appendage, hoisting and displaying an urn that appeared identical to the one harboring Joan's ashes; he carefully set it down inches from Liam's tethered hand.

Liam wiggled his digits reflexively in the urn's direction.

"Normally," the beast explained, "I'd be more inclined to flush these precious ashes down the shitter with other societal rot than share them with someone as unworthy as you."

Forming a loose circle, the airborne bots eddied about each other acrobatically. A fourth, then a fifth, and finally, the remainder of the swarm joined their counterparts in an aerial ballet suggestive of M's graceful El Camino choreography. A score or so of them had gathered when they simultaneously sprouted tiny lasers, some of them red, others blue, and others white.

"But as it stands," the serpent bloviated, his round, bloodshot eyes still fixed on Liam, "Joan had abilities she naively believed that it would be immoral to or that she was simply too frightened to exploit for a higher purpose."

Higher purpose?

The bots congregated into a tidy rectangle that encompassed the entire ceiling, forming a display of the approximate dimensions of a sport-bar's screen.

"Because she knew," the serpent nattered, its vocal pitch rising, "that accessing your channel, reading your thoughts, caused you discomfort. Because you were unwilling to sacrifice your ego and cede her space to fully explore her gifts, she suppressed them."

Liam stared at a mirror image of himself lying on the table that had appeared on the ceiling.

"At enormous cost to herself."

Except no shackles appeared in the picture.

"She misguidedly and tragically allowed them to atrophy through disuse."

Liam flexed his wrists. The straps arrested them, but the

display only showed him shaking them spasmodically, hinting at some kind of palsy.

"The stress she endured from suppressing her true nature caused her extraordinary, mutated immunities to fail her and left her vulnerable to the abominable plague of cancer."

"Let me go, you crazy fuck!" Liam screamed. This time, he heard himself.

"There's nothing stopping you, my friend." The serpent inclined his head to indicate the shackle-free ceiling display. "You're free to go. God forbid I would ever so much as consider confining someone against his or her will."

"Is that why you were drugging Maria in the wee hours in your slash lab?"

The beast heaved a weary sigh. "I need your help right now. We'll discuss Maria later."

A loud, remote thud shook the room, reverberating in Liam's addled brain. A light shower of dust drifted down from the ceiling like flour through a sifter.

"They're fighting out there, Liam," the serpent noted, "over the future. I alone can stop the killing, Liam, yet here I am forced to deal with you instead of embracing Jesús, my son, my anointed successor."

His son…?

DAILY NEWS

BREAKING NEWS

Militias launch assault on MillTown.

Liam gaped as the ceiling display fractured into twin, equilateral rectangles.

On the left, Jared Jeberische and his fundits watched and commented on the contents of their own split screen, on one side of which Liam appeared in real time on the table; the other side was an aerial shot of the gun battle taking place as militias attempted to fight their way into the compound. An inset in the half of the screen displaying the combat showed the pilot who'd downed Lance Rancette's PNS drone firing a grenade from a launcher perched on his shoulder.

The images repeated themselves endlessly in ever tinier windows, even as the ceiling display itself scaled down into smaller and smaller rectangles until every single drone bore the same image.

I've gone insane.

A cold, rigid device seized Liam's cranium and jerked it to the left, where he found himself looking into the mad, deep-set eyes of Ouroboros, who was wriggling his bloody way out of the serpent's midsection like an alien spawn.

Liam felt the gurney to which he was bound to begin descending slowly through the floor as if borne by a pulley device lowering a casket into the earth.

"I gave myself the sacraments," Ouroboros announced, his voice seeming more distant, "which led me to the epiphany that the self-administration in itself was insufficient to imbue me with the full spectrum of Joan's abilities."

He tootled some exotic, suspenseful notes on his flute, then continued his account.

"I experienced, however, an epiphany that revealed to me that it was only through your channel, wretched as you are, that I could access Joan's telepathic ability."

The serpent's elongated neck traced Liam's descent.

"Under the extraordinarily inopportune circumstances," Ouroboros continued, "I was obliged to break with my usual protocol and administer slash without preparing you with an initial psilo-only session."

"Fuck you!"

"Best not to adulterate your journey with hostility," his nemesis advised coolly. "It could engender some truly unnerving episodes."

Stay calm and meet his gaze, a voice implored from somewhere in the recesses of Liam's feverish mind.

He was stunned to suddenly find his extremities free to rub his eyes for relief. Sitting up suddenly, his head grew progressively lighter; he grasped it with his hands to stop it, he fancied briefly, from floating away.

A sun exploded far above him as though someone had shone a

floodlight in his eyes. His heart raced as it had so recently underground. He fought to remain conscious.

The serpent's scaled muzzle began peeling away into shards of scaly flesh that fluttered downward, alighting on a verdant plain; moments later, they morphed into a blaze of flowers, lining a dirt trail winding through a meadow that suddenly lay before Liam or some avatar of himself, and Joan, whose hand he miraculously found squeezed in his own.

Sun fell on their shoulders as they strolled from the parking lot down the trail to Lake Ray Hubbard, entwined digits swinging in rhythm.

Liam sobbed.

"You found her!" his captor exulted.

Liam was vaguely aware of several points of slight pressure on his patchy scalp but felt nothing directly on his skin. He intuited that Ouroboros was pressing the tips of his prosthetic digits against some kind of sensor.

Electrodes!

DAILY NEWS

BREAKING NEWS

Florida governor condemns ads urging its citizens to move to Costa Rica.

After making love in the tall grass carpeting the lake shore, Joan gazed at the gold-plated pawn shop ring Liam had slipped on her finger. Liam smiled dreamily as Joan recited with feeling the entirety of Shakespeare's "Shall I Compare Thee to a Summer's Day?" He found himself murmuring the lyrical verses in concert with her, aware on some level that he was somehow recalling line after line of exquisite poetry he had never actually read.

His eyes closed, and he saw lines of blurry text.

Fragments of her photographic memory?

Like a murmuring from a distant room, Ouroboros avidly

recited the same words, punctuated by another thud and the distant wailing of an infant.

Liam was scarcely aware of Joan delicately and unhurriedly untangling herself from his sleepy embrace before slipping back into her bra and panties. *Why put on underwear to go swimming?* Wading into the water, she momentarily sank below the surface before popping up again a few scary moments later and dog-paddling further from shore. As the wind kicked up suddenly, he shouted at her to be careful; she wasn't a strong swimmer.

She waved.

Pleasantly fatigued, he dozed on the grass, the fading sun caressing his lazy, stubbled smile.

He found himself humming a favorite Dan Hill song of hers, "Never Thought (That I Could Love)," that he, never a fan of schmaltz, had always tuned out, if not outright mocked.

Asshole! he cursed himself.

Then he sang it, putting words to it of which he had no recall. Maestro's haunting voice hummed and then sang along with him, while in the background, he heard more baby cries and the unintelligible chatter of a group of anxious people on the move.

Ouroboros suddenly stopped singing to exult.

"It's working, Liam!" he cried. "It's *working!*"

What?

"I'm in your *fuckin'* head, man!"

Liam opened his eyes to inky darkness. A drone, red lights blinking, hovered low over the lake, apparently monitoring him. Joan had vanished. He found himself suddenly on the far side of the lake, striding up a mountain trail in search of her in the dark as the drone silently lit his way with a spotlight. The rocky dirt ribbon led to a ledge receiving the first rays of the day from the sunrise. Joan, angelically radiant, floated above a narrow promontory on a facing cliff.

He called her. She smiled at him but said nothing.

She's so young.

He wept.

"I love you," Joan's voice purred in his head.

"Go to her, Liam," ordered the hovering drone in the voice of its apparent controller.

"It's too far to jump," Liam protested.

"We have no choice, Liam," the drone argued.

We?

"It's not a choice, Liam," the drone countered. "Your proximity to her strengthens me, strengthens my ability to enlighten humanity, to end the carnage."

He's insane.

"Are you deaf to the explosions out there, Liam?" the drone inquired. "It's because you mistreated Joan that this," —the drone spun its lights around as if to indicate the unfolding shit show— "was necessary."

As if on cue, Liam heard another great thud. The room shuddered.

"Now meet your fear and redeem yourself," ordered the drone, its controller's voice acquiring an edge.

Setting his jaw, Liam backtracked a few yards, turned, and faced the precipice. Joan grew more ephemeral even as she thrust her arms out before her, seemingly beseeching him.

But.

"Close your eyes, Liam, and run to her!"

Liam counted to three. Opening his eyes for a last, quick glimpse, the scene appeared as a film negative. He bolted for the cliff's edge, which seemed to recede the closer he got to it. A swell of desire swept over him as Joan shed her garments.

Reclosing his eyes, he tried to convince himself he was prepared to die; he'd read that people tripping on mushrooms testified to hallucinating their deaths before being seized by a euphoric feeling of unity with the universe. He sprinted forward blindly, trusting intuition would alert him to the optimal instant to leap. An updraft told him he was over the edge. His heart soared as the wind appeared to bear him up. His weightless self neared the far ledge. He opened his eyes to see Joan's lips moving but couldn't understand her words.

And then he plummeted into the void like a sack of rocks.

I'm dying.

"You're transitioning," the drone informed him. "Now we can stop the carnage."

Liam plunged into the canyon's depths. What looked like a ribbon of the highway below transformed as he plummeted toward a foamy torrent raging through the chasm. Joan's eerie, rippling reflection met his eyes.

The roiling, rushing water exploded into a miasma of intense color, like a deep space image, as it rose to meet him, swallowing and dissolving his disintegrating flesh. A mist arose of which he euphorically found himself apart. The spray engulfed him and Joan before dissolving into sunshine; they exchanged wedding vows before the affable, comb-overed justice of the peace and his chatty, middle-aged secretary, who gushed over Joan's floral print elopement dress.

Radiant as any conventionally gowned bride, Joan joined Liam in swiping at joyful tears.

The cramped county office dissolved into a laboratory in which a little girl shorn of hair, who looked a lot like Joan, gasped with sobs; she lay loosely tethered to a gurney with electrodes affixed to her scalp; wires spanned from them to an analog monitor. A man in a white lab coat stood on either side of her, questioning her about photos and pictures they held up to her face.

Mounted on a tripod a few feet in front of her was a movie camera, its red recording light blinking.

"I want my mother!" she shrieked.

"I told you she's coming, Joanie," the interrogator on the left, a short, burly older man, insisted tersely.

"My name is Joan, not Joanie!" his subject snapped between sobs. "And I'm tired. I want to sleep. In *my* bed."

"You need to finish your work, Joan," he snapped, "before your mother gets here. Otherwise, we'll have to send her home alone."

"*No!*" she screamed.

"She'll be really upset."

"Your parents are so proud of you," the man on her right interjected, "for helping our country. We'll get you home as soon as we possibly can, honey."

The older man nodded irritably.

"Don't call me that!"

Joan closed her eyes. Her features were set in an eerie, grimly adult cast.

"Did you know your partner has been questioning your Project EXTRACT protocols, Dr. McCarrihy?" she asked icily.

She smiled grimly as the men gaped at her and each other in evident astonishment.

"What in the name of God? What the hell is she talking about?" McCarrihy exclaimed. "How does she know my name? That's confidential."

Confidential?

"What are you so afraid of, Joseph?" His colleague held McCarrihy's widened eyes. "That she can read your mind?"

"My God, you're sabotaging me, you son of a—"

"I merely communicated to the director," his colleague explained calmly, "that you'd produce better results if you treated these prodigies more like children rather than telepathic lab rats, McCarrihy ."

"This is *my* project," McCarrihy declared. "I'll fire your back-stabbing ass."

"Not if they fire you first."

The electrodes affixed to Joan's shaved head suddenly peeled off.

"That's impossible," McCarrihy's colleague marveled.

"Yes, it is," McCarrihy concurred with grim satisfaction.

"That adhesive has never failed."

"She's extraordinary," McCarrihy said, "Too bad she's such a brat."

"She's eight years old, Joseph."

McCarrihy shrugged. "I'll be on the right side of history."

Liam recognized with a jolt that the older man was the one pictured in the Project EXTRACT report: McCarrihy. And he was a dead ringer. Liam was additionally stunned to note, for Ouroboros, a.k.a. Ignatius Adler, a.k.a. Maestro, a.k.a. the crazed leader of the El Camino cult.

El Camino. The Way. *Ouroboros's way.*

"I see you recognize my grandfather, Liam," said Ouroboros. "Joseph McCarrihy was a genius, a visionary. He somehow learned of and located Joan and recognized her at once as a prodigy among prodigies. But his fanatical patriotism and hatred for Communism led him to excesses. He allowed himself to be set up."

"*Set up?*" Liam heard himself roar. "He destroyed families, for Christ's sake. Four of his guinea pigs killed themselves."

Joan's face morphed into his own and McCarrihy's into Ouroboros's.

"The *company* destroyed families," Ouroboros countered. "They crucified him and buried the truth. He recognized my abilities and told me about the project, Joan, and the Mayan curanderas he'd studied. He told me it was critical that I continue his studies. He said the future of humankind depended on it."

Liam listened, dumbfounded.

"Of course," Ouroboros continued with a rueful laugh, "I knew the old boy was crackers.

"But I dug up his files after he shot himself and learned of Joan's extraordinary abilities. She should have been the prototype of a new human, with her capabilities optimized, but you, in your profound ignorance, fucked up everything."

Joan was in her hospital bed in their dusky living room, her body ravaged by cancer. Liam watched from above, sobbing helplessly as he observed himself struggle to ease—*somehow*—the agony of her final hours.

The house shuddered from what felt like a nearby bomb blast.

<u>DAILY NEWS</u>

<u>BREAKING NEWS</u>

White House mum on rumors of 'trillionaire's'
lunar lair.

"Shit!" Ouroboros exclaimed.

Liam gaped in hallucinatory astonishment as his nemesis screamed in agony. A bony, wrinkled, tattooed old man with Mayan features rhythmically poked his chest with what appeared to be a rigid, pointed reed dipped in pigments.

The living room evaporated to reveal the dim interior of a hut in which a grubby, bronzed young man sporting dreadlocks and thick glasses sat on a dirt floor, legs folded over each other. Across from him in the same attitude was a tiny, boldly tattooed, crepe-fleshed curandera who bore a striking resemblance to an aged Maria. Flanking her were two assistants, or apprentices, similarly inked; one of them played a mystical air on a primitive flute crafted from what appeared to be the bone of a large bird.

After singeing some herbs in a toad-shaped vessel and muttering unintelligibly what Liam supposed were prayers, the curandera explained to Ignatius Adler that they were all about to receive the sacrament of the k'aizalaj okox, the psychedelic mushroom that would lead them to entheos, or spiritual transcendence. Once their spiritual journey was underway, she said, those worthy of it would ingest the ashes of an ancestor whose unique essence they would learn to harness in service of their kin.

From a well-worn terra-cotta bowl, whose lip depicted the tail-swallowing serpent Ouroboros, the medicine woman doled out some fungi resembling round dollhouse tables of approximately equal sizes. They all partook evenly. Following their cue, Adler masticated energetically to break down the fungi's leathery texture and absorb the mind-altering psychotropic compound within.

Trembling with excitement, he watched as the medicine woman made an elaborate, deliberate ritual of lifting a weathered bowl of opaque, odious liquid to the lips of her assistants, who closed their eyes and tilted their heads back to somberly receive it.

Eyes squeezed shut, Ignatius Adler leaned forward eagerly, his lips curled upward in a rapturous, anticipatory smile to receive the sacrament: a slurry of ashes, presumably from one of his companions' ancestors. Mouth agape and head tilted back, he awaited the sensation of the liquid dripping onto his outthrust tongue.

The women exchanged glances and, at a solemn nod of the curandera's head, rose as one and silently exited the enclosure.

Feeling and hearing nothing, Adler opened his eyes questioningly after a few moments to find himself abandoned. He blinked rapidly, incredulity and outrage registering across his dark features. Shrieking his rage at the perceived betrayal, he kicked the weathered brazier in which the old woman had burned the herbs.

Clanging off a large stone, the receptacle scattered its embers. Aromatic smoke rose into the void.

"Get the *fuck* out of my head!" Ouroboros shrieked in his ear as Liam's vision retreated to the cramped space where he'd initially found himself. Smoke was filling the room, along with a rhythmic pounding like a sledgehammer on a wall.

Through the haze, Liam watched a man he assumed to be Miguel bending over Maria's bare midsection. She appeared to be unconscious. In Miguel's right hand was what looked like a plastic syringe.

"Me lo agradecerás algún día, mi amor," the man intoned. "Dar a luz al hijo del maestro es un regalo increíble."

Oh my God.

Liam knew enough Spanish to understand that Miguel was telling his unconscious lover how fortunate she was to be chosen to give birth to the Maestro's child.

As the thickening smoke erased his vision and forced his eyes closed, Maria made herself heard in his head.

Get on the floor, señor.

"The straps," Liam gasped, coughing.

"They're loose," she cried. "Get on the floor. We're almost in."

Liam heard and felt distant booming and muffled voices.

Ouroboros, or his avatar, had vanished into the billowing, choking haze.

Woozy from the smoke, Liam felt oddly at peace. Whatever had been accomplished, he'd given it everything to recover those precious remains. He'd seen Joan, felt her, talked to her, even *made love* to her. She was at peace. He experienced an inkling of communion, of being a tiny part of an infinite consciousness of living *and* dead, just as he'd been a part of the mist and sunshine.

"Get away from the door, Liam," a female voice called. "We're coming in."

Lying on the floor, he closed his eyes, exhausted, and passed out under the gurney. He'd stopped respiring when the door was bashed open moments later.

Hoisting his limp form onto the gurney, M and Jess wheeled him from the smoke-choked space out into an alley that ran behind the back of the mill as Maria, Jesús clamped in her arms, trotted alongside, murmuring in his ear.

Some kind of explosive landed behind them, leveling the shed they'd just fled.

"Holy shit!" Liam heard T exclaim, as if from a distance.

Liam was dimly aware of gliding down a long tunnel, less frightening somehow than the one they'd so recently used, toward a luminous, indistinct figure that might have been Joan. He was ecstatic. The nearer he got to the glowing figure, the faster he seemed to move.

"I'm losing him," a faraway voice cried. "Give him air."

He continued his blissful journey toward oblivion.

He felt an annoying, rhythmic thumping against his chest, and something pressed against what seemed to be his mouth. The light receded, and his progress stalled.

Something cool pressed against his face. A rich flow of oxygen suddenly filled his lungs. The tunnel vanished as he convulsed and coughed. Gasping, he gulped oxygen and opened his eyes, blinking in the daylight. Faces peered back at him.

"OMG," T exulted. "He's back."

"Thank God," Jess muttered, "wherever she is."

"Welcome back," M greeted him, beaming.

A mixture of profound sorrow and gratitude washed over him as he lay there, panting.

"Look," T said in apparent awe. He pointed skyward.

A fleet of drones appeared above their heads, broadcasting an electronic cover of "Glory, Glory Hallelujah" in English and Spanish, projecting a giant holo of Maria, like the Madonna, cradling the infant Jesús. Maria's Mayan features were subtly anglicized, and her and Jesús's black hair and flesh tones lightened.

Crawling along the bottom of the display were running totals of donations to an apparent account titled "The Jesus Fund" in dollars, pounds, and Euros. Absent was any information identifying the account's founders. Contributions ran in the tens of millions.

Above the chyron, the holo split into four separate images, including the original of Maria and three others of crowds in cities around the world supposedly ecstatically celebrating Jesús' birth.

"Good *God*!" Jess exclaimed.

"I know," said Sister Sadie, who had sidled up to the group. "Isn't she a beautiful peacemaker?"

Liam was now present enough to notice that the gunfire and explosions had ceased. Ironically, Ouroboros seemed to have fulfilled his pledge to stop the carnage, such as it was.

"That footage could be deepfaked," Jess noted, "or been taken anytime, anywhere."

Favoring her right leg, Sadie dabbed with a towel at the blood trickling from an array of tiny cuts on her face.

"Blast blew out a bunch of fuckin' windows," she said matter-of-factly.

"Where's Ouroboros?" Liam asked, rubbing his eyes with his hands.

"Disappeared."

"He set off a smoke bomb to cover his escape," T said.

"Are you positive it was him?" Jess asked.

Liam looked at her in astonishment.

"You *were* wasted, Liam."

"Coulda been a holo."

"Or a hallu."

Liam shrugged dismissively. "Whatever," he said. "I saw what I saw."

"T thought he saw a hole in the back wall while we were putting you on the gurney," M said. "Looks like he had an escape hatch painted over and probably disguised himself after to blend in with the locals.

"He was *really* paranoid."

Liam gave her a look.

"The ashes?" he inquired after a pause.

"Ashes?"

"He had the urn with him."

His companions exchanged glances.

"You mean he slashed you?" T ventured.

Liam glanced at each of them in turn.

"Didn't see 'em when we grabbed you," T said. "If the asshole didn't take 'em, they must have been blown to hell along with the shed."

They fell silent. Jess sat down next to Liam and side-hugged him awkwardly.

"It doesn't matter," he said pensively, wiping away tears. "I saw her, held her, talked to her. She knows how hard I tried, how hard we all tried."

"I know it sounds like a cliché," he concluded, "But I feel genuinely at peace for the first time since she died.

He looked around at each of his stolid companions before realizing their young healer had vanished.

"Where's Maria?"

Ellie, who had turned toward the swelling, murmuring crowd gathered beneath the free-floating display two stories overhead, looked back at the group.

"She was furious about the augmented holo and the money crawl," she said. "I think she went to demand they kill 'em."

"They who? By herself?" Liam persisted.

They exchanged concerned glances.

"So it would appear," Jess lamented.

"Ouroboros wants them!" Liam exclaimed, wincing at a sudden jolt to his bones. "And she's in pain."

He willed himself shakily to his feet, grimacing. "We gotta find 'em!" He suddenly convulsed and collapsed on the ground, writhing.

"You look like you got tased!" T declared as they all knelt to help him.

"*Find them!*" Liam shrieked through clenched teeth. "Go! All of you!"

As he closed his eyes and went as limp as he could to ride out the spasms, a fresh, white-hot shock of additional pain registered in his torso. What felt like a metallic claw slapped across his mouth, cutting off his screams. His eyes flew open to a glimpse of swarthy skin, penetrating blue eyes behind a mask, and a sliver of neck tattoo.

"See how *you* like being kicked around, asshole," a familiar, mellifluous voice uttered from behind the mask.

The muffled sound of a wailing baby was audible from a swollen bundle attached to a broad strap slung around his assailant's arm and shoulder.

"Thanks for delivering Jesús, so to speak," Ouroboros continued. "I'd love to unpack our recent trip with you, but I gotta bounce."

"Maria was tased!" Jess suddenly exclaimed in Liam's ear.

Liam groaned in agony.

Tasing him again, Ouroboros hurried away in the opposite direction from whence he'd come.

"Who is that, Liam?" Jess asked.

"Tased," he groaned.

"*Yes*, she *was!*" Jess said. "And *Jesús* is gone!"

"I know."

"You *know*?!" she exclaimed. "My god, that bastard just tased Liam!"

We're gonna need a plan.

A thin smile on his lips, Liam blacked out.

END

Book 2 of Psychotropia Coming Soon

ACKNOWLEDGMENTS

Thanks to the following people for their assistance in the arduous, it ultimately satisfying, process of independently publishing this book.

A deafening shoutout to Stacey Smekofske for her support and expertise in helping navigate a most challenging venture. I have learned an enormous amount about how the indie industry works from our convos and her straightforward, highly insightful video course.

Thanks to my copy/line editor Krysta Winsheimer, who called out my penchant for using a few short words to excess, along with highlighting some inconsistencies and redundancies. This book is much better for her efforts.

Thanks also to Marco Gamino, who helped ensure that my use of conversational Spanish, pronounced in a few passages, passed muster as he proofed the manuscript.

Thanks as well to the artists at Damonza, who transformed the cover concept I gave them into vivid, awesome imagery that improved on my own vision.

And thanks, finally, to my book-loving, sharp-eyed partner, Lori McMillan, who read and annotated the entire manuscript, improved the product, and supported me along the way.

ABOUT THE AUTHOR

Bill Reinert is a retired journalist and teacher who spends his "seven-day weekends" writing satire, playing the piano, working word puzzles, and torturing his cats with a laser pointer. Born in Rhode Island, he's spent most of his life on the Left Coast, mostly in Portland, Oregon.

PSYCHOTROPIA GLOSSARY

A, B

Anarchist: A person who rebels against any authority, established order, or ruling power

antibis: Slang for antibiotics

aud-sim replication: Audio recording paired with poor-quality video of the speaker

BBQ Chirps: A Ground Bounty snack product containing insect-derived protein

Bezos Lunar Research Station: A privately owned and managed advanced research facility based on the moon

Bloregon: Pejorative nickname for Oregon—a mashup of (politically) blue, boring, and Oregon

Big One: Slang for a major earthquake that shook the Pacific Northwest in 2028

Bug Bar: A Ground Bounty snack product containing insect-derived protein

Bugburgers: A Ground Bounty snack product containing insect-derived protein

C, D

Caminos: Denizens of El Camino, a cult of homeless people occupying two closed Portland neighborhood schools

capiche: Expression used to ask if a message, warning, etc. has been understood

Chocicadas: A chocolate-covered Ground Bounty snack product containing insect-derived protein

Chirps: A Ground Bounty snack product containing insect-derived protein

Covid (19): An acute disease in humans caused by a coronavirus, characterized mainly by fever and cough but capable of progressing to severe symptoms and, in some cases, death

cremains: a person's cremated remains.

Cricketacos: A Ground Bounty snack product containing insect-derived protein

curandera: (Spanish) a female folk healer or medicine woman who uses herbs or psychoactive plants, magic, and spiritualism to treat illness, induce visions, impart traditional wisdom, etc.; a female shaman

deepfaked/deepfakes: a deceptively realistic but fake piece of media created by altering existing video or audio material

deefs: Slang for deepfakes

DNATek: A device able to identify DNA from bone fragments in human ashes

Doomsday: A social media platform that streams violent videos accompanied by Chat commentary that depicts them as cautionary

down-low: a state or condition of secrecy —usually used in the phrase *on the down-low*

dreads: Slang for dreadlocks, a hairstyle consisting of dreadlocks

dudette: Liam's slang diminutive for his trans neighbor Miriam, suggesting a female "dude"

E, F

El Camino: (Spanish) The Way (English): The name of a cult of homeless people occupying two closed Portland neighborhood schools

Election Day Quake: A big earthquake that rattled the Pacific Northwest in 2028

EndDaze: A live-action role-playing game (LARP) in which human players and holograms streamed by AI drones fight against and or alongside each other

enth: exaggeration

entheos (Greek): Spiritual transcendence

EyeRIS (Eye Retina Information Scan): Trademarked, fashionable eyewear that displays information to the wearer using a <u>head-up display</u>. Wearers communicate with the Internet via voice commands.

E-ZVR: Virtual reality headset

Fade-A-Wear: Camouflage that renders the target virtually invisible by bending light waves around the target. The material removes not only the wearer's visual, infrared (night vision), and thermal signatures but also the target's shadow.

flies: Slang for drones

FOMO: Acronym for "Fear of missing out"

fundits: Pundits whose main purpose is mocking, rather than analyzing, news reports

G, H

Gabbel: A chat platform rivaling Meta, X, and other large social media applications

gchat: Generic term for an AI function

GearUPPrint: A 3-D printer

Ground Bounty: Snack company specializing in treats made with insect protein

hallu: Slang for hallucination

Hunab Ku: An ancient Mayan symbol believed to represent the Supreme God or the One Being, with *Hunab* meaning "one state of being" and *Ku* meaning "God," encompassing all opposites in the universe

holo: Slang for hologram, a three-dimensional image formed by the interference of light beams from a laser or other coherent light source

holomap: A 3-D holographic map that can be projected from a digital device such as a smartphone or watch

Homeless Studies Department: Fictional department at Portland State University

Hydrant: A polyethylene water vessel worn on the upper back with tubing that runs to the user's mouth

I, J

Idaho Department of Border Security: Agency responsible for security at the state's borders with Washington and Oregon

Idunnoans: Woke pejorative for Idahoans

I-Dash: Internet car dashboard screen

Instapoll: Public polling organization

invisifabric: Generic name for stealth garments like Invisiwear

Invisitote: Trademarked label of tote bag manufactured using Invisiwear

Invisiwear: Prototype of highly light reflective garments that render the wearer nearly invisible

I-Ware: Bargain, unreliable knockoffs of EyeRIS eyewear

K, L

k'aizalaj okox: Hallucinogenic mushrooms often consumed during ritual ceremonies

LARPing: Abbreviation for taking part in a live-action role-playing game

Lowd Boyz: white nationalist, Christian, anti-woke paramilitary

M, N

Mayhem: A social media platform that streams violent videos accompanied by AI commentary that depicts them as cautionary

megachurch: A church with an unusually large congregation, typically one preaching a conservative or evangelical form of Christianity

Metaverse/Metaversal/Metaversity: A hypothetical, immersive 3-D environment where you can experience life in ways you would not be able to in the physical world

moonbase: A facility on or below the surface of the Moon that enables human activity on the Moon

Neo-Luddites/Ludds/Luddites: A person opposed to new technology or ways of working

Nextdoor: Community website/social media platform

NiteEyes: Trademarked compact night vision goggles that use image intensification technology

non-dom: Pejorative slang for a homeless person, derived from the bureaucratic term "non-domiciled"

O, P

Onewheel: A single-wheeled, self-balancing transportation device with pedals or footrests that the rider stands on, relying on their balance to control the device

Patriot Congress: Congress representing a confederation of Red states

Patriot News Service (PNS): Major online and broadcast news outlet

pols: Slang for politicians

Project EXTRACT: A classified CIA program that conducted tests on children (ages 6–10) who displayed characteristics of extra-sensory perception, possibly involved the administration of mind-altering drugs

psilo therapy: Psilocybin therapy

Q, R

Redantz: A Ground Bounty snack product containing insect-derived protein

respies: Slang for respirators

rezzies: Slang used by homeless people to refer to domiciled residents

S, T

Satirev (Reverse spelling of veritas): Media organization and website that functions as a clearinghouse for classified or otherwise privileged information

schizo: Slang for schizophrenic

Sheermask: Transparent, breathable, particulate-filtering facepiece respirator

slashists: Slang for individuals who support the use of psilocybin for enlightenment

slashholes: Pejorative slang for individuals who exploit the hype around slash therapy for their own profit

slash therapy: Guided psychotherapy involving the ingestion of psilocybin and human ashes (cremains)

slow-moed: Action that is made to appear slower than normal by replaying a recording at a slower speed

SOUNdR: A long-distance eavesdropping device

TerBites: A Ground Bounty snack product containing insect-derived protein

Transcendence Lab/TLab: A small room with gurneys in which Ouroboros administers slash therapy to his followers

tweaker: Slang for a methamphetamine user

unchipped: A person who has not received an implanted microchip

unvaxxed: A person who has not been vaccinated

U, V

veering: Slang for participating in a virtual reality function

W, X

WikiSpex: Nonprofit, decentralized website specializing in the analysis and illegal publication of patent applications and other intellectual property

Y, Z

Youth Party: Loosely organized, youth-oriented, Portland-based group known for vandalizing property controlled by Red State residents